ORACLE BONE

A CHUANQI 傳奇 NOVEL

LYDIA KWA

ARSENAL PULP PRESS
VANCOUVER

ARSENAL PULP PRESS
Suite 202 – 211 East Georgia St.
Vancouver, BC V6A 1Z6
Canada
arsenalpulp.com

The publisher gratefully acknowledges the support of the Canada Council for the Arts and the British Columbia Arts Council for its publishing program, and the Government of Canada (through the Canada Book Fund) and the Government of British Columbia (through the Book Publishing Tax Credit Program) for its publishing activities.

This is a work of fiction. Any resemblance of characters to persons either living or deceased is purely coincidental.

Cover and text design by Oliver McPartlin
Edited by Susan Safyan

Printed and bound in Canada

Library and Archives Canada Cataloguing in Publication:
To come

For the outcast
still sustained by love

MAP OF
CHANG'AN

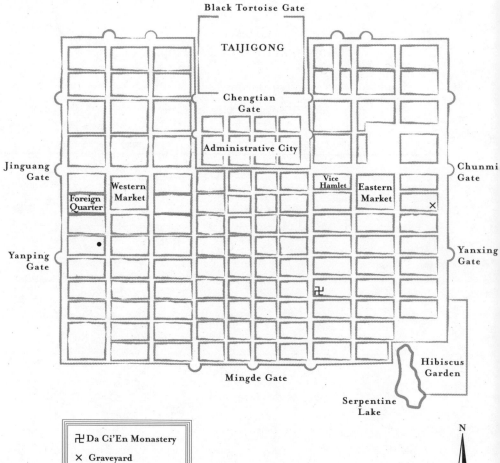

FORBIDDEN PARK

Black Tortoise Gate

TAIJIGONG

Chengtian
Gate

Administrative City

Jinguang
Gate

Foreign
Quarter

Western
Market

Vice
Hamlet

Eastern
Market

Chunmi
Gate

×

Yanping
Gate

Yanxing
Gate

卐

Mingde Gate

Hibiscus
Garden

Serpentine
Lake

N

卐 Da Ci'En Monastery

× Graveyard

• Da Fa Temple

THE MAIN CHARACTERS

LING
Orphaned girl

QILAN
Daoist nun from Da Fa Temple

WU ZHAO
Empress Consort to Li Zhi

LI ZHI
Emperor

XIE
Qilan's father; lover to Wu Zhao

GUI
Demon

XUANZANG
Abbot of Da Ci'en Monastery; translator of sutras

HARELIP
Monk, herbalist, and healer at Da Ci'en Monastery

ARDHANARI
Sculptor

PRONUNCIATION GUIDE FOR SOME CHINESE NAMES

This is meant to be a rough guide to how to pronounce these names. I've transliterated them according to common ways of sounding vowels and consonants in English; this is not at all related to the Pinyin system, which is the basis for how the names have been spelled in the novel. The all-important tones have not been indicated here either.

Qilan is pronounced "Chee Lan"
Wu Zhao is pronounced "Woo Chow"
Li Zhi is pronounced "Lee Tzeh"
Xie is pronounced "Si-ieh"
Gui is pronounced "Goo-we"
Xuanzang is pronounced "Sh'-yuan chang"

To live is to die, to be awake is to sleep, to be young is to be old, for the one flows into the other, and the process is capable of being reversed.
—Heraclitus

PROLOGUE

This is a tale set during the rise of Wu Zhao in the court of Emperor Li Zhi, in the country known as Zhongguo, the Central Kingdom. That was during the latter half the seventh century of the Common Era, back when humans thought of time as a linear construct.

I was strolling down a narrow corridor in the ancient sector of Xi'an one insufferably humid summer evening when a woman's hypnotic voice rose above the ordinary noises of the city, compelling me to search for her.

After turning many corners, my clothing soaked with sweat, I chanced upon the magic. The storyteller sat in a secluded corner at the end of a narrow alley lit by a single kerosene lamp, surrounded by her rapt listeners. Her mouth had only a few teeth left and she, showing no shame about it, spoke in a loud, bright tone of voice.

She seemed unperturbed by the bustle and.dust of travellers. She and some older members of the audience were engaged in a kind of singing repartee. First, she would sing—as if bellowing across a mountain pass—and then a member of the audience replied to her. I took my seat on a low stool at the back of the sizeable crowd.

After many rounds of this melodic exchange, the singers and the audience grew quiet. We sat listening to this precious silence. Waiting, it seemed to me, although I wasn't sure for what or whom.

"This is a fable," she began, "and hence, spiced with all kinds of outrageous lies." She cackled, and the audience applauded vigorously. "Definitely not sanctioned by officials." More clapping.

"Of course I'm not a famous liar. And I might never achieve fame in my lifetime. I consider myself inferior to the great Masters. But I'm happy as long as I can tell stories to audiences like you. Call me the Imperfect One!"

I was pleased by such humility. Imperfections, especially in this new era of erasures, are rather quaint yet subversive.

Thus began the first of twenty-one continuous nights of storytelling.

I share these interwoven intrigues here in approximately the same sequence. Dear reader, may your persistence be rewarded. As for me, it remains true that free and easy roaming fulfills me like no other activity.

—Unknown Wayfarer

BOOK ONE

Gu - Poison

Toward the end of Xianqing 顯慶 reign period
Xiaoshu 小署 Jieqi, Slight Heat,
Sixth Lunar Month,
New Moon

Ling flung herself into the murky, cold water.

The water engulfed her. She opened her mouth and forced herself to swallow, despite her instincts. *This must be what dying is like*, she thought, *no longer aware of having a body, no longer separate from everything else.*

As the torrent of water rushed into her lungs, she heard the voice admonish her, *No, you mustn't die.* Her mother came to her, the blood gash across her neck a clotted scar. She wrapped her arms around Ling who welcomed the embrace and smiled. Just before she lost consciousness, she felt her body surge upwards.

When she came to, she was back on the barge, tied up. Her captor scowled, "Foolish girl, why did you do that? If I hadn't noticed your beautiful eyes … " He grasped her chin with his grimy fingers and jerked her face up. He made her kneel on the rough and uneven boards of the barge. She looked past him and saw the other bandits huddled at the back of the barge, smoking. She counted, *one, two, three, four, five.*

"Eyes like that, you're not quite normal, are you? I want to know what it's like, to be taken by such a creature," he mumbled as he loosened his pants and lifted his member toward her mouth. She felt his hands' rough, greedy taking.

She choked and coughed. Nothing she could do. Kept glancing at the shadows in the back. Kept counting. *One, two, three, four, five.*

That admonition yet again, *No, you mustn't die.*

She disagreed. Dying would have been better. She stared at the tattoo on his arm—a blue mountain with a few jagged crags, but within it the face of a tiger with jaws open, revealing teeth. Moments later, she heard the others utter his name, fear in their throats. Shan Hu. So that was what the tattoo was about, 山虎, Tiger in the Mountain.

There were two carts close to the edge of the canal. The goods from the barge were loaded into one, then the other, leaving a tiny space in the second where she was shoved, just another piece of stolen property. Ling crouched in the cart, crammed in with crates of jade vessels and rattan cylinders of tea. Her body hurt from cuts and bruises, her fine clothes were soiled and torn. The only window in the cart was a hole as wide as her face. Crates sat between her and that tiny gap, but she managed to catch glimpses of the passing landscape as the team of horses galloped away from the barge toward the centre of town.

As the cart rattled over the rough road, her body tossed back and forth, Ling grew numb to the physical pain, gripped instead by memories of the raid. She and her parents had started out from their tea farm in Hubei outside of the city of Jingzhou, and after travelling by land, took the Grand Canal northward on the Yangzi River to Shaanxi province. They finally arrived a few li outside of Huazhou town just at sunset. Her father had decided they would transport their goods via the canal the next day. They were all tired, especially the horses and men. A trip along the canal would be a welcome change after weeks of travelling overland. They would rest overnight before their final journey to the Western Capital.

That night, sleeping between her parents, Ling felt excited at the prospect of visiting Chang'an for the first time. She was lulled to sleep by the soft slapping sounds of water against the sides of the barge.

A few hours before daybreak, mayhem ensued when their barge was invaded by bandits. Ling glimpsed her father's terror-filled eyes as he was stabbed in the back. She and her mother were dragged from their sleeping cabin up to the bow of the barge. They were forced to watch all the slain men being thrown overboard. Her mother tried to shield her as they huddled on the deck, but Shan Hu dragged her mother away while one of his henchman held on to Ling.

She could never forget how her mother looked when she was brought back, her clothes torn, her hair dishevelled. Shan Hu laughed and threw her down next to Ling. Her mother, sobbing, whispered to Ling, "Forgive me." She grabbed the knife from Shan Hu's belt and slit her own neck.

In the cart, body racked with pain, Ling sobbed at the memory. There was no more reason to live. Where was Shan Hu taking her? What would he do with her? A life enslaved to someone so vile was not a life she wanted to live.

When they entered Huazhou, the sunlight came through the tiny window of the cart at an angle. Ling glimpsed streets with people moving about, unaware of her captivity.

Had she imagined it—her mother coming to her in the water and embracing her? Did her mother bring her to the surface, willing her to return back to the land of the living? *No, you mustn't die.*

The butterfly was minuscule, its wings a creamy white. The tips of its forewings seemed razor sharp. The butterfly flitted through the dusty haze of the town's public square. Ling imagined that the creature must have come from some other world, far purer than this tainted place she was in. It had navigated rough terrain, slipped past thorny branches in some distant forest.

The market was unbearably loud. Ling wished she could shrink down to the size of that butterfly and fly away. Her face and arms hurt from bruises and cuts. But the worst pain was inside her throat and in her chest. Even if she escaped, where could she go? She sighed heavily, noticing that her mouth was dry and tasted like metal.

It was still scorching hot, even though the sun was past its peak. She guessed, judging from the angle of the shadows, that it must be around mid-afternoon. The rays of sunlight slanted in, striking faces and bodies with merciless intent. Men's bellowing voices competed with one another, jostling for the attention of onlookers, their shouts a constant hammering inside her skull. She'd been brought here early in the morning, when the air was still cool. It seemed interminable, being inundated with this barrage of sound, waiting for hours on end, not knowing what her fate might be.

Among the buyers and sellers at the auction, there didn't seem to be any taking of turns or orderliness, merely the chaos that came with the momentum of greed. Men yelled out prices as the children for sale were paraded on the platform, one by one.

The smell of others' fear engulfed her; the older boys, the women, and the rest of the children all reeked of panic. But she couldn't smell her own fear. Although it was hot, her teeth clattered against one another. Ling curled her hands into fists, determined to show an unwavering dignity.

She looked down at her feet. There was a cut on her right big toe that stung. Her captor had poured some wine over it earlier, joking that spirits cured every ailment. She ached from hours of being forced to stand with her hands tied behind her back, her body bound by ropes. Ling hated the loose brown trousers and sleeveless top she had been made to wear. She felt dirty, inside and out.

Ling looked up to see where the butterfly was. It had disappeared. She closed her eyes, imagining how its sharp-tipped wings could cut through the ropes that bound her. When she opened her eyes again, it was as if the butterfly had heard her longing and materialized, this time flitting behind the head of the oily-skinned tavern owner. The unsavory man had taken time out from bossing his servants around and stood in front of the entrance of Prosperity Tavern, legs planted solidly on the ground, soft, doughy fingers perched on his generous hips. His eyes scanned the auction merchandise. An uneven patch of grease marred his chin. Behind him, the three-storey tavern was packed full of rowdy customers. Ling noticed a few on the upper floor leaning against the railing, wine cups in hand, surveying the action below.

The tavern owner rested his foot atop one paw of the tavern's stone guardian, opened his mouth wide, and used a blade of straw to dislodge the detritus between his two remaining top front teeth.

"Oily Face", mumbled Ling under her breath. Her stomach growled. Occasionally, Oily Face shouted out an amount of money that he was willing to pay. He was cheap and had yet to win a bid.

A servant cradling a clay basin was about to feed chicken bones with shreds of meat to the stray dogs, but Oily Face stretched his arm out in a gesture of warning and shouted, "Stinking wastrel, save those bones! For the soup!"

Interspersed with boys and girls and the occasional labourer being auctioned off were beautiful birds that Ling had never seen before. They had large hooked claws and brightly alluring green, red, blue, and yellow feathers. There was even a stunning-looking horse with a slate-grey coat speckled with chalk-white markings; its appearance was met with shouts of approval and head nodding. After much yelling between the auctioneer and interested buyers, it was sold for a high price.

Shan Hu soon took over the proceedings. Stacked along one side of the market were large crates of goods. Ling winced; the crates were marked "Tribute Tea" with the insignia of her father's business. Other crates were being opened as Shan Hu called out the items to be sold. Raw turquoise, garnets, and rocks with gold veins—goods that her parents had brought with them from their county in Hubei. Ling hated that Shan Hu's filthy hands were scooping up the precious stones to show off to the bidders. All the goods sold quickly. Then there was only Ling left.

"How much for this rare specimen?" shouted her captor, pulling her closer to the centre of the market with the rope that wound around her torso. He sniggered suggestively. "She's not going to bite! Come on, get closer for a look-see."

Ling bit her lower lip. Only dead things were specimens.

"When has anyone in these parts ever seen such a pair of eyes?"

Ling shuddered. What a fake, sweet tone. She gritted her teeth. Maybe it was good that she hadn't died. If she managed to escape, she vowed that she would return someday and avenge her parents' deaths.

Oily Face stepped toward her and unabashedly stared. Ling pulled away, mustering as much saliva as she could, aimed at Oily Face's forehead right between his bushy, unkempt eyebrows. His face took on an even more disagreeable countenance as he grimaced and wiped off the offending gob with the back of his hand.

Ling felt the hard slap of Shan Hu's hand against the side of her head. "Good-for-nothing turd! This what I get, keeping you alive?"

Even though her body was confined, she refused to be cowed. She spun around and clamped her teeth down hard on his arm. Shan Hu let out a loud yelp of pain and, with his other arm, yanked hard at the rope.

Ling was pulled backward, and her body smashed against the opened crate of precious stones. She struggled to get up, but didn't see the planks and tripped. She felt a sharp pain at her right ankle. Shan

Hu stood over her, waving a blade close to her throat. He snarled, "Behave, or I will have to slice up that tongue of yours and make a pickled delicacy out of it."

A few men in the public square laughed. But an elderly woman called out in a quivering voice, "Don't hurt her! She's a child."

Waves of tremors overcame Ling. She choked back tears, which pooled in her eyes and blurred her vision. Her hands were tied behind her back, but they discovered the edges of a stone on the ground. She closed a fist over it.

She looked past the auctioneer and saw a strange mist appear. It shimmered a light yellowish-gold. A slight movement of air stirred across the reddish-brown earth.

"Arrgh!!" Shan Hu screamed, his eyes widening as he clutched his belly and groaned. Pushed back by some mysterious power, he flew past Ling until he hit his head against some crates. Shan Hu moaned, pressing a palm against his left ear. Blood trickled from his ear down his neck.

"Sir, how much for this creature?" The voice seemed to have come out of nowhere. It carried silence within it, shattering the rowdy atmosphere. The hairs on the back of Ling's neck stood up. She turned her head to look in the direction of the voice.

Her serene face beamed down at Ling. The woman had a long mane of thick black hair that she wore in an unusual fashion, partly braided, partly coiled like a snake at the back of her head. She wore white robes with a thin purple border, black trousers underneath, and hemp sandals. She wasn't tall, but her body seemed to radiate an intense strength. It was hard to guess how old she might be. Her skin was a honeyed brown—it made Ling think of certain kinds of amber, the ones that were a darker shade. The woman wore a pendant that hung in front of her heart, a yin-yang symbol.

Shan Hu dusted himself off and turned to face the woman. "Where did you come from?" he asked. "What in Heaven's name are you talking about?"

The woman raised her tone, her eyes suddenly wide and fierce. "I said, how much for this creature?" Ling shivered when the woman's lips flared back to bare her teeth.

"I'll give her to you for a thousand strings of cash," he replied, eyeing the woman suspiciously. He took out his handkerchief and wiped the blood away from his face and neck.

"Aren't you conducting an illegal sale? She looks like a Chinese to me, not a foreigner or an aboriginal from the South. You know very well that's a capital offence."

Oily Face was grinning and nodding his head. "That's right. Execution by strangulation."

"How dare you!" Shan Hu snarled.

"How about we settle the sale with this? I promise I won't report you to my friends in the Tang court." She pulled out a silver ingot from within her left sleeve without hesitation.

Shan Hu's eyes widened in surprise. He stared at the yin-yang pendant on the woman's chest. "Aren't you clergy? Some kind of nun? Must be, dressed like that. You religious folk have peculiar habits. None of my business how you spend your money."

The woman said nothing but looked firmly at him.

"A holy person like you comes to a dirty, polluted market offering so much money for a young girl?" Shan Hu leered at the nun with a sly, suggestive look. He lost no time in reaching out for the ingot in the woman's open palm, but she pulled her hand away too quickly.

"Is that meant to be a yes?" The nun's eyes flashed brightly at him. He grunted.

She opened her palm again, the sliver ingot catching a gleam of sunlight. "Either you take this, or we'll be standing here all day playing stupid games, Insult-the-Nun or Snatch-the-Emptiness."

"Good one, good one!" came a voice from the crowd. A few onlookers laughed loudly.

Shan Hu snorted, his face puffy and red. Oily Face, watching from a safe distance, yelled out, "She's right. Those eyes are too weird. Maybe she's possessed. Do you want to risk getting caught for banditry? You know the punishment. Strangulation, huh?" He scurried back into the inn as soon as he shouted this out.

Shan Hu pursed his lips together tightly. He should take the silver. He was no fool, but he didn't like being insulted. And who in this town would dare report him anyway? But this dark-skinned woman was an outsider. Was she lying when she said she would report him?

The square became hushed as people waited to see what Shan Hu would do. He scowled and fumed in silence. Oily Face had a point. The girl had been nothing but trouble from the moment she was captured. He wasn't going to risk dragging her around to the next town.

He stretched out his hand and nodded. "All right, uh ... your ... Your Reverence."

The nun threw the silver up into the air, and Shan Hu caught it in his mud-caked hand, then bit into it, just to make sure. He sliced the ropes off Ling's hands and feet with his knife. The woman didn't lose a moment and grasped Ling's arm firmly to guide her away as Shan Hu tucked the ingot into the purse on his belt.

"Oww, oww!" Ling cringed. A sharp pain travelled up her right heel, along the outside of her calf. She lifted her foot off the ground. It hung down at an awkward angle, as if unhinged.

The nun squatted down, and gestured to Ling to climb atop her back. Ling hobbled forward. Still clutching the small stone in one hand, she wrapped her arms around the nun's neck. She was hoisted up, her legs firmly held against the nun's hips, and swiftly taken away from the auction. Ling looked back, wondering what had happened to that Heaven-sent butterfly. It had vanished, almost as suddenly as it had appeared.

When they reached a quiet alley, the nun paused at a water pump. She bent low so that Ling could climb off. Ling did not put much weight on her injured foot and limped toward the water pump. Her mysterious rescuer cupped some water in her hands and offered it to Ling who took a tentative sip then quickly drained all of it. She hadn't realized until then how thirsty she was. She drank two more offerings of water in the same manner.

The nun sat on a rock and wiped her forehead with a handkerchief. She picked up a stick and with it wrote two characters in the reddish-brown earth, 奇蘭, saying as she did, "My name is Qilan, Rare Orchid. You may call me by this name only when we're alone. But in front of others, please call me Sister Orchid."

Ling simply nodded, aware of an inexplicable feeling welling up in her chest. What was it? It was soft and tender, that sensation. She looked at the characters written on the ground. Without a doubt, there was only one meaning for Lan, which was Orchid. But the first character was an entirely different thing altogether; it could mean either rare or strange. Wasn't it sometimes the case that a strange thing was also rare, rising above the ordinary, making it much more noticeable? But not all strange things were rare, surely.

Qilan passed the stick to Ling. "Now, show me your name."

"Ling," the girl replied in a brisk tone and shook her head in refusal. She withdrew her hand and clasped the small stone more tightly in her fist behind her back.

"Yes ... but which one?" Qilan politely insisted.

More head shaking. Ling gingerly passed the stone to her other hand but was still unsure. She cast her gaze toward the ground and thought of her mother admonishing her never to reveal the actual word behind the sound of her name. Her mother had told her to let others assume which character it was. *To let others know your true name is to let them have power over you.*

She looked at Qilan's face, which seemed to radiate irresistible warmth. It was hard to say no to that.

"I ... I ..." Ling blushed, feeling awkward. Her hand reached out and took the stick. She finally wrote her name next to Qilan's, 靈.

"Ah ... Spirit or Soul."

Head still lowered, Ling felt a slight smile come to her face, despite her nervousness. She would leave it at that. Let the nun think whichever one was right.

"Come on, hop back on. I'm going to take you to a quiet inn where I will tend to your injury. Then we must eat." Qilan bent down so that Ling could climb up.

As Qilan walked, Ling closed her eyes and leaned into Qilan's back. She was dizzy with hunger and pain.

Behind them, a light movement of air passed over the ground and erased their names, lifting the hem of the nun's robes ever so imperceptibly.

They wound their way through what felt like a dizzying maze of alleys. Only an occasional breeze provided relief from the heat. Ling felt buoyed along, as if the nun was not so much walking as floating. A light, sweet scent wafted from Qilan's hair. It made Ling think of apricots.

Ling looked at the long shadows cast against the wall by the last rays of the sun. She and Qilan formed a silhouette of a beast with two heads and a large curved hump on its back.

By the time they reached a teahouse off the main path, Ling's face felt hot, and she wheezed a bit from the heat and dust. Unlike Prosperity Tavern, the teahouse was a modest affair, its thatched roof in disrepair. A rough piece of wood for a sign above the entrance read Idle Tea 閒暇茶.

The innkeeper rushed out from behind his counter and greeted Qilan with several bows in quick succession, his hands clasped together in deference in front of his heart. The man looked pronouncedly desiccated and reed-like, and his bows were so vigorous that Ling thought he just might break into two at any moment.

"Sister Orchid, it's been a while since you passed through! So honoured. How auspicious. Please give my greetings to Abbess Si."

This zealous deference intrigued Ling. *You'd think she was some kind of royalty*, she mused, *the way the old fellow was bowing.*

The teahouse had five tables, but only one was taken up by a couple of elderly men. Dried Reed seated Qilan and Ling at the back near the windows that looked onto an inner courtyard. Ling gazed out at a young boy who was picking at his nose with relish, while half-heartedly minding his charge of two chickens and a pig. Behind him was a stable. Through its open doors, Ling spied a donkey and two horses—one chestnut-coloured, the other a soft grey—and an old man with a sparse goatee tending to the horses. He caught Qilan's gaze and nodded at her.

Qilan addressed Dried Reed in a firm tone. "We will leave immediately after our meal." She licked her lips and furrowed her brow. "Let me think ... bring chicken fried with leeks, steamed salted fish with egg, green beans with fermented soybeans, three bowls of millet. Any summer garlic? Add a dish of your house pickles." The innkeeper nodded then scurried off to the kitchen.

Ling placed the unpolished turquoise on the table.

"Your pet?"

Ling didn't answer. The intimate tone made her uneasy.

"Place your foot here," gestured Qilan, patting her lap. "I warn you, this will hurt, but I must fix your ankle."

Ling cautiously lifted her right foot onto Qilan's lap. She gripped the sides of the stool in preparation. Qilan cradled the heel with one hand then rotated the foot with the other, at first gently, then swiftly, resulting in a sharp clunking sound. Ling gasped loudly. The room began to spin. She steadied her hand against the table, sat up straight, and took a deep breath. She felt her heart speed up. She looked away from Qilan, trying to distract herself with the antics of the boy in the dusty courtyard. He was scattering millet husks and clucking, as if he too were a chicken.

Dried Reed approached their table with a tray holding a large clay teapot and two cups. Ling's nose picked up the strong smell of the tea as it was poured. It was not the same tea as the one she'd lived with all her life, but it was close enough. It had hints of pine, slightly smoky. It reminded her of home.

Ling shook her head vigorously. "I can't ... the smell ..." She threw up a watery mess into the spittoon beneath the table.

Dried Reed snarled disapprovingly. "Your friend has no tongue to wag, but look how well she retches." He bent down cautiously and extricated the filled spittoon.

"Quite the aim."

Ling wiped her mouth on her sleeve. She lowered her forehead onto her hands on the table.

The innkeeper returned with a large tray filled with dishes of food along with three bowls of steaming millet.

She raised her head off the table and stared at the food. Her stomach rumbled loudly. "Nuns eat meat?"

"Why, that's the most you've spoken so far!"

Ling's lips quivered. She tried to stop herself, but the sorrow rose up to her throat, and she began to heave in long, loud gasps. She bent forward and covered her face with her hands, then gave herself up to unrestrained sobbing.

"Merciful Heaven." Qilan pulled out a mala from inside one of her sleeves and began to chant. Satisfied after doing a round of repetitions, she smiled and stood up and sniffed the array of food loudly.

Next, she scooped portions of food and millet into a bowl and beckoned to Dried Reed. "Give this to my trusty assistant." Then she turned back to address Ling. "About the meat—let's just say that I'm not the usual kind of nun. I do indulge occasionally. Especially when I'm away from the temple on some errands." Qilan's eyes gleamed as she dipped a finger into the sauce and licked it clean.

Ling wiped off her tears and stared intently at the speed at which Qilan picked up pieces of chicken dripping with sauce and stuffed them into her mouth, grunting as she chomped.

The tiniest soft crease formed on Ling's forehead, just between her eyes. She stammered, "Wh-where are you from?"

Qilan, mouth full, replied, "Da Fa Temple in Chang'an. And you?"

Ling turned her head away to look out at the courtyard. "Far from here." She shuddered as the flood of memories welled up.

"Come, drink this cup of hot water before you feel the urge to throw up again."

Ling took a sip of the hot water. A tremor passed through her.

Qilan put her bowl and chopsticks down and sipped some tea. "Ah, I feel better now." She burped twice. Loudly. "What happened to you? Where is your family?"

"Gone." Ling stared into the cup of water.

Qilan waited. The silence stretched on.

"Attacked. Father ... murdered. My, my m–m-mother, she ... the bandit, he ... and then ... she slashed ... " Ling brought her hand up to her throat and gestured to Qilan what had happened. She felt an ache press against her chest. For an instant, she was her mother, and the pain of dying overtook her.

She coughed uneasily and stared at the darkening sky outside the inn. The centre of her being felt hollowed out, as if she was no longer there physically, no more than an unfettered spirit. Ling reached for the piece of turquoise on the table and clutched it in her right palm. It was the only thing she had that reminded her of life with her parents.

"No other family?"

Ling shook her head. "What's next? Where ... " Words had deserted her.

"Give me your hand." Qilan pointed to Ling's left hand.

Qilan lightly pressed the fingers of her own hand at Ling's wrist. Then she released and waited while Ling transferred her pet turquoise to the left hand. Qilan took Ling's pulses on the right wrist.

Qilan gently gathered both of Ling's hands, cupping them between her own, so that their hands closed in together, the turquoise securely in the centre of Ling's palms. Ling felt a vibrating pulse travel up both arms.

"Now, keep your hands closed." Qilan used her thumb to press a spot halfway up between the wrist and elbow on the inside of both of Ling's arms. Qilan burped three times in succession, then stood up, went behind Ling, and placed her thumbs on either side of her neck at the base of her skull.

Ling closed her eyes and felt her breath grow deeper. The nausea slowly subsided. "More water. More. Thirsty," she mumbled.

The donkey in the courtyard brayed. The boy nattered on to his chickens. Up and down in pitch went his voice, the boy imparting the most important details in soft, round sounds. Ling drank all the water. She looked out to the courtyard and saw that the old man was now sitting on a wood stump and eating.

"Feel better?"

She did feel better, but she didn't want to look at Qilan or answer her. She looked down at the cup nestled between her palms. She was nervous, all kinds of thoughts racing through her mind. "Why did you save me?"

Qilan smiled. "If someone needs help and I can assist, I don't hesitate to act."

Ling's voice wavered with emotion. "I ... don't know ... how I could repay you."

"No need to repay."

"Where will I go?"

"I'll take care of you. I didn't rescue you from the auction to then abandon you," Qilan assured her. "Eat up now. Before the food gets cold. Then we'll start our journey toward Chang'an."

Ling blurted out, "I must return here some day. To kill ... "

"Kill?"

"The murderer."

"Was it that foul man I took you away from?"

Ling nodded.

"Your thirst for revenge might not remain this compelling as time passes." Qilan took a slow, loud sip of tea.

"I must."

"If you still feel so insistent in a few years' time, I promise you, I'll bring you back to Huazhou."

"Help me kill him?"

"Didn't say that. I'll bring you back to ferret out that despicable lout. Then you'll have a chance to decide what you want to do."

Ling was dumbfounded. The only reason she would seek him out would be to kill him. Or at least die an honourable death while trying to do so.

"Your parents would want you to be happy, rather than be poisoned by your sorrow and anger."

Her body quaked. *How would you know what my parents want?*

"Your task now is to get strong."

"Will you help me become strong?"

"Yes."

Ling put the cup of water down on the table because her hands were shaking too much. All that she had known was now lost to her. She resolved that, with Qilan's help, she would get strong, so strong she would be able to slay Shan Hu one day.

THE INNER PALACE AT TAIJIGONG, NORTH CENTRAL CHANG'AN

Your Majesty," the Empress coyly whispered as she sidled up to Li Zhi on the couch, "you know how hard it's been, since those awful women ..." She took a quick breath in and held it for a few moments.

The Emperor grimaced. He did not like to see Wu Zhao unhappy. She could be so lovely when she was in a good mood, but when she was displeased she was capable of the worst rages. He shuddered at the memory of her last episode.

He dismissed the maids-in-waiting and turned his attention to placating her. He carefully repositioned a sable cushion behind Wu Zhao's head and stroked her left hand. "My dear, what else do you wish me to do? After all, I let you have your way with them."

The sides of Wu Zhao's rouged mouth turned downward in a dramatic show of displeasure. "There's something else you haven't done! You know what it is, surely?"

This made him nervous. He leaned back against the couch, a cleverly constructed frame of tree limbs in the shape of a dragon. "Tell me, my precious plum." He raised her hand up to his lips and kissed each finger tenderly. "Anything. Anything for you."

"We need to assign Luoyang as the permanent Eastern Capital. You know that, and still you delay! We must formally recognize it as on par with Chang'an. Then we could move everyone there—the court, the palace—and rule from there."

"But why would that be necessary? Such a costly move! I don't understand."

"Don't you see how being here is taking a toll on me? The lack of sleep, the nightmares, those ghosts."

"I have only your word that the ghosts even exist. Are you suggesting we uproot the whole court and palace just because of your nightmares?"

Her face clouded over with displeasure, and she pulled her hand away, then glowered at him. "You can't afford to stand by while I continue to suffer. Look at your health lately. Not doing so well with your eyes—and the dizzy spells. You need me to help you, don't you? Why do I have to lecture you about the obvious? Can you afford to see my health suffer too? Where would you be without me?" She straightened up and added, "Besides, my sources say that Luoyang is astrologically more preferable."

"Your sources?"

Just then, the drum from the tower north of Taijigong began to beat the rhythm for the Hour of the Pig, the ergeng night watch.

Wu Zhao didn't answer Li Zhi's question. "You've been spending too much time and attention on that foolish monk. All that money wasted on translation of the sutras."

Li Zhi frowned. "Xuanzang?"

Wu Zhao pursed her lips. "We should return to our heritage.

Daosim. Laozi. Long before Buddhism came here. Let's not waste time on this religion that isn't even ours, anyway."

"It was my mother's religion. And it remains mine," replied Li Zhi, in a flat, firm tone. "Besides, our Buddhism is different. It retains our Daoist beliefs. Change, flow, timing. But of course you know all that, my dearest pearl."

He cautiously reached out and tucked a stray hair back in place behind her ear. The tension in Wu Zhao's face softened and she sighed, resting her hands in her lap. "Much to consider, isn't there, Your Majesty? But we have to leave the discussions for another day since it's getting late and I must retire to my chambers."

"Not staying here tonight?" He pouted.

"Oh, I can't. I must look in on our infant son and see if he needs me. And then I must rest afterward in my own private chambers."

Li Zhi stifled a sigh. She wasn't as interested in relations with him lately. Was it because she had another child last year? Strange, being pregnant with child or bearing children had done nothing to stave off her sexual appetites before. Maybe her sexual energies were being diverted elsewhere. He wondered with whom she was dallying. He must have his spies check on her.

He resented how much power she wielded over him. But what choice did he have? She was right, of course—he needed her. He watched as she walked out and thought that she seemed rather impatient to leave tonight. They hadn't even shared a cup of wine together.

The eunuch on sentinel duty glanced to his right along the zigzag corridor, as far as his eyes could see, counting the lanterns hanging from the eaves. He noted that there was one lantern which was battered from the festivities of the night before, its rice paper torn on one side, the frame slightly warped. An image of one of the palace ladies-in-waiting danced through his mind. This caused a shiver to overtake his body.

He was still bound up with his mind's fanciful twists when a clump of bamboo leaves to his left suddenly stirred. The eunuch felt a momentary abrasion on his smooth cheeks, as if a rough cloth had been passed over his face. He shuddered and shook his shoulders this way and that, as if protesting. His armour jangled lightly about his torso from the movement. How did that wine taste? If only he could have been allowed; but no, he was a mere palace guard and not allowed such indulgences. He sighed.

Silly, snickered the travelling funnel of energy. It wanted to laugh, but then that would have alerted the eunuch to its presence. Once the wind reached the Empress's private chambers, it swerved adroitly around the first screen, past the outer receiving chamber, then down a short hallway, past a second screen and through a long hallway just before arriving at a final screen. Safe from spying eyes, the wind next spun out like a vortex, casting off its invisibility. It unfurled the shell and entered from the top, filling out the human form.

Xie strode lightly across the room to where the single lamp was lit on the round marble table. To where Wu Zhao sat waiting.

When she saw him, she laughed. "You know, you have the tally that you could use to enter Taijigong. Why resort to your trickery?" It never failed to delight her—how he could enter the palace and escape detection.

"The usual way? It's too obvious and, you must know, rather boring."

Xie was dressed all in black, but his eyes shone brightly, reflecting the light from the candle at the table where Wu Zhao sat. His skin was pale and glowed with youthfulness, even though he was past fifty sui.

With his slender fingers, he pulled out a small red silk pouch from inside his sleeve to present to her. She stuck her fingers into the pouch and felt the object. It was cool to the touch. She closed her eyes to concentrate better. Some kind of animal. She pulled it out of the pouch and exclaimed with delight, "A xuanwu tortoise! How clever of you!"

The jade creature fitted in her palm so perfectly that when she closed her fingers over it, the stone seemed to warm on her skin. It had the body of a turtle but its tail looked different. All coiled up, like that of a snake.

"Yes, the Dark Warrior will assist us in conquering our enemies."

Wu Zhao studied the outline of Xie's face. It was changing with each progressive day of his experiment, and she was enthralled and enticed by his mysterious capabilities.

Xie held her gaze. She trembled, her whole body knowing that he was completely unafraid of her.

"My calculations are that we will reach the most auspicious moment for a grand public ritual for you in about six years' time." He smiled and wrapped one hand around her neck, drawing her closer to him. The edges of his mouth turned up ever so slightly. "Many things need to happen before then," he continued.

She gasped at how intently he was staring at her throat. He could choke her. He could do anything. Her face flushed with excitement and she groped for his member beneath his gown. He moaned and nodded his approval.

"For a start," he said, "we need to acquire a certain oracle bone. It belonged to your father."

"You know about it?"

"I've heard, yes."

"And?"

"I believe it could be useful." He paused and tilted his head slightly, as if trying to release a knot of tension in his neck.

"It's being kept at my half-brothers' uncle's place. Most know him as Hsu the Elder, who runs a martial arts school in Huazhou. Some of my father's belongings were moved there when he died."

She felt the thrum of her body resonate with his rising desire. He undressed her and carried her to the kang. "What do you want to do with it?"

Xie's eyelids fluttered, half distracted by the waves of pleasure moving through him as she stroked his thighs. He didn't answer.

She persisted. "Tell me why you'd care about a piece of bone."

"You know it isn't just a bone."

She glared at Xie and stopped her fervent stroking. "Alright. I won't lie to you if you don't lie to me. The bone was unearthed in a pit near Mount Li. My father was given the bone by Gaozu. Now it's your turn to tell me—why are you interested in it?"

"I believe we can use it, Your Highness. Six years from now."

"Use it for what?"

"Feng and Shan rituals." He smiled lewdly at her.

Wu Zhao's eyes widened. The shape of her lips told Xie that she was now quite aroused. He parted her thighs and used his fingers to penetrate her. His jade stalk now fully engorged, he grasped it at the base and entered her without delay. He dug his fingers into her buttocks and began thrusting.

After they climaxed, Wu Zhao pushed Xie off her. She wiped the glistening film of sweat off her breasts with a linen handkerchief.

"This oracle bone ... and the idea of Feng and Shan rituals ... how exciting," she whispered breathily, then turned to face him. "I've been sitting dutifully behind the veil, acting demure, when in fact, everyone knows I make much better decisions than he ever could! I'm sick of the fake deference. How much longer before the pathetic man becomes totally useless? I must become ruler of this empire." She sighed softly to herself, as if she were envisioning that day.

"It is a simply matter of timing," Xie said. "Your fate was forecast. How could any human stand in the way of Heaven's decree? Those old diehards need to get used to you making more and more of the important decisions. You also will need to have the Emperor publicly sanction you as his equal between now and the time when you assume full power. What better way to do it than in conducting the rituals at the most auspicious moment?" Xie took her hand and laid it back on his jade stalk. She resumed her rhythmic stroking.

"That hasn't been done since Emperor Guangwu of the Eastern Han."

"Not in the past six hundred years, no, not since his reign. But you, my dear, will succeed." His tone wasn't tender, but determined and unapologetic.

"Just a few obstacles ... a few," she murmured, thinking of those who stood in her way, seeing the faces of the men who were part of the aristocratic bloc, the supporters of the former Empress Wang, men who continued to despise her victorious elimination of the competition.

She climbed on top of Xie, closed her eyes, and placed her palms against his bony shoulders. "You will obey me. Most definitely." She bent down and licked his nipples, then bit down hard on each orb.

He writhed, pretending to be in pain.

HUAZHOU

Why don't you stay overnight and leave tomorrow?" offered Dried Reed.

"We mustn't delay." Qilan offered Dried Reed more copper cash.

The innkeeper took the coins, enough to buy a few more chickens and pigs, and bowed deeply at the waist.

Old Chen was already waiting with the horses in front of the stables. Qilan took the brown scarf from around Old Chen's neck and wrapped it around Ling's head, tucking her shoulder-length hair underneath it.

"You'll be a boy for the rest of this journey, until we reach the temple."

Qilan mounted the grey stallion and hoisted Ling up to sit behind her. Old Chen rode beside them on the chestnut mare that looked almost as old as her rider with its wobbly gait and deeply curved back.

The sun was just about to disappear below the horizon. Instead of taking the direct route, Qilan led them upward, on a narrow path. The landscape was barren with hardly any shrubs or bushes. Large rocks loomed on either side of the path. Qilan tilted her head to draw their attention to the swirl of dust below, on the lower road. Three men on fast steeds raced down the road heading toward Chang'an.

Ling could tell by the look in Old Chen's eyes that he was surprised. Yet he said nothing. They continued to ride slowly, at an ambling pace.

Up ahead to the northwest, a grove appeared like an apparition, an anomaly in the dry landscape. Qilan signalled them to stop about a hundred paces away and dismount.

"A magical forest," remarked Qilan, in a matter-of-fact tone. "We will travel through it."

Qilan walked toward the grove, leading her horse by the reins. Ling looked at Old Chen, uncertain. But Old Chen simply shrugged and gently touched Ling on her shoulder, urging her to follow.

Draped from the lowest branch of a tree was a strip of cloth. It flapped in the dim light, as if waving to them from some other realm.

"What does it say?" asked Old Chen.

"Just a Daoist charm. It says that this forest's magic will lead all our fears to become manifested as strange beasts."

"What?"

"Oh, I knew that." Qilan continued, "We will travel through the night until daybreak."

Ling and Old Chen looked worriedly at each other. They walked into the woods just as the very last rays of light in the sky faded. Ling could smell the change. *What was it?* she wondered. She felt the air caress her face, the back of her neck and wrists.

They walked for a long time. The moon was several days past new, not quite half yet. They heard the cry of an owl but couldn't see it.

"Let's now mount our horses and ride at a steady pace. Follow me," said Qilan. She helped Ling get back in the saddle then mounted her horse. Ling wrapped her arms around Qilan's waist.

"Stay calm and don't stray from the path. Old Chen, we must control the animals and not let them bolt. Remember—this is a forest of illusions. It will read our deepest fears and create visions from them. Yet none of these visions will hurt us as long as we treat them as mere illusions."

Even though it was summer, the night turned remarkably cold. The partial moon soon disappeared behind clouds, and it became nearly impossible to see ahead. Waves of soft scuffling sounds occasionally travelled through the underbrush.

Qilan began to chant. Her voice was clear, its deep timbre carrying far ahead of them. Ling had never heard such a chant before, but it soothed her.

A winged creature swooped toward Old Chen. His chestnut mare took fright and reared back. Old Chen held the reins firmly and managed to subdue her. The raptor swerved just a hair's breadth away from his face, swiftly disappearing into the darkness. Panting heavily, the old man could barely find the breath to whisper to his mare, "Quiet now, steady."

Qilan continued to chant, unperturbed. Apparitions assaulted their senses, one after another. They pierced through the surrounding darkness, as if they were being illuminated from within. A spotted deer suddenly materialized, blocking their way. Its mouth opened to expose the faces of countless human babies. Qilan bade her horse to proceed. Ling felt a strong urge to scream but remembered Qilan's admonition to stay calm. She covered her mouth with her arm. They passed through the deer apparition. Ling looked back. Nothing but darkness. She caught her breath in sharp, shallow bursts.

Were those visions simply a product of their fears? Just as Ling had that thought, a serpent unfurled its length from a branch, its forehead bearing a tattoo exactly like the one on Shan Hu's arm. She had to do something. She reached down to the small knife tucked into the side of the saddle, pulled it out, and raised herself up, intending to slash at the hateful vision.

Qilan grabbed hold of Ling's hand. A burning sensation at her wrist forced Ling to release her grip and drop the knife. It fell to the ground with a muffled thud.

They were almost out of the woods when Qilan stop chanting.

"That piece of cloth caused all that trouble, didn't it?" asked Old Chen.

"No, it merely told the truth. The real danger resides in our minds," answered Qilan.

Old Chen scratched behind his left ear. Having been frightened out of his wits, he was grateful that they were all unharmed. And he was going to take Sister Orchid at her word without understanding how a forest could have such magic.

They found shade and let the horses drink from a stream. They must have travelled many hours, for there was a small hint of approaching dawn in the lightening sky. Qilan sat against the trunk of an old tree.

Ling's body trembled with an overwhelming force. Her legs wobbled when she dismounted, so she carefully made her way toward Qilan. Without saying a word, Ling lay down on the ground and rested her head in Qilan's lap. The last thing she felt was the comforting brush of Qilan's hand against her cheek.

When Ling woke up, the sun was peeking out from the edge of the forest. She noticed how sunlight brightened the dew on the lichen that spread across the bark of the tree.

"We're not going to proceed just yet," announced Qilan.

"But Chang'an is so close. I mean, I understand why you took the upper route just now, but ..." Old Chen raised his thick white eyebrows. They wriggled about, like two worms with disparate identities. It seemed to Ling that they were like brother and sister on the old man's face, quite at odds with each other. This made Ling smile.

"I need to spend a few hours alone to regain some energy before we can proceed. We may have to linger here yet another night, until the next morning. I will have to see how long I might need."

"How about ..." Old Chen began to say something.

"Those men on the lower road?"

He gulped nervously and nodded.

"We'll be safe here. There'll be no one here to attack us, human or beast. Safer to linger, in fact, than to rush back to the city now."

Qilan left them and clambered down a trail at the edge of the cliff until she found shade under a large overhang. She sat cross-legged and seemed to sink into an immobile state.

Old Chen disappeared for a while, carrying a spear he'd fashioned from a branch. Ling, meanwhile, fell asleep once again. By the time Old Chen returned, the sun was halfway past its zenith. He'd killed a hare and brought it back slung over one shoulder. He flung the carcass down unceremoniously near Ling, startling her awake. He then threw down a handful of wild mushrooms.

Next, he went to one of his saddlebags and fished out a gourd. He handed the gourd to Ling. "Fill this with water."

Ling carefully made her way back to the stream, took off her straw sandals, and rolled up her pants. She walked into the water. The ankle that had been injured was still slightly swollen, but at least she could put some weight on it without excruciating pain. The stream's cold water came up to just below her knees.

Small fish nipped at her feet, which began to tingle, a ticklish and slightly uncomfortable sensation, but it pleased her that she could feel her skin, rather than remain numb. She splashed water on her face and arms, filled the gourd, and walked back.

Old Chen had collected some rocks and made a circle with them. He threw in some dried twigs and started a fire with flint and metal. "Luckily for us, I had another spare knife in my other saddlebag," he quipped to Ling. "And look, some taro and hazelnuts."

They munched on a few nuts while Old Chen worked. He stripped the hare of its fur, sliced it open, and removed the viscera before washing it out with water. He rubbed the inside of the hare with coarse salt, which he kept in a pouch that hung from his belt, threw in hazelnuts and mushrooms and the taro that he had sliced into rounds. He plucked about ten peppers from another small pouch.

"Here, smell this. Sichuan peppers."

Ling drew close to Old Chen's open palm and inhaled. The spicy smell was intoxicating and made her choke.

Having finished his preparations, he wrapped the carcass with twine and secured it along a sturdy branch, which he rested between the pronged branches he had fashioned and driven into the ground. He fed the fire with more twigs and broken branches, then beamed with pleasure at his makeshift spit.

By now it was dusk and there was still no sign of Qilan.

"Why won't she say ..." Ling whispered to Old Chen, huddling close to his rugged form as he roasted the hare.

"She's not like the rest of us. Knows lots, but likes to keep things private."

"Why?"

"'Cause some folks are dumb. Got to keep the wisdom away from the stupid, that's why."

Ling admired his simple faith in Qilan. She relaxed, leaned against the old man, and inhaled deeply. She liked the smell of his clothes. She didn't mind the stains on his sleeves, still fresh with blood from the kill. She could trust that smell; death and life all mixed in together, undisguised.

Old Chen took a swig from his goatskin flask and spat the liquid out in a fine spray onto the roasting carcass.

Ling was startled. "What was that?"

"Toad Tumulus. My favourite."

She must have looked puzzled because Old Chen continued. "Bet you don't know what a tumulus is, do you? It's a burial mound." He chortled loudly. "Imagine, what a name for a delicious ale! I say, life is made juicy with death. Here, try some."

She shook her head vigorously.

"Suit yourself. More for me then." He took a large gulp of the ale.

Ling stared at the hare's carcass roasting in the flames. The smell of the meat seasoned with nuts and mushrooms made Ling feel even hungrier.

Old Chen took the hare off the roasting spit and placed it on a rock. He sliced the grilled meat with his knife and placed a piece on a large leaf, then scooped some of the stuffing onto the leaf. Steam rose from the cooked food, visible by the light of the flames. He cooled it down by blowing on it before passing the leaf to Ling. A nice breeze stirred in the night air, and it nudged at the scarf covering Ling's hair, revealing a few loose strands. Old Chen smiled wistfully. When he finished eating, he got up and walked over to his mare. Speaking softly to her, he fed her and Qilan's horse a few hazelnuts.

Old Chen returned to the fire with a wooden xiao flute and sat back down. He began to play the flute, his eyes fully closed. The melody that emerged was like water flowing. It reminded Ling of the stream nearby. The melody was punctuated with occasional full, sharp notes, interruptions in the peaceful and pleasant flow. *Nothing is beautiful forever*, she thought. It made her sad. She quickly wiped her tears away, not wanting Old Chen to see.

When Old Chen finished playing, he dropped the flute into his lap and cut another piece of meat for the girl and one for himself.

"I know Sister Orchid for about six or seven years now. Way back when she was about twenty-one sui. Much older than you are now." Old Chen looked quizzically at Ling, half-expecting her to tell him her age. But Ling stayed silent.

"The brave girl ran away from home. Proud to say, I was the one who heard her knocks and opened the side door for her." Old Chen looked around him cautiously, checking to see that the nun was not within earshot. He continued, sinking his voice into a whisper. "I get bits of gossip from the other nuns. Don't you go repeating that I told you."

Ling shook her head adamantly.

"Her father is tight with the Empress. I mean, she *really* likes him." He winked. "People say he was a nobody before that. Struggling scholar, paid little—so many of those types nowadays, all the brains, but useless. He worked in the department of music and astronomy, collecting star charts. Tidied up all those sheets of music they have stashed in the bureau in the Eastern Sector. Heavens, all those dusty scraps of paper. Some bamboo scrolls in fragments. I don't get it, how come music and stars in the same department? But that's the gossip. Who knows if it's true."

Ling licked her fingers as she ate, listening with rapt attention. Old Chen paused to chew the meat. He murmured his approval and smacked his lips with satisfaction. "Mmm ... I'm a good cook, don't you think?"

She nodded and smiled with a quizzical expression. "And then?"

"Here's what I heard." Old Chen paused with a faraway look in his eyes, lit by the flames of the fire. "Before Qilan showed up at the temple, when she was a girl, she dreamt that her father was lost one day in some strange, isolated place. She told him about the dream, saying she feared for his life. She begged him to retire from serving the government so that they could move to a small town far away from Chang'an. But Xie took no heed of his daughter's dream and refused." Old Chen took a large swig from the water gourd, and burped not once but three times.

"You ... you burp a lot. Then you talk. So slowly."

"Hush now with your complaints. You're not too talkative yourself."

Ling bit her lip and lowered her eyes. Old Chen seemed not to notice Ling's sudden change of mood.

"Patience, girl. You're not going to be going anywhere fast."

Ling blushed.

"As I was saying, Xie didn't take her warning seriously. You know, some folks are too smart for their own good. It's pride. Poison—all you need is a titch inside your body—it spreads like a disease and soon it slays you. Invisible-like. The man's the head of his household, and here's his daughter telling him to drop a stable government post, just because of a dream? So he thinks it's ridiculous." Old Chen chortled and almost choked on a piece of hare, but gulped down some water just in time.

"So then ..."

"What do you know—next thing, she falls ill. And I mean she's hanging on for dear life. Fever for a hundred days. Isn't that something? The rest of us would have died after a week. Doctor came to the house, tried his best, but you know how bad it was when even he shook his head and couldn't say much more than 'make her comfortable.'"

Old Chen lowered his gaze, took another gulp of water, and thumped his chest twice. His voice sank to a whisper. "Heaven got angry. She tried to interfere with Fate by trying to pull that undeserving father away from his destiny. That's why some big sacrifice had to be made. In the end, he knew he had to do it. He went to a temple to pray for her recovery. She'd have died if he hadn't done that. Had to be." He nodded his head with a weighty solemnity and grunted.

Ling stared hard into the flames, the heat stinging her eyes. Was that really the reason Qilan fell ill? Because she didn't go along with Heaven's will? She reckoned if she asked Old Chen whether he thought Qilan deserved to fall deathly ill, he would say no. And yet he was invoking the traditional idea that Heaven punished or rewarded based on wrong or right actions.

"You're not making sense. First you say he was poisoned by pride, ignoring his daughter's advice. Then you tell me that Heaven punished Qilan for interfering with Fate. Which one is it?"

"Whoa—that's the most words I've heard from you!"

A shudder passed through Ling and her face burned with rage. What if she applied the same logic to her life? What had her parents done to deserve their deaths? Was Qilan guilty of interfering with Fate when she rescued her from the auction? Maybe Heaven had no say in punishing or rewarding; maybe it was human beings who decided whether there was going to be hatred or mercy.

Ling stared into the darkness. Qilan was somewhere out there, but what exactly was she doing? From a distance came the faint hoot of an owl.

"They say," Old Chen continued, "that the temple was haunted, and Xie sold his soul there in order to save his daughter's life. A pact with the Spirit World." He suddenly looked worried, his bushy eyebrows furrowed. "Qilan recovered. But when she opened her eyes, she no longer saw the man she'd known as her father."

"What do you mean?"

Old Chen shrugged his shoulders. "I'm only telling you what I heard."

Ling frowned, deep in thought. What had Qilan noticed about her father? Did he look completely different? Or was it something less obvious but still noticeable by those closest to him? Ling had many questions. She vowed that one day she would ask Qilan.

"Instead of feeling happy that she didn't die, our friend Qilan was horrified to learn that her father had sold his soul to save her life. How did our beloved Sister Orchid decide to view the whole disaster? She believed that she was made to fall ill by the demon, and that was how her father ended up getting trapped into losing his soul!"

"You know how Sister Orchid thinks?" Ling was skeptical. Would Qilan have shared these thoughts with others?

Old Chen nodded and took another swig of the ale. "That's what I heard. Sister Orchid told Abbess Si recently that she believes it was her father's love for her that was at the root of the tragedy. She was saved from death and, in return, her father was lost. I just don't know ..."

Ling was wide-eyed. Why would Qilan feel guilty? Her father had made his choice! Ling took a drink of water and accepted more food from Old Chen. "Is he dangerous?"

A rustle of leaves overhead led them both to suddenly look up, although it was too dark to see.

"Of course the fellow's dangerous. If you're possessed by an evil spirit, you're going to do more harm than regular bad folks."

This made Ling recall Shan Hu's menacing presence and the way he used his whole body to threaten everyone around him. Was he possessed too?

"So you're saying that if a person sells his soul, that means he gets possessed?"

"Uh-huh."

Old Chen caught sight of Ling's puzzled look in the glow of the fire. "You know what else? Xie got promoted two years ago and is no longer slaving away in that music and stars department. There's juicy gossip, uh ... her father isn't really working for the Emperor. He's ... he's ... oops, wait, wait, maybe you're too young to hear this." Old Chen paused and stuffed more food into his mouth.

Ling had had enough. She poked Old Chen in his ribs with her elbow. He pretended to double over, clutching at his sides in a mock show of agony. She liked the way he did that so convincingly. She gently slapped him on the top of his bald head. There was a moment in which they both froze, watching for a reaction from the other, then Old Chen giggled.

"Tell." She poked him again.

"What?"

"Tell me everything!"

"Xie is the Empress Wu Zhao's lover."

"Oh?"

"They're up to no good."

Old Chen picked the remaining meat from the bones and wrapped the leftovers in a large leaf. He secured the packet with twine.

"Remember, it's none of our business. Just gossip, is all."

They were silent for quite a long time, then were startled when Qilan appeared. She said nothing to them and refused the meat that Old Chen offered to her.

Old Chen threw some blankets on Ling as she settled in for the night. It didn't take long for her to fall asleep. It was as if her body still craved sleep. She roused for a brief moment when she felt Qilan stroke her hair and adjust the blanket around her.

Later that night, Ling saw a wild dog come up to her and circle three times around her. She wasn't afraid, just aware that this animal was watching her intently. Was it a friend or an enemy? She couldn't tell.

The Inner Palace at Taijigong, North Central Chang'an

Surely it was an illusion, something she misperceived in that half-asleep state, when she stirred momentarily and glanced into the mirror next to her kang. Her image seemed not to be entirely tethered to her; suddenly its outlines quivered. Wu Zhao could have sworn her reflection started to enlarge. It leapt out from the mirror toward her. She crossed her arms in front of her face and cried out, "Ah Pu, Ah Pu," her voice stripped of artifice, exposed and vulnerable.

The maid appeared, not betraying any sign of surprise or anxiety. In silent obeisance, the devoted maidservant patted Wu Zhao's shoulder. She was used to Her Highness's nightmares. She fetched a cup of water for her mistress who sat up straight, eyes wide with alarm.

"It always passes," murmured Ah Pu.

"Another bad dream. Although I wonder ..." Wu Zhao's voice trailed off before regaining a firmer tone. "Keep the lamp lit," she commanded Ah Pu.

After making sure she had tended to her mistress's needs, Ah Pu left the room to return to her sleeping chamber behind the screen. Wu Zhao didn't want to fall asleep. She willed herself to stare into the mirror. Her mind struggled, trying to make sense of why this was happening. Was this all a figment of her imagination? Was Li Zhi correct to imply it was all in her mind?

She screamed. Ah Pu came rushing back in. "What is it, Your Highness?"

A dirty red streak stained the front of the mirror, and the smell of blood permeated the room. Ah Pu gasped at the sight, stunned.

"Summon the guard, quick!"

Ah Pu scurried out and in short measure, the eunuch guard arrived. Even he was shocked, his face ashen. His legs felt weak as he bowed to Wu Zhao, bending down to the floor on one knee.

"Get rid of that mirror. Now!" She was furious but didn't know whom she could punish. "I cannot rest until this is taken care of," Wu Zhao mumbled to herself after the guard left.

The candle on the far table suddenly sputtered and its flame lengthened to three times its height. Wu Zhao grabbed the cup next to her and flung it at the candle. Both the cup and the candle fell to the floor.

You think you got rid of us, did you? a woman's voice whispered in Wu Zhao's ear.

On the kang, Wu Zhao curled her knees up to her chest and wrapped her arms tightly around her legs. Her mind raced back to the time when the former Empress and the concubine Xiao were killed. An idea soon came to her. "Summon the guard who got rid of the former empress and concubine Xiao!" hissed Wu Zhao at Ah Pu who shook her head in confusion.

"Ignorant woman!" Wu Zhao said. "The head guard! The one I demoted to position of gardener. He's now somewhere in the workers' quarters. Ask anyone guarding the corridor! They will know. Immediately!"

Ah Pu once again ran out, relieved to be away, if only temporarily, from her mistress's chambers, which now reeked of rotting flesh.

Wu Zhao wanted to punish someone. Would it be the former head guard? She shivered as the memory of that fateful night came to her. She had seen her enemies' decapitated heads—he had brought them in a box to show her. All the body parts had been burnt down to ashes. How then could the women have returned when their heads were separated from their bodies?

She remembered the Abbess Si at Da Fa Temple. The muscles in her neck stiffened, and her face flushed with annoyance. The nun had been far too obliging to be believable. Hadn't the Abbess reassured her that the exorcism would work? Wu Zhao scowled.

It seemed to take forever, but finally the former head guard appeared before her. He prostrated before her. "Your Highness."

"Do you know that the women formerly know as Empress Wang and concubine Xiao continue to pester me as ghosts?"

"A guard showed me the mirror with the blood, Your Highness."

"How did you get rid of their bodies?"

"I burned them as you had instructed, Your Highness."

"What did you do with their ashes?"

"I took them outside of Taijigong and scattered them into a tributary of the Wei River."

"If you are lying to me, you will lose your life."

"I give you my oath, Your Highness." The former head guard clasped his hands together and said in an unwavering voice, "It is my duty to serve Your Highness in whatever way you see fit."

After the gardener left, Wu Zhao gritted her teeth together. She was not going to be defeated by these stubborn ghosts. She was the one who was alive, who had the power to do as she saw fit. *Ghosts are merely ephemeral*, she told herself. But a shiver passed through her, nonetheless.

THE VICE HAMLET,
EAST CENTRAL CHANG'AN

There was not much you could tell from the outside, except that a gold insignia emblazoned on both front doors proclaimed that the current owner of the mansion had the last name of 謝, which meant gratitude. Some people joked that the ideograph was actually 邪, insinuating that the Empress's current favourite, Xie, was less than honourable, or worse, evil.

The previous owner had been an official who had fallen out of favour with the Court and exiled far to the south, to an inconsequential outpost. Ever since claiming his mansion, Xie relished creating a private world of meaning and pleasure, a dreamscape to fulfill his particular needs. He cared about decorative details, such as the gold insignia on the front gate doors. He stripped the rooms of all evidence of the previous owner and replaced the art with his favourite calligraphic pieces. He named his home Rogues' Mansion, a name shared only with his inner circle. Those bold enough to gossip about Xie would comment that his appearance had been undergoing unusual changes in the past few years, insinuating that only a sorcerer could make himself more youthful and stronger with the passage of time.

The Vice Hamlet was accustomed to deviance, but even so, to suspect that a sorcerer lived in their midst was unsettling for some—but not those who benefitted from vice. The Hamlet contained the city's quota of brothels and was resplendent with various tattoo and drinking establishments. It wanted for nothing. Even spiritual appetites could be indulged here; the area included places of worship for Buddhists, Daoists, Nestorian Christians, and Zoroastrians. The respectable existed alongside the bawdy and illicit; which was why Xie felt so at home here in the Vice Hamlet. Unlike the rest of Chang'an, the dusk curfew was never in effect. It was as if the Vice Hamlet was a whole world unto itself. Xie knew he was scrutinized while at Taijigong. But the working residents of this special hamlet weren't trying to be anyone but who they were.

The mansion's large reception hall faced south across the outer courtyard. This was where Xie received visitors. Two guards always stood watch at the hall and answered knocks on the large main gates.

In the middle section of Rogues' Mansion was an area accessible only to his special guests. In the hall facing the middle courtyard, Xie had commissioned an enormous mural stretching three bays wide. It depicted a magical paradise, inspired by the classic *Shanhaijing* 山海經, the background of clouds rendered gorgeously in delicate shades of blue, grey, and cream. In the foreground drifted maiden fairies in diaphanous gowns, riding deer. Beasts like the Nine-Tailed Fox, the Awestruck, the Banereptile-Niece, and the What-Not Fish, roamed forests, mountains, or oceans across the impressive mural.

On that evening, the cicadas were particularly loud. Xie stood in the middle courtyard, facing the mural in the large hall, lit up with hanging lanterns. He watched the writhing figures of his guests entangled with one another.

"Master Xie, why won't you come join us?" cried out one of the women.

He laughed. "Not yet. I'm waiting for some people to arrive."

Soon after the drums had sounded the Hour of the Dog, he heard the echo of the secret knock from the side entrance.

Three men in dark trousers and tunics entered, their faces concealed by large bamboo hats. They followed him along a series of corridors to a room in the northern part of the mansion, far away from the orgy.

They removed their hats and bowed to Xie.

"Where is it?"

The senior man clasped his hands together in front of his face. "Master, we were overcome by a powerful asphyxiating mist when we entered Hsu the Elder's school."

"You dare return without the oracle bone?" He slapped the man, who went flying sideways across the room.

"Tell me everything!" Xie roared.

The two other spies fell to their knees and kowtowed frantically, hitting their foreheads on the stone floor to show their need for the master's forgiveness. The senior spy crawled on his knees to join the other two, his lower lip bleeding.

"When we reached the school," the senior man said, "a freakish golden smoke rolled out past the open doors of the entrance. It ... made the air around our bodies so damp we didn't know what was happening. Our skin felt like it was being stung by a thousand bees. We couldn't breathe. We all got very dizzy."

Another spy added, "We stumbled through this smoke and crossed the courtyard into the main hall. Hsu the Elder was slumped over in his chair, and every one of his students was either slouched forward or lying down on the ground, dazed. We threw water on Hsu's face, but he was barely able to tell us where the vault was. The vault door was open without any signs of forced entry. There were jewels inside. Jade pieces. Some gold. An opened mahogany box with a yellow velvet-lined interior. But no oracle bone." The spy hung his head low, looking ashamed.

Xie frowned. "None of the other precious objects were taken?"

"No, Master."

"Did you search for clues in town?"

"We asked around, but no one could tell us anything."

One of the other spies piped up. "The owner of Prosperity Tavern said there were a few odd occurrences at the auction that same afternoon ..."

Xie had believed these men to be the best, yet here they were offering him irrelevant tidbits. This should have been straightforward. He dismissed the spies and returned to the middle courtyard, but his mood was ruined. He sneered at the pile of inebriated bodies in the hall. Leaving them, he entered a corridor that took him to the very back of his mansion, where he unlocked the doors to his private study. No one else was allowed here.

Xie shut all the outer windows, making sure none of the servants could look in. Sitting down on the edge of his daybed, he bent forward, whispering as if to himself. "I'm still, still not ..."

You promised me. Don't be silly.

Xie gasped, feeling his throat tighten. He shuddered violently.

I don't like how you have these episodes. Relapsing to your former self.

Xie struggled up from the daybed and stood in the middle of the room. He wrapped his arms around his torso and began to spin until he dissolved into a whirlwind. A funnel of mist escaped from the top of his head. Xie's form collapsed to the floor, a hollow shell.

Bluish-white and hazy at first, the demon streamed out with a low hiss, showing its true form as it landed on all fours on the floor. It was fearsome, yet its form was not solid. It was a contradiction, both menacing and insubstantial.

The demon crouched low, its gangly limbs shivering as it shook its large head, riddled with bony, black protuberances. Its mouth emitted a constant smoky hiss of air and left a film of dew on whatever it encountered. The demon's ears were large, awkward peach-coloured flaps that could lay flat against its head or perk up straight. Its front limbs ended in long, scythe-like claws, and its back limbs bore cleft-shaped hooves. The demon's eyes were cavernous absences from which orbs of bluish-green light occasionally glowed.

The world is dirt, it whispered to the air as it scurried around the room caressing the legs of chairs and furniture with its front claws, and making rasping sounds as it searched the shadows. It took comfort in being outside of Xie's body. The man still had a few stubborn episodes, resisting his progressive transformation.

The demon hissed. Only the oracle bone would catapult its transformation to the ultimate and irreversible state. These past few years, disguised as Xie, it got close to the Empress, winning her confidence and learning the whereabouts of the oracle bone from his informants—all that had been rather simple if tedious. But acquiring the bone was supposed to have been straightforward as well. Who was the culprit who had beaten the spies to it? What was to be done? How would it find the bone?

The demon had needed time to fulfill its wishes. There, at that abandoned and ruined temple, it had suffered for eons, waiting and waiting to attract the human who would accept the bargain. In the meantime, it had performed acts of mischief by roaming far and wide in its invisible state, whispering unsettling thoughts into the ears of humans, tempting them to darkness. But those interferences afforded a small measure of satisfaction compared to having found the human who'd agreed to a full possession.

It mustn't lose sight of its ultimate mission. Now that it had the use of Xie's body, it would succeed eventually. With time and the progressive infusion of potions, it would gain complete power of this human's body and turn it into something far more powerful than each of them would be on its own. The transformation might take a few more years, but what was that compared to the length of time it had already been waiting?

I almost had it, the demon growled. Vexed, it crept back into the centre of the room and once again became a hazy vortex that re-entered Xie's shell through the top.

Xie came to very slowly and shook his head, covering his ears with his hands. He heard a loud humming that was almost deafening, and shivered as the cold wind inside his body surged through all his cells. Xie blinked several times then sneezed loudly, not once but four times in quick succession. He pulled out his handkerchief and blew into it, then looked at the border, where it was embroidered. *Such a fine piece of handiwork.* He sighed as a memory arose, unbidden. He heard a faint whirring in his brain, as if some wheel-like contraption was set into motion. *There you go again, being nostalgic for your past life.*

The muscles in his chest tightened and he felt a touch of queasiness. Xie went to the large dark rosewood cabinet in the far corner and opened its doors. He pulled out a leather pouch and, reaching into it, broke off a chunk of the resinous material; using tongs, he passed it over the candle flame until it smoked. Then he dropped it into the palm-shaped bronze vessel on the table behind him. He sat down and waved the smoke toward his face, inhaling deeply.

He sniffled and blew his nose again on the handkerchief. The demon complained, *Why do you still fall prey to old habits? Sentiment does not befit a vessel of mine.* Xie felt tremors throughout his body, compelling him to take action. He rose from his chair, pulled a knife from a drawer, and shredded the handkerchief. Xie felt a sudden wave of sadness. A tear streamed out of his left eye.

Your human heart is a troublesome beast.

A muscle along his upper right cheek started to twitch. Xie took a few more deep breaths of the smoke. How long would it take before all traces of his memories and his love for others were eliminated? He didn't mind forgetting many things, but there was one person he especially didn't want to forget.

Of course he'd been desperate to save her.

He had trusted the scholar, whom he'd mistakenly regarded as a friend. "There's an enchanted place," the scholar had disclosed. "Go there, for only that kind of power will save her. Just be prepared to sacrifice, for this will cost you."

Xie rode off in the direction of the temple. By the time he arrived, it was dusk. *Curious,* he thought, *hadn't it been only late morning just moments ago? What had happened to the usual progression of time?*

It was Feast of All Souls, the fifteenth day of the seventh lunar month. He had expected the temple to be busy, but it was instead shrouded in a sullen darkness. He dismounted from his horse, recalling the scholar's instructions to do so, and walked along the path leading up to the temple entrance. The path was at first barely visible, obscured by thick, gnarled creepers, but these gave way as he headed toward the temple.

"To the Demon God of Literature" read the dusty, cobwebbed sign atop the entrance. Xie stepped through the threshold into the cavernous space. Light from the full moon streamed into the hall. A low murmuring reverberated through the temple, followed by a wind that stirred the cobwebs and tickled Xie's right ear.

I've been waiting for you.

The voice sounded disconcertingly like his, except that it possessed a jagged edge, like a knife that could sever bone in an instant. The strength drained out of Xie's legs, and he fell to his knees. He couldn't budge. He wished he could flee. As soon as he thought it, the moaning wind in the temple roared, *You cannot escape me.*

The teeth in Xie's mouth began to chatter loudly. He folded his arms in front of his body and gripped his elbows.

Chilling, aren't I?

"Wh ... who are you?" Xie stammered, asking the question with what little energy he could muster. He felt a force descend onto him and push him down until the side of his face smacked the stone floor.

I am Gui.

"What, what do you want from me?" sputtered Xie, as he curled up into himself, feeling the force hold him down.

Your allegiance. Henceforth, my voice will be your voice. I'll spare your daughter on one condition. Let me fully inhabit you and alter you. You won't complain if I make you very famous and powerful, surely?

"What do you mean, inhabit me?"

Your family will not recognize you any longer.

He winced. How could he do such a thing? And yet, how could he live on if his daughter died from her illness? Sweat formed at his brow, and he felt a chill travel down his spine. "You say this will save her life?"

I never lie. And you will become very powerful.

Xie swallowed hard and nodded.

Was that a nod of assent?

Xie's heart raced with fear and urgency. His life was at stake. But his daughter lay dying. He couldn't ignore this chance to save her. He nodded again, very slowly, deliberately.

A blue shadow rose up in front of him. Then he felt a piercing sensation at the crown of his head, as if he were being split apart from the top down. He screamed as an indescribable pain shot through his body.

Xie lifted his head from the table, returning from the recollection. The resin had completely burned down, and the sweet haze hung in the air, continuing to cast its effect on him.

In the distance, the bell from the eastern tower sounded, and there were cries from the alleys outside the mansion, announcing the time. Already the fourth watch.

He left the room and returned to the middle hall. Everyone slept or lay in a drunken stupor. He surveyed the bodies. A prostitute's face was momentarily lit by the flickering flame above her. *She has such a sweet, serene face,* he thought. It reminded him of someone. His jade stalk stirred. He closed his eyes and dug his fingernails into his trembling thighs.

OUTSIDE THE FOREST OF ILLUSIONS

Still cool out, and not even dawn yet. Ling rubbed her eyes and saw Qilan smiling down at her. "Time to get up, we're heading out soon."

Like Qilan and Old Chen had done, Ling wrapped a scarf around her face so that her nose and mouth were covered.

Qilan set a fast pace now. The route took them through a landscape of dry, wide regions, the low hills in the distance pockmarked with cave dwellings.

They approached Chang'an, their clothes covered with a layer of red dust, as the sun was just rising above the horizon. In the distance, the city of terracotta walls loomed. There were travellers ahead of them—carriages and caravans, as well as those riding horses or donkeys. As they drew nearer to the large Chunming Gate, Ling could see the burly guards questioning incoming travellers before allowing them to pass.

They entered the city and rode along the main east-west thoroughfare. Qilan said, "They say that this is the largest city in the world."

Ling had never encountered anything like this. Chang'an was unlike Jingzhou city, close to her parent's tea farm. Here the city walls were so tall that they cast long shadows. Heat emanated not only from the sun overhead but from bodies both human and animal, jostling for space on the wide avenue. Such noise! So many colours! Different kinds of faces: men with turbans and thick beards, women in bright, flowing robes wrapped around their bodies, and unfamiliar fair-skinned people who rode in caravans. Large buildings lined the main thoroughfare, some with signs she could read. They passed many places of worship that looked grand and overwhelming, like beasts that were dormant but might rouse given the right encouragement.

They continued to ride along the thoroughfare, passing through gates in the high walls that separated one ward from the next. Soon they entered the Western Sector and passed by a large market, noisy with thronging crowds. They turned into side streets, travelling at a more relaxed pace. Here were narrower wooden buildings, most of them two storeys high. Many front doors stood open, and children and elderly folk milled about in the alleys. A sprinkling of ground-floor shops sold wares or offered cooked food. A strong whiff of fried spices followed by a trace of sweet tobacco smoke made Ling sneeze. There were clean, earthy smells as hot water evaporated from just-washed cobblestones, in contrast to the rank odours of stray dogs.

When they turned into a deserted alley, Qilan angled her body back to speak to Ling. "Do you know who now reigns on the Throne?"

"Emperor Li Zhi."

"He has been ill. His Empress rules in his stead."

Old Chen snickered. Qilan continued, "The Emperor was never a strong man, from his youth. He has made it worse for himself by indulging in vices. His current Empress is one of his greatest vices."

"What are vices?"

"Things people do to waste their vital essence."

"Why would people do that?"

"Because we're stupid. That's why," piped in Old Chen.

Ling stared at Qilan. "Do you have ..."

"Of course."

"Like ..."

"Most of my vices are invisible to others."

"Like?"

"If I told you, they wouldn't remain invisible." Qilan winked at Ling.

Ling blushed and felt awkward. "Where does the new Empress live?" she asked to change the subject.

"North of the city. Right at the very edge, outside the northernmost wall. The Imperial Palace Taijigong is its own walled city."

"Have you ... seen her?"

"No. Our Abbess has, though. I hear that she is quite beautiful."

"You're beautiful," Ling whispered, leaning forward against Qilan's back.

"Girl," Old Chen mumbled, "stay away from that murderous vixen. She killed the Emperor's former empress and concubine after having them viciously tortured."

"Shhh!" admonished Qilan.

Ling recalled Old Chen's story. She wondered where Qilan's father lived. Was he also at Taijigong?

At the end of the alley, they turned right onto a wide street with a few residences between rows of shops. In the middle section of this long street, on their right, was a large compound fenced in by low walls of unfired bricks. Inside, partially visible above the walls, was a square structure with a domed roof.

Qilan and Old Chen dismounted and helped Ling off the horse.

"What's that?"

"It's a fire temple," replied Old Chen.

Ling followed Old Chen and Qilan as they led the horses to the compound across from the fire temple. The compound was ringed by walls made of slatted wood. She looked up at the large sign above the entrance. Da Fa Temple 大法寺.

The doors at the entrance were open, which afforded a view of the beautiful garden inside. Ling's attention was quickly drawn to the formidable temple guardians on either side of the entrance—larger-than-life wooden figures that resembled neither human nor beast, one with its mouth wide open, and the other with mouth closed.

Old Chen led both horses around to the back, where the stables were. Qilan and Ling stepped through the main entrance.

Ling was startled by the silence. There was a mynah bird on the roof and a few chickadees on the gravel path, feeding on small seeds.

She looked around. "Where is everyone?"

"They are likely doing a quiet meditation at this time of day."

"Is it always so quiet?"

"Often. Sometimes there is chanting, or the bell is rung." Qilan pointed to the bell tower to their right.

Qilan walked ahead, and Ling followed her through long hallways, as they turned many corners.

"Here," Qilan said, stopping at a large set of vermillion doors. "The Abbess Si's study. Let's wait here. When they are finished with their meditation, she will return here."

The Abbess was not long in arriving. She was an older woman, her hair already all white but kept tidily in a similar kind of braid as Qilan wore. There were many wrinkles around her eyes, but her smile was warm.

"Sister Orchid, welcome back. You've brought a visitor." The Abbess opened the doors to her study and they followed her in.

"Abbess Si," Qilan clasped her hands in front of her chest, palms together, and bowed deeply. "Look who I found."

The Abbess looked amused to see the bedraggled young girl sitting on the low couch, biting her nails. She studied Ling's face intently. When she noticed Ling's eyes, she exclaimed, "The Langgan!"

"Exactly."

This made no sense to Ling. *Who, or what, was this Langgan?*

"Welcome, my child."

"Her name is Ling."

The Abbess placed her hands lightly on Ling's shoulders and continued to beam warmly at her. "Ling, since Sister Orchid has brought you, she will be the one to have primary responsibility for you. Of course, everyone here will also look after your needs and teach you the ins and outs of our daily life."

Then she turned to look at Qilan. "Did you succeed ..."

"Yes, Abbess."

"Good."

DA CI'EN MONASTERY,
SOUTHEASTERN CHANG'AN

Halfway into the Hour of the Snake, Harelip paused in front of the open doors of the Translation Hall at Da Ci'en Monastery, the Monastery of Great Maternal Grace. He'd been on his way to the apothecary with a basket of hops, sweet wormwood, and lily buds, but he felt a powerful need to halt and listen. The young monk was mesmerized by the deep yet chime-like voice of the Master.

On a dais on the raised platform at the front of the hall was the Venerable Master Xuanzang, the Abbot of Da Ci'en, the famous monk who had returned to the country after sixteen years away. Around him, sitting in a circle, were the twelve monks appointed by Imperial edict to assist him with the work of translation. Below Xuanzang and his group of learned monks, seated on cushions on the floor of the Hall, were twenty-four monks in eight orderly rows of three. Right behind Xuanzang hung three gigantic scrolls. The scrolls outlined the requirements of those who assisted in the vast translation of the Tripitaka—the collection of Sakyamuni Buddha's teachings—that Xuanzang had brought back from India.

Xuanzang struck the brass bowl, letting the sound echo through the spacious hall until its reverberation completely disappeared. He struck the bowl a second time. Once again he waited until silence set in, before the third and last strike of the brass bowl.

Harelip's ears welcomed the rich and melodious drone of Xuanzang's voice reciting the lines that always began each day of translation work in that Hall.

The unsurpassed, profound, and wonderful Dharma,
Is difficult to encounter in hundreds of millions of eons,
I now see and hear it, receive and uphold it,
And I vow to fathom the Tathagata's true meaning.

Xuanzang turned his attention to the slim palm leaves resting on a low stand in front of him. He cleared his throat and took a deep breath. He placed his finger on the first line on the top of the palm leaf and delivered aloud his translation from Sanskrit into Chinese at a slow, deliberate pace, pausing at the end of each line. His circle of monks then proceeded to do their work: One monk transcribed what the Master said in Chinese, and then the two monks next to him checked their copy of the sutra to verify whether Xuanzang had read the Sanskrit in the correct order and not missed anything. The fourth and fifth monks verified that the correct Chinese ideograms were used. The sixth monk in the circle was Huili, Xuanzang's esteemed assistant and biographer. He faced Xuanzang directly; the rest of the monks on the platform, as well as Harelip, could see only his back. Huili and three other monks conversed with the Master, responding to the lines with questions about the meanings of the translated sentences. After the Master and these monks were satisfied with the resulting line, the whole process was repeated with the remaining lines on the palm leaf. Three monks served as sentence arrangers, making sure the lines thus recited were written in correct order. Huili, using the third available copy of the sutra in Sansrkit, also served as the overall revision supervisor who oversaw the whole process.

Harelip observed a lot of energetic debate between Xuanzang and his team of translators, who rustled papers and scribbled lines. He was fascinated by the process. After Xuanzang and the twelve assistants finished the work of translating lines, the final and approved sheet of

Chinese translation was brought down to the copyists sitting on the floor below.

The first monk in the first row copied the text, then passed the original translation to the monk to his right. Hence, each translated sheet travelled like a snake, winding its way along the row of three copyists to the next row behind them. Meanwhile, each row of monks had produced three copies of the original. These were collected by a junior monk. The original translation, after passing through the last and eighth row of monks, was collected by another monk. Two monks laid out the papers in a grid on a long table, replicating the seating arrangement in the hall, so that they could keep track. In this way, Xuanzang's translations were transcribed then copied, resulting in one original copy and twenty-four others.

Harelip lost track of time, mesmerized by the repetitive rhythms that pervaded the hall. It was not the first time he'd witnessed this ritual. He mumbled a few lines that he could hear the Master say, trying to follow along. It was the long version of the Heart Sutra, and this was the first time it was being translated from Sanskrit into Chinese.

While the copyists focused on their tasks, Xuanzang continued with his translations, adhering to the same orderly process in the circle of twelve monks. Whenever Xuanzang completed a translation of a palm leaf, he turned the leaf over and placed it on the empty cushion to the right. There was a pause as the Master took a long sip of tea.

Xuanzang's thunderous voice suddenly rattled Harelip out of his reverie. "You, back there! Gawking at me? Looks like you're mouthing my words. Come here and show me what's in your basket!"

Everything came to an abrupt halt. All brushes were laid down. Silence in the hall.

Harelip swallowed hard and with his free hand felt for the smooth beads of the sandalwood mala under his robe. With the thumb and first finger of his right hand, he advanced from bead to bead as he meekly walked up along the narrow aisle on the left, approaching the Master.

A whiff of incense tickled his nostrils. He squinted, pressing his eyelids tightly together. *No, it mustn't happen*, he said to himself. Despite his resolve, the impulse overcame him, and a loud volley of sneezes echoed through the spacious hall. Harelip wiped his nose on his sleeve. The monk to his right giggled.

Xuanzang stared hard at Harelip's face. "So, you're the one they told me about, the one gifted with knowledge about herbs."

Harelip knelt down before the venerable monk, and freeing his arms of the basket and mala, flung himself down to make three prostrations, after which he knelt. Keeping his gaze lowered, Harelip replied, "Venerable Master, I am the one who now occupies the apothecary near this hall. I just moved in there a few months ago. I used to work in another section of the monastery."

"I've been told you have great ability."

Harelip blushed, feeling awkward. His teacher, who had taught him so much, was now far too old to work. Yes, he knew how to listen to the complex workings of bodies. He was told he had a talent for concocting brews and infusions. But he never boasted about his abilities.

"I have been receiving assistance from the Imperial physician, but to no avail. I want to see what you could do for me," said Xuanzang.

Harelip couldn't conceal his surprise. Choosing him over the Imperial physician?

"I don't mean right now. As you can see, I'm busy. But soon."

"Yes, of course, Venerable Master. You may summon me when it is convenient for you."

Dashu 大暑 Jieqi,
Great Heat,
Sixth Lunar Month, Full Moon

DA FA TEMPLE,
WEST CENTRAL CHANG'AN

L ing sniffed the air. The dormitory smelled of incense. *Must be in their robes and even on their skin*, she thought. She liked the smell of the incense. As far as she could tell, everyone else in the large room was asleep. Moonlight streamed in, and it made her feel restless.

It had been two weeks since she first entered Da Fa Temple. By now, Ling was familiar with the various sections of the temple, the kitchen next to the common eating area, the three meditation halls, small study rooms, and the dormitory in which almost all of them slept. Then there was Old Chen with his son and daughter-in-law and young granddaughter, who lived in the small building next to the main temple building. Old Chen and his son did all kinds of chores for the temple—buying supplies, caring for the horses and donkeys, and doing repair work.

Ling surmised that three nuns held the most power at Da Fa Temple: Abbess Si, Sister Lizi, and Qilan. Their quarters were separated from everyone else's, and aside from that first day when she sat in the Abbess's study, she had yet to enter any of their private rooms.

Ever since she'd arrived at the temple, she had not shared a private moment with Qilan. She wasn't sure why not, after all they had been through. But Qilan always smiled at her whenever she saw her. Yesterday, Qilan had come up to her at the mid-morning meal and said that they would soon spend some time together.

Everything still felt like a dream to her. A very painful dream. She cried herself to sleep most nights, thinking of her parents. She didn't know how long it would take before she could feel entirely at home here, if ever. And yet, from the very first day, the nuns seemed to treat her as if she was one of them. She could call half of them by name now and was discovering their quirks and preferences. Ling had always been a good observer; she learned best that way.

She'd grown more comfortable following the nuns' schedule. For each of the three daily chanting periods she sat in the section with all the novices, even though she did not wear nun's robes but an off-white hemp gown they'd given her. Qilan sat with the Abbess and Sister Lizi on the raised dais, facing the rest of them.

More than once she'd wondered who would succeed the elderly Abbess Si. Would it be Qilan or the Abbess's assistant, Sister Lizi? Was that her real name, or did the nuns name her that because of her appearance? She had a smooth, small face and a firm, curvaceous body with generous hips—like a pear.

Ling was getting used to sitting on a cushion on the floor. There were always sheets of paper on the tiny, low, angled table placed in front of each of them. Xu, one of the novice nuns, sat on her right and showed her what to do. Tonight's sheets had been different, like nothing she had seen before. She tried to read the words, but she didn't understand the kinds of sounds the nuns made. Why did they pronounce the words that way? Some words weren't even legible to her. So she surrendered herself wholly to the sounds, not knowing what they were chanting. Time disappeared, and she'd felt herself carried along on the rhythms of their voices.

Ling stared at the moonlight streaming through the window lattices. The shadows cast on the sleeping forms in the dormitory made them look not quite human. She heard the sound of cicadas from the garden. The room was stiflingly warm, yet she shook from head to toe from an inner chill. Ling wished she could be close to Qilan now, soothed in her embrace. Would that ever happen again? Ling sighed. She needed Qilan. There were still so many things she wanted to tell her, things she did not dare to utter since she'd lost her parents. She touched a hand to her cheek, recalling how it had felt to be asleep close to Qilan and soothed by her presence after they had emerged from the Forest of Illusions.

She tossed about on the straw mat. The nun in the bed next to her was talking in her sleep. It was a mantra, perhaps, repetitive and droning, but given a passionate delivery.

Ling rooted inside the pocket on her gown and felt the edges of the small turquoise gem. It was the only thing she possessed that was connected to her past life with her parents. It had become a quiet friend, one who didn't speak the way humans spoke; nonetheless, Ling felt a close, wordless bond with the stone.

She reluctantly surrendered to her sleepiness and closed her eyes. Her inner field of vision was hazy at first, as if obscured by mist or veils. Her mother came to her. She climbed into the bed with her and placed her arms around Ling, snuggling close. *Remember why we chose that name for you? You exist beyond this form.* Ling jolted out of her half-asleep state and sat up, heart pounding hard in her chest. She drew up her legs and clasped her hands around her knees, looking furtively about the room. Had her mother actually come to her?

Her mind cast back, as it often did, to that fateful night on the canal. She could have sworn that she hadn't imagined it—that her mother had swum toward her and pulled her back up to the surface of the water in the canal. *No, you mustn't die.* Those were her mother's words. She was meant to survive—she could feel that in her bones now. She mustn't tell anyone. Not even Qilan. No one would believe her. But she believed what she had experienced.

Ling took in the hushed sounds around her, and after feeling calmer, lay back down. Close to dawn she fell asleep and quickly descended into the dark, murky water, drowning yet again. She woke up covered in sweat. A sliver of cold air sliced into the skin of her neck, and she cried out.

"What's the matter?" Xu came to her side and squeezed her hand.

"Where are my parents?" Ling demanded. "What have you done with them?" She lashed out at Xu, hitting her, but Xu remained calm and shook her vigorously by the shoulders.

"Wake up, Ling. You were dreaming! You're here at Da Fa Temple. Remember?"

After the midmorning meal, Sister Lizi, with her usual dour expression, led Ling through many corridors and across two inner courtyards until they reached a wing of the temple at the northeastern corner. They saw no one else as they walked down the corridors. Ling watched the nun's shapely body jostle ahead of her, her straw sandals slapping the stone tiles. Sister Lizi knocked on the door, and Qilan's voice responded quickly. "Enter." Sister Lizi opened the door for Ling and left immediately.

Qilan stood facing what looked like a tiny courtyard. She turned around slowly and asked, "How did you sleep?"

Ling shook her head briskly. "I ... I didn't sleep well."

"So I've heard. Seems you've been having nightmares almost every night since you came here."

Ling didn't answer but looked keenly at everything in the study. She then craned her neck to look past Qilan. She could see past the lattice doors; outside the study was a small garden and beyond that, the wall that demarcated the temple from the outside world. Other than the occasional human voice, Ling heard the braying of an unhappy donkey interrupt the plodding rhythms of horses' hooves and the frequent rattling sounds of cartwheels travelling the cobblestoned street.

Qilan motioned to Ling to follow her into the garden. They sat there side by side on stone stools. Qilan silently pointed out a caterpillar on the underside of a camellia bush and extended a finger out to it. Soon it crawled onto Qilan's finger. She looked at Ling. "You're like this caterpillar, still early in the cycle of transformation."

Ling stared at the creature. She didn't like that she was being compared to an ugly worm. She crossed her arms in front of her chest. "Don't get it."

"The *Daodejing* says, 'To become whole, let yourself be partial. To become straight, let yourself be crooked.'"

The caterpillar crawled up Qilan's hand to her wrist and under her sleeve.

"Oh wait, what if ..." Ling's face softened.

Qilan took Ling's hand. "Reach for it underneath my sleeve—palm up, like this. Slide your hand up."

Ling was nervous but did as she was told. When she was almost at Qilan's elbow, she felt a tickling sensation against her fingers, then the creature crept into her palm. She withdrew her hand.

It was a miniature orange butterfly with bright blue eyes on its lower wings.

"How could that—?"

The butterfly disappeared into thin air.

"Where did it go?"

"Look under the camellia leaf."

Instead of the butterfly, Ling found the caterpillar, its pliable yellow body moving across the leafy surface.

"How did you do that?" Ling leaned forward, hands holding onto the top of her thighs.

"I transformed the caterpillar into the butterfly it would become. Then I changed it back into its original form, and moved it to the leaf. These are spells of transformation, crossing time and space and form."

Ling was stunned. Never in her life had she ever encountered such magic.

"You see, the cycle of life is not necessarily straightforward and predictable."

"But ... but, this is—"

"Impossible?"

Ling nodded, then quickly shook her head.

"Do you reject what you've just seen? Or would you consider letting go of all those notions you've grown up with?"

"Do you mean what I'd been taught?" What Qilan was saying frightened her. "This magic ... Can you bring my parents back to life?"

"That would require an enormous disruption of the patterns already laid down."

"But is it possible?"

"Yes—but it would mean upsetting the very fabric of destiny. Including yours and mine."

Qilan's solemn, slightly ominous tone frightened her and kept her from asking more questions.

"It isn't my place to bring them back. They've crossed into another realm, Ling."

Ling felt her throat constrict and tears begin to well in her eyes. "Am I meant to stay here?"

"Remain at the temple for a few years and decide later. You can take vows later if you wish to make this your path."

Sadness burdened her heart, but she looked up at Qilan. "The nuns ... say this phrase a lot, 'serve the Dao.' What does that mean?"

"It means to act in accordance with what is natural in the Cosmos."

"Was what you just did with the caterpillar ... would that be in accordance with, with the Dao?"

"That was of a different form of reality altogether. A sublime one. Yes, it was in accordance with the Dao. The great philosopher Zhuangzi said, 'South of Chu there is a caterpillar which counts five hundred years as one spring and five hundred years as one autumn.'"

"So there are things that happen outside of natural laws?"

"Outside of what most people consider as natural laws. Note the difference." Qilan raised a finger and continued. "Certain phenomena exist according to other laws. The Dao flows through us, Ling. We aren't separate from Earth and Heaven. We choose—we always choose whether to live in accord with the Dao or against it."

"And some people, like you, can do ... unusual things, but they are still natural."

"Yes."

Ling was dumbfounded. She clasped the sides of her head and bent forward so that her head was almost between her knees. She felt the blood rush down to her head, then straightened up quickly and felt a spell of dizziness. When it passed, Ling stood up from the stool, her hands clenched into fists at her side. "My parents are gone. Why did I survive?"

"I don't have the answer. Some day, you will answer your own questions. Besides, your parents aren't gone."

"What?"

"Their physical bodies are no more, but they aren't gone."

Once again, Ling felt her whole body start to tremble with the enormity of what Qilan told her. *Life and death were not separate? Death wasn't the end of life?*

"Evolution of forms is infinitely occurring," added the nun.

Ling didn't know how she felt about such a fancy comment. In truth, she felt puzzled as well as angry.

Ling squinted her eyes at Qilan. "Can you do that?"

"Do what?"

"Transform like that caterpillar. I mean, not just an illusion. I mean really change."

Qilan smiled. "It could be done. But I couldn't hold it for too long, otherwise I might not be able to return in this form."

"Will you show me how to do it?"

"Maybe. Ask me in a few years' time."

"You promised me you would take me back to Huazhou some day so I can search for my parents' murderer."

"I haven't forgotten. I will train you how to fight. In a few years' time, when you are ready to face the killer, we will go in search of him."

Ling nodded, feeling slightly calmer. That was something to look forward to. She would train her mind and body, prepare for that day, when she could slay Shan Hu. She must avenge her parents—her spirit couldn't completely be at rest until she accomplished that.

THE VICE HAMLET, EAST CENTRAL CHANG'AN

Gui liked to leave Xie's body at the beginning of the wugeng fifth watch. Late night romps were necessary. Halfway between midnight and sunrise was the time of grief for humans, when all energies in the ether were soaked in the ache of being mortal.

Comforting, Gui thought as it sniffed the damp air. The inebriated took solace in shadows, in the recesses of alleys, while the occasional thief lurked about, hoping for an easy victim. A handful of women trolled the streets in desperation. Gui paid no mind to these. Instead, with its extraordinary sense of smell, it ferreted out the pregnant women sequestered in dimmed interiors, in the midst of labour pains.

This particular night, as it crawled along the roof, spying on the brothel quarters below, Gui detected the salty scent of an imminent birth. The water had already broken, and the rusty tang of fresh blood and tissue rose up to its nostrils. The demon assumed a vaporous state and stole in between the slats of the walls, swirling along the floors.

The woman lay on the kang, legs splayed, the head of the newborn half-emerged. A midwife cupped the tiny head firmly and urged, "Just a bit more. Come on, one big push. Another one, yes ..."

The demon drew close but hovered in the shadows, waiting for the right moment. It sprung forward just when the infant emerged from the sanctuary of the womb, reached past the midwife's hands, tapped the top of the newborn's head, opening a hole into its crown, and sucked the precious hun cloud-soul away.

All the midwife saw was a fast-moving mist dart between her and the infant. One moment, the newborn was warm and alive; the next, cold and dead, a vapid, blue shell. She shrieked, causing the mother, still in a stupor, to raise her sweat-drenched head up to look.

Just as the women raised the alarm with their screams, Gui escaped through a gap in the ceiling and was back on the roof. It then made a quick tour of the city's small gardens and wooded sections, where it collected all of the spiders, snakes, frogs, lice, and centipedes it could find.

Returning to Rogues' Mansion, the demon went to the garden in the northwest corner and flung its collection of tiny creatures into a large glazed urn. A heavy iron lid kept the victims from escaping. Gui snickered with glee as it listened to the biggest snake devour the others. When the time was right, the gu poison that it would extract from the dead snake would come in handy.

It had been a fruitful outing tonight. Gui heaved with satisfaction and emitted a single long belch.

Da Fa Temple,
West Central Chang'an

Qilan walked to the southeast corner of the tiny courtyard outside her study where a cast iron claw-footed vessel sat. It was filled to the brim with water. The moon above was just past full, partially hidden by clouds. Qilan looked down at the surface of the water. She could see the stern expression she wore as she studied the movement of the clouds in the reflection.

When the moon was no longer obscured, she cupped her hands together and blew into her palms. The tiny clouds formed by her breath coalesced into a swirling sphere that she released into the water. The water's surface became taut. The reflection of the moon and clouds disappeared. In their place was an image of Xie's lifeless form propped up on the kang.

Qilan mumbled a few words into the first two fingers of her right hand and pointed them at the water's surface. She shut her eyes tightly, and her mind entered Xie's room while her body still stood at the urn in a trance. She drew near to Xie who lay limp like a person in deep sleep. She scanned his body with her eyes. His soul was missing, as it had been all the other times. Seeing Xie like this never failed to disturb her.

Whenever Gui left on one of its expeditions, it always took Xie's soul. She used to wonder if she would be able to recover her father's soul, but with each visit, her hope wore away.

There was a change in the air. Her ears pricked up and her nose detected the unmistakable scent. She exited just in time. Back in her body at the urn, Qilan watched the scene displayed on the water's surface.

Gui entered Xie's bedroom, its body glowing a bluish-green. The protuberances on its jaws bulged and throbbed as it climbed up on to the kang and re-entered Xie from the top of his head. The lifeless shell gradually became enlivened. Xie stretched his arms and legs out. He yawned, as if just waking up, blinked rapidly several times, then gave the room a cold stare.

Qilan sighed. Her father's physical form had changed so much. He had become exceedingly handsome and alluring. The illusory man looked even younger than her father had been. His skin was elastic, his whole being seemed youthful and radiant. On the water's surface, she watched as Xie's expression darkened.

He looked around and growled, "Who's been here?"

Qilan withdrew the spell from the water's surface and stood looking up at the moon to calm herself.

DA CI'EN MONASTERY,
SOUTHEASTERN CHANG'AN

Harelip awoke long before the monastery bell sounded for morning ablutions and prayers. He was anxious about having to examine Xuanzang. Last night, tense with anticipation, he drifted between wakefulness and a light rest, skirting just below the surface of awareness, and tossed back and forth on his straw mat, wishing for more sleep.

He was not going to have his way. The bell tower in their ward sounded the approach of dawn. He groaned and forced himself to get up. Glancing around in the dim pre-dawn light, he noted that his neighbour to the right wasn't in his bed. *Trust him to be so industrious.* Not even the head cook was up at this hour.

The first thing he did when he reached the apothecary was light the candles and burn incense on the small altar. He took out his mala and said mantras, tapping out the rhythm with a short stick on the wooden frog. After three rounds of the mala, he stopped and made buckwheat tea. Inhaling its mellow earthy aroma, he felt grateful.

Harelip surveyed the interior of the apothecary with satisfaction. It had taken considerable work to clean up this long-abandoned storeroom, but he was content with what he'd accomplished so far. On the shelves that ran along two sides of the room were ceramic jars and pine boxes labelled with the names of herbs. Beneath the tables were wooden boxes of herbs, also neatly labelled. On his long table, below the room's one window, were two mortar and pestle sets, a measuring scale, several wooden spoons of various sizes, and a sharp slicing instrument mounted on a sturdy box.

Harelip closed his eyes and hummed softly between sips of the tea. He sat perfectly upright on his high stool, his body becoming more relaxed by the moment, and swayed rhythmically back and forth ever so slightly as if moved by a force from within. By the time the young novice came to summon him, he was absolutely calm. He collected his satchel, stuffed it with a few essentials, and followed behind the apprentice at an unhurried pace.

Xuanzang's rooms were in the western wing of the monastery. There was a private library-study, a bedchamber, and a modest-sized reception hall where he received disciples and distinguished visitors. Harelip had never entered the Venerable Master's private rooms before. The room was faintly lit by a single candle. Now, as he approached the monk, he could smell a slight body odour. Xuanzang reclined on the divan, still wearing his night clothes. He looked very pale and tired and had a blanket wrapped around his shoulders.

Why hadn't he detected the odour that morning in the Translation Hall? He was puzzled. Perhaps the incense in the hall had masked the smell. Harelip tried to sniff inconspicuously. It made him think of radishes left out in the heat too long.

Harelip bowed low and waited.

"Come." Xuanzang's voice wavered, betraying a vulnerability that startled Harelip.

Harelip approached the divan, carefully pulled a stool next to it, and sat down.

"May I take your pulses, Venerable Master?"

Xuanzang nodded, but Harelip made sure he didn't rush. He took several deep breaths before he reached into his satchel and brought out his tiny pulse cushion. He gently took Xuanzang's right hand and positioned it on the cushion. He waited. Nothing materialized. The pulse was empty. As he took Xuanzang's left hand, he lowered his gaze to conceal his expression. When he felt the strong emotion pass, he raised his head and motioned to Xuanzang to open his mouth. "Show me your tongue."

It was pale.

"I've been feeling so weary lately. And having heart palpitations."

"Night sweats?"

"Yes. Sometimes, even during the day, I suddenly break out in a sweat. I feel very nervous. Dizzy."

Harelip thought to himself, *Kidney Yang deficiency, now becoming long-term qi stagnation in the chest.* "Have you taken herbs for your condition?"

"Of course I have, dear boy! Many kinds, over the years. Sometimes they have helped, sometimes not. Your teacher treated me, when you were a mere sprite, when you were off in some other part of this ridiculously huge monastery, training, learning, whatever you were doing."

"Yes, Venerable Master. I also served at another monastery for some years before I entered Da Ci'en." Harelip answered minimally; he concentrated on taking Xuanzang's pulses.

"Seems that nothing is helping me much these days. I'm easily tired. Terrible toll to sit all morning in the Translation Hall. It's as if my mind is mired in mud. What mud! And I'm cranky all the time, as you can judge for yourself."

Harelip withdrew his hands and placed them in his lap. He needed to be quiet for a few moments. Surely the other healers had suspected what he was finding as well. He stared down at the floor between his feet.

"Tell me the truth! How serious is it? The Imperial physician never tells me the whole truth."

"Your qi is very low, your pulses weak. It would be helpful if ..." Harelip wasn't sure how to put it.

"Go on."

"It would help if you took a long period of rest from your strenuous work. How would you wish to spend the next few years? No one can ever predict how long ... but ..."

Xuanzang gasped. "You—you dare to be honest with me. Finally, someone ..." He stopped speaking in mid-sentence, a faraway look in his eyes. "Sometimes I feel well. But then I suffer setbacks."

Harelip checked Xuanzang's pulses again. Two of them had turned wiry, like the tight strings of an erhu. "Do you feel pain anywhere?"

"Yes, but the pain doesn't stay in one place; it travels—my lower back, my knees, sometimes, or the balls of my feet. I had an attack of this burning pain two days ago."

"Do you feel cold sometimes?"

Xuanzang sighed. "All the time. Would you believe it, looking at me now, that I used to be a hardy one?"

"Yes, I believe you, Venerable Master. How else could you have endured all those years of travelling and such tremendous physical exertions?"

"I haven't been well ever since we crossed the Tian Shan range on the way back from India. Horrific doesn't even begin to describe it. Biting winds, blizzards, ice on our faces, snow all around us. Three out of ten frozen to death. That trip almost killed me. Well, it's been slowly killing me, hasn't it?"

Xuanzang fell back onto the cushions behind him. His eyelids fluttered and he sighed softly several times. His breath grew shallow. "How have I managed to tolerate it? Work distracts me, at the very least. What's the point of complaining?"

Harelip spared no time in pulling out his needles and sticking them into Heart and Lung points on either side of the Master's wrists and halfway up the inside of his forearms. A few miao later, Xuanzang began to breathe more easily.

"I can't stop," Xuanzang said, not so much addressing Harelip as himself. "I went all the way to India to get those precious sutras, all six hundred and fifty-seven of them. No time to rest. Do you understand?"

Harelip nodded. *It must be hard*, he thought, *to be so driven.*

"So don't tell me to work less. Though I appreciate your honesty."

Harelip wasn't going to argue with Xuanzang. He concentrated on periodically twisting the needles and paying attention to the sick man's breathing, the feel of his skin, changes in the various pulses he took. Only when Xuanzang's pulses stabilized and he fell asleep, starting to snore, did Harelip get up from his stool. He studied a hanging scroll on the opposite wall. The calligraphy was beautiful.

It was a stanza from a poem called "Return to Gardens and Fields," attributed to Tao Yuanming, a poet who lived more than two hundred years before their time.

Since my youth I have loved hills and mountains,
Never was my nature suited for this world of men.
Mistakenly entangled in this dusty web,
Thirteen years now.
A fettered bird pines for ancient forest,
Fish in the pond recalls its original pool.

Harelip liked how the poet used his name, 淵 yuan, in reference to the pool. How clever of him to allude to the homonym, 原, which meant "origin." He sighed, thinking of his parents and his brother.

Xuanzang stirred awake, mumbling as he did so, "Find that section quickly." Harelip turned around and caught sight of a small silk drawing on the table to the left of Xuanzang's daybed, slightly behind it. The drawing sat next to palm leaf pages of the *Mahaprajnaparamita Sutra*. It depicted a creature that looked like a turtle but without a shell. An unrecognizable script adorned the inside of the creature's body and the space around it.

"Caught your attention, hasn't it?" wheezed Xuanzang again, coughing a bit. "It's something I obtained on my pilgrimage."

"What kind of script is that?"

"It's a magical charm. I've had it all these years. Now ..." Xuanzang stopped talking.

Harelip drew closer to the diagram and peered at it more carefully.

"Beautiful drawing. Did you, uh—may I ask?—obtain this in India?"

"No. When I was delayed in Khotan."

"Curious." Harelip ventured. His head was filled with questions. He returned to the stool next to Xuanzang and took the pulses again. *Slight improvement. But only temporary*, he reminded himself. He removed the needles, sticking them into a small pincushion. He thought fondly of his mother who had made it for him many years ago.

Xuanzang launched into a story about having to linger in Khotan for eight months, waiting for replacement scrolls to be sent to him for the ones he had lost while crossing the Indus. Harelip could tell that Xuanzang relished telling the story—the storm, the calamity of fifty manuscripts falling into the river. The King of Kapisa had chided him for including the seeds of many kinds of flowers in his cargo. Xuanzang hadn't been aware of the curse—every boat that had attempted to cross that river with flower seeds in years past was subjected to similar misfortunes. Even a river could be cursed or be subjected to some kind of a spell. Xuanzang's face grew quite animated while a film of sweat formed on his forehead.

"So this was true of anyone trying to cross the Indus with flower seeds?"

"It seemed so. King Kapisa met me on the other side of the river at Hund and was surprised I hadn't known of the legend. Imagine the cost of my ignorance!" Xuanzang slapped his scalp loudly with the palm of his hand, causing a slight reddening of the skin.

Quite the storyteller, thought Harelip, *he has skilfully diverted our conversation away from the turtle diagram.*

"Venerable Master, I hope you don't mind my curiosity. I'm always full of questions."

Xuanzang nodded, a slight smile on his lips. "Exceptionally observant for a young one. Reminds me of myself when I was young."

"If you would allow, Venerable One, I will do my best to reduce the pain and weakness. But I cannot cure you of this condition. Follow my advice, and we might prolong your life a bit longer." He regarded Xuanzang with a sombre expression.

"Not only curious, but slightly impudent too, I see." A big smile stretched across the monk's face, revealing his missing teeth. A whiff of something odorous escaped. Harelip blinked and held his breath.

"All right, all right. How about I sleep a few more hours each night, meaning I won't arise as early. How's that?"

"How about you go to bed a few hours earlier? Might I also suggest more deep-breathing exercises? In addition to what you already do, of course. In that time between the second and third watch?" replied Harelip, with a suggestive tilt of his head toward the palm leaves lying on the table.

"You know my schedule, do you?"

"I am only surmising that you don't go to bed too early."

"Well, because my mind is engrossed with all the work I have to complete."

"Unlike our Emperor, who is kept up late for other reasons."

Xuanzang feigned a look of surprise, but Harelip detected a mischievous glint in his eyes.

"Do you know this exercise?" Harelip stood up and demonstrated the movements, starting with his palms facing each other in front of his belly, then separating them, stretching the arms out until one palm faced Heaven, the other faced Earth, then bringing the hands toward the centre, close to his dan tien, reversing the position of the hands as his arms stretched out once again.

"Is that all?"

"This one as well." Harelip stood in a wide stance and placed his hands on his upper thighs, twisting his torso as if to look up and back at the ceiling. "This one will help your breathing."

"How many times?"

"Start with six of each. Then work up to twelve, if you can."

Xuanzang huffed, "Of course I can."

The main drum tower in the north sounded the hundred and eight beats for the dawn watch—eighteen fast beats followed by eighteen slow beats repeated another two times. This was echoed by the bells in the central, east, and west towers in the city. The bell tower in the monastery's main courtyard soon responded with clanging. It was time for morning prayers in the Great Hall, yet Xuanzang showed no indication he wished their visit to end.

Harelip tucked his things back into his satchel, adjusted his robes, and cleared his throat, trying to hint that he needed to leave soon.

As if guessing Harelip's thoughts, Xuanzang said, "Don't worry about the morning meditation. I've already sent word we will be late."

Harelip nodded, not sure what to do next. He stood where he was, feeling awkward. What else did Xuanzang wish him to do?

"My whole life's work. I dragged those precious Buddhist scriptures back, with so many tribulations along the way. Now we're rendering them into Chinese, so that many can hear and read the Dharma and have the chance to become liberated. I know there's never any guarantee. People turn a deaf ear all the time. That's none of my business, though. I know what I have to do. So you see, dear boy, I need to live long enough to finish the work of translation. I simply must." His voice faltered, and he wheezed from the exertion. He took a few sips of tea. "And yet ... there's something in me that longs for a return to that sanctuary on Mount Shaoshi ..." His eyes stared past Harelip.

Harelip sensed the power of Xuanzang's longing. It made him think of his own.

"You know that the Sanskrit word 'tatha' means 'thusness'?"

"Yes, as in Tathagatha."

"One who has discerned the truth of emptiness. You see, I'm consoled whenever I meditate on emptiness. Especially in these trying times." He raised his right index finger. "I do meditate, or else where would I be? Dead, ages ago!" His voice sank to a whisper. "So much I don't know. Will I finish my translation work before I die? Will the Emperor continue his support of the project? I just don't know." A sigh shook his chest.

Harelip felt a twinge of affection toward the monk. "Venerable Master, in your struggles, the Dharma has given you much comfort."

"Refusing to get swept up in fears. Aren't I one to talk?"

"Your candour is admirable, Venerable One."

Xuanzang made a flourishing gesture in the air. "Never mind the flattery. Go make up some brews for me."

"Most certainly. But please remember—the brews would be more effective if you reduced the amount of strain."

Xuanzang stared at Harelip and made some clucking noises. The young monk had a healthy backbone. Other monks would be quaking in their sandals at the slightest increase of volume in his voice. They would never dare ask him such personal questions.

After Harelip left, Xuanzang felt morose and his mind drifted. He turned to lie on his side, trying to find a comfortable position. He was utterly drained. He didn't want to be Abbot any longer. The city was noisy with too many people, and then there were his endless obligations. Duty, it was always about duty for him.

The Inner Palace at Taijigong, North Central Chang'an

Cries of alarm rang through the hallways of the Inner Palace. "The Emperor! The Emperor!" shouted a eunuch guard. Other guards speedily echoed the first alarm.

Wu Zhao had been sleeping in her chambers across the pond. She ordered the maidservants to dress her and prepare her quickly. The chief guard soon arrived in the outer reception hall.

"Your Highness, the situation is dire."

"Have the Imperial physician summoned immediately!"

"It has been done, Your Highness."

When she arrived at Li Zhi's chambers, the first thing she noticed was that his gaze was different; his eyes were glazed over and failed to track her presence. Li Zhi's left side was dramatically contracted, and drool issued from that side of his mouth.

The Imperial physician's arrival was soon announced. He rushed in and hastily bowed to the Empress before checking the Emperor's pulses and breathing. He unfurled his pouch of needles, laying them out on the side table. One needle, two, many around his head and on his arms. When he was finally done, the Imperial physician's face was pale from anxiety, and beads of sweat formed above his upper lip. He furrowed his brow as he wrote out a list of herbs on the prescription sheet, which he then handed over to his assistant and dispatched him with haste to the Imperial apothecary.

Kneeling before the Empress, the Imperial physician said with a faltering voice, "Your Highness, the Emperor has suffered a serious setback. He had regained some strength after suffering the last episode, but he is now completely paralyzed on his left side. His eye on that side is unable to focus well, and he is unable to speak at this time."

Wu Zhao looked past the kneeling physician to the limp body on the bed. *This reminds me of the time his father lay dying*, she thought. She had been on her way out of Li Shimin's bedchamber with the basin of water, and Li Zhi had brazenly blocked the corridor. She could see that he was aroused, his jade stalk pushing out against his gown. She quickly knelt before him, close to his erection, and splashed herself with some of the water from the basin. "Your Highness, your golden dew blesses my humble presence." Hearing his moan of approval, she reached under his gown and worked him to a suitable climax.

Wu Zhao brought herself back into the present and regarded the Imperial physician with as solemn an expression as she could muster.

The Imperial physician threw himself on the floor and hit his head against it as a show of obeisance. He lifted his face up just enough to clasp his hands together in reverence. "Your Highness, I am indeed no longer sure I can do much more."

"I see."

She contemplated what to do next. She must appear shocked. Devastated. She went to Li Zhi's side and sat on the kang. She wrapped her hand around his limp wrist and thought of things that saddened her—men at court who had failed to support her, women who plotted her downfall. And the worst—having to wait for several years before the Feng and Shan rituals.

A dull pain crept into her gut, just below her ribs. There was so much she needed to express. Yet no one could really understand her private anguish. Her lower lip trembled, and the tears began to flow.

DA CI'EN MONASTERY, SOUTHEASTERN CHANG'AN

Rain muffled the sounds filtering in from outside. The hard staccato of clappers drifted in, accompanied by the voices of those whose occupation was to call out the passage of time. Harelip listened to the soothing rhythm of raindrops hitting the tiles of the roof. He wished that he too could be deep in sleep, but try as he might, all that he had managed were a few twists and turns on his straw mat. He listened to the bullfrogs out in the dark marsh and wondered what they were saying.

He got up from his mat and walked outside to stand under the eaves, shielded from the downpour. The canopy of water reminded Harelip of a small waterfall he had accidentally discovered as a boy. How he had loved stepping on the mossy stones, then climbing upward by slow increments as his fingers pressed into the rock face, searching for the slightest indentations, the reassuring textures he could cling to. This tender recollection brought a slight smile to his lips.

That boy of nine sui had taken a break from digging for the roots his father was expecting him to find when he reached a cave behind the waterfall. He had stood inside the mouth of the cave, his clothes and sandals soaked from the spray, his mouth agape, watching that forceful rush of water, a veil that separated him from the forest. *That was such a long time ago,* Harelip thought, as he stretched out his left hand and closed his eyes to better enjoy the cool drip of water against his open palm. His feline friend Maya pawed at his sandals. Harelip bent down and scooped the cat up in his arms. It was past midnight. Maya's green eyes were slits at this time of night. He studied her face, white-whiskered with a black forehead and nose. He closed his eyes for a few moments, relishing the purring of the cat's body against his own. When he opened his eyes, he looked out again at the rain.

His parents had taught him how to know the world of plants and minerals not only by looking at them, but also by touching them, to sense what they were like beneath their outer appearance. It was perfectly natural that he would extend his exploration to humans—the textures of skin, muscle, sinew, and bone, and what lay beneath—energy, blood, and qi.

Harelip sighed, remembering that he first entered the monastery at fifteen sui. His parents wanted to spare him—but he wasn't sure whether they or he had a harder time with the taunts of others. It wasn't easy at first. He wasn't happy at the first monastery, an offshoot of Da Ci'en, in the small town Huaxian, close to Mount Hua. Being in a religious order was no guarantee against cruelty from others. And being in a small monastery made it a lot worse; there was no anonymity, and no one took his side against the bullies.

Despite the taunts, it was clear that he had inherited some gifts from his parents and knew a great deal about the healing power of herbs. He welcomed the invitation to travel to Chang'an and apprentice with the master herbalist at Da Ci'en. He learned so much from that monk, who had been in charge of the apothecary for thirty some years before he passed on. At least he'd had twelve years with his mentor.

The last time he saw his parents, they'd come to the monastery to make offerings at Autumn Equinox. That was last year. He'd noticed how much they'd aged over the years and was grateful that his younger brother was taking care of them.

Harelip scratched Maya between the eyes, which made the cat purr even more vigorously. "Are you happy, Maya?" he asked, enjoying how the rhythmic hum travelled up his arms.

Truths are seldom simple. He supposed he had been reasonably happy. Or was it more a matter of uneventful peace? At Da Ci'en, he had gained a certain freedom. Free of bullying, he even gained respect. What he despised were the rules and edicts issuing from the Emperor that seemed to be about his whims and impulses, changing from time to time, depending on His Majesty's moods. His thoughts turned to Xuanzang. What would the Master actually do? Would he simply accelerate his pace of work for fear of not finishing his project before dying? He didn't quite believe that Xuanzang would work less. Harelip didn't envy Xuanzang having to juggle Imperial requests with his commitment to the translation work.

Forks of lightning tore through the darkness. Harelip started to count, under his breath, "one miao ... two miao ... three ..." before the rumble sounded ever closer. The cracks of thunder reverberated through him, unsettling him. Maya wriggled out of Harelip's embrace and wandered off to her next adventure. Harelip withdrew his hands into his sleeves and shuddered.

Was it the city that made him lonelier? He recalled Tao Yuanming's poem. Did he long for hills and mountains too? The answer was clearly yes. Sometimes he went to Mount Hua to gather certain roots and herbs. He had encountered spirits there and encountered the mountain's magic. It was the mountain of his youth. The spirits recognized him and weren't unkind to him.

How did the poet Tao Yuanming refer to the world of men? *This dusty web.* Chang'an was reputed to be the largest city in the world, a place filled with many kinds of temples for as many kinds of worshippers as one could imagine. It was truly a web of tremendous complexity and colour. For the most part, he liked living in a sanctuary while being able to venture out into that swirl of activity and variety. Still, there was too much noise here. The moments of pure silence were rare. Even the announcement of time was an assault on the ears—the drums, the bell, the wooden clapper, and then the chanting out of the passing moments. So much anxiety over time passing. At least on nights like this there were pure sounds from nature that provided some soothing comfort—the rain, the chorus of bullfrogs, the occasional call of a mynah.

Harelip pictured Xuanzang travelling for all those years across barren landscapes, through mountainous regions, perhaps fighting his own inner demons on cold winter nights while shivering next to the dying embers of a fire. Had the famous monk longed for the warmth of another's body? *He must have lusts, surely, Venerable Master or not*, thought Harelip. He was a man, and hence prone to carnal stirrings. Before he could think about his own cravings, Harelip shivered and then stifled a sneeze.

He felt a tiny jab on his right forearm. Instantly, without a second thought, he brought his left palm down on the spot and swore loudly. Too late—the mosquito was killed before Harelip remembered that he was supposed to observe the precept of not killing. That made him swear a second time.

So who had said he had to be above reproach? He helped alleviate the sufferings of the monks, yet he killed little creatures that annoyed him. Now and then, a few unsavory words escaped from his mouth. That was just the way he was.

He yawned. He had better get some sleep. He mustn't worry too much about the famous monk.

Xuanzang felt the hiss of their hot tongues at the back of his neck. He sprinted up the mountain with speed and agility, then scaled the precipitous peak while keeping a hair's breadth ahead of the long-tailed creatures chasing him. Their mouths spewed far-reaching flames. The sulphurous odour entered his lungs. He coughed and choked as he barely kept ahead of them. His feet seemed to float on air as he ascended the cliff face. He found himself groping along the walls of a dark cave, though light beamed from the animals' eyes and pierced the darkness, allowing him to see his way as he ran farther inside. Numerous labyrinthine twists later, he stumbled on a large mural painted on one wall, a magnificent painting of Buddha surrounded by countless arhats and disciples.

He shivered awake. Only in his dream could he, a man of fifty-nine sui, be capable of such stupendous athleticism. He shook his head vigorously several times as if to dislodge the creatures from his mind. Those beasts were gigantic, and their vicious jaws had snapped just a few cun shy of his robes. He struggled out of bed, his knees stiff and painful.

At the wash basin, while removing sleep from his eyes, he realized that the monsters in his dream looked familiar to him, with their multiple eyes and long tails. *Why would that be?* he mused.

The bell from the tower signalled it was time for morning meditation. He walked over to his cabinet of old books, pulled out the copy of the *Shanhaijing* 山海經, *The Classic of Mountains and Seas*, and quickly flipped to the section called Great Wilderness. There it was, a drawing of the Zhulong with an accompanying description:

> *Beyond the northwest seas, north of the River Scarlet, a mountain*
> *exists shaped like the tail of the creatures that live on it. When*
> *the sun rises, the light reflects on the mountain as if it were a*

luminescent tail, hence its name Brilliant Tail. Creatures that live here are half god and half human with human faces and crimson serpentine bodies. They are called Zhulong, Torch Dragons. These Zhulong beings have a row of five vertical eyes that form a seam or scar on their faces. When a Zhulong deity closes its eyes, there is darkness. When it opens its eyes, there is light. Zhulong neither eat nor sleep nor breathe. They subsist on elements in the atmosphere by absorbing nutrients through their skins. The winds and rains are at their beck and call. Zhulong deities shine their torches over the ninefold darkness, bringing light to darkness.

Xuanzang wrote the characters for the name Zhulong—Zhu, 燭 a torch that brings light, or illumination. Then the character for dragon 龍. He stared at the second character and pursed his lips. Why would there be dragons? He sensed that the dream was important, but what was it trying to tell him? So many times in the past, dreams had guided him, granted him wisdom for making critical decisions. Some of his dreams had saved his life. He felt dizzy, as if on the edge of a cliff, about to lose ground. He swayed and grabbed onto the back of a chair and cleared his throat loudly several times. Then he burst out laughing, made nervous by his own vulnerability.

He lit a stick of incense on the altar. Yet another morning when he lacked the energy to make his way to the large hall for the group meditation. He would stay here, in private, and rest until it was time for the translation work.

He sat on his meditation cushion, but his mind was restless, and he kept recalling the reply that Li Zhi had made to his request only two-and-a-half years before: "Let it be said of you as was said of the wise men of antiquity, 'The Great Recluse never leaves town!'"

Xuanzang had so longed to have some time away from the city, to continue his work with only one or two disciples at the temple on Mount Shaoshi. He recalled how vulnerable he'd felt, begging the Emperor to be allowed to leave Chang'an for Mount Shaoshi. He had been sorely disappointed at the Emperor's reply. But not surprised.

He fidgeted on his cushion. It was difficult not to feel bitter about being a captive in the city. But a voice inside his head urged, *Take the precipitous path and you will be rewarded.* He opened his eyes in astonishment. There was no time for bitterness about an unfulfilled wish, especially when his life's calling had been far more compelling.

Later, at the Translation Hall, meeting with his elite group of disciple translators, Xuanzang sat in the centre of the circle. Huili was the first to speak up. "Venerable Master, we have been discussing the *Mahaprajnaparamita*. We think it preferable to translate only certain portions, not the whole six hundred fascicles. We will make an abridged version."

"Why would you think this?"

"Master, your health ... We mustn't overtax you."

Another disciple spoke up. "Besides, some portions are obviously repetitive. Redundant."

Xuanzang's face, usually pale and grey, turned a shade of red at this dismissive tone. "You are only paying attention to the superficial structure of the words. There is a purpose to that so-called 'redundancy.'" Xuanzang proceeded to relate his dream to his disciples. Then he added in a definitive tone, "I believe we ought to undertake to finish the remaining 100,000 lines. Only then will I be able to enter the cave and fulfill my destiny."

His disciples were speechless and bowed their heads. Their Master had been guided and protected all those years through dangerous places and treacherous situations to bring the sutras back from India.

They knew he had fought off countless ghosts and demons, that he'd heard the voices of bodhisattvas. There was no arguing with such a determined and strong spirit.

Xuanzang added, "I'm not going to let worry about my health stop me."

Huili bowed deeply at the waist, made his way to the gong to the right, and struck it three times, signalling the retinue of copyists waiting outside to proceed into the Translation Hall.

Qixi 七戲 Festival,
Seventh night of the Seventh Lunar Month

DA FA TEMPLE,
WEST CENTRAL CHANG'AN

Beyond the walls of the temple, crowds gathered to view the stars. Sitting in her inner courtyard, Qilan heard people gossiping and the sharp, jubilant squeals of children. Firecrackers exploded sporadically.

She directed her gaze upward. It was easy to find the Weaver Girl in the upper northwest with the Cowherd star in the south.

A young girl's singing voice carried above the noise, sweet yet firm.

The reeds flourish, lush
White dew still falling
My beloved, so dear
Wanders lost along the shoreline
Upriver I search for him
The journey, long and tortuous

An ancient song from the Han Dynasty sung by the common folk for hundreds of years. Qilan hummed along. She imagined herself on the other side of the wall, one of the common folk, happy to be part of the celebrations. She wasn't capable of such fanciful, romantic notions; she'd never been like the other girls her age, longing for a future husband who would be loyal. There was no one she needed to be reunited with.

Wait, a voice whispered, *how about your mother? And your father?*

"My father is no longer a man," she mumbled under her breath. But it was true; she did long to be reunited with her mother, even though she knew it was an impossibility for as long as she remained in Chang'an. Every year at the time of the Qixi Festival, since her departure from the family home, she had felt a particularly strong tug at her heart, thinking of her mother. *Where is she now?* Her mother had told her to hide, to cultivate her strength, to wait for a sign. But no sign had arrived. Qilan recalled her mother's words before they bid each other farewell: *You must wait for the eleventh anniversary of your father's departure.*

She and her mother had a wordless kinship that extended beyond their human forms. Her mother had shown her how to transform herself, to disappear into the air and travel about undetected by others. From her father, she had learned much from ancient scholarly texts: the sayings of sages such as Zhuangzi, the vast records of history, the poems from the *Shijing*, the ways of the *Yijing*.

When Father travelled into Chang'an to work, Mother would take her out to forests, to rivers, to all kinds of magical places. She learned that there was a mind in nature that exceeded human limitations. She learned from her mother how to awaken that mind of nature within herself and how to unite with the greater mind that existed in nature.

You are my dear heart, her mother used to say.

The voices of the celebrants on the other side of the wall brought Qilan back to the present. She looked up at the Weaver and Cowherd in the sky. Strife between dark forces and life on earth might last for another two thousand years or more. It wasn't entirely clear to her how it would all play out. All she knew was that this earth would no longer exist in the same way in that future era.

There would be wars within the invisible realms of the mind and deep inside the bodies of humans and animals. An overwhelming greed would overtake the hearts of many, causing them to abandon acts of love and generosity. Deception would become the veil that separated many people's minds from truths.

It was inevitable—the human race would cease to exist. Miraculously, the earth would survive, along with creatures invisible to the eye, those who could proliferate in extreme weather conditions, parasites, and those that could transform themselves to adapt to changing circumstances. The chimeric creatures would triumph, the ones whose minds and bodies could transform in response to adversities, become two or three creatures combined, resistant to the diseases that had decimated purer variants. It would be the fulfillment of *The Classic of the Mountains and Seas*, all time collapsing and myths becoming fact.

The girl's song from the other side of the temple wall brought her back to the present.

The reeds luxuriant, green
White dew turns to frost
My beloved, so dear
Drifts beyond the waters
Upriver I search for him
The journey, long and arduous

She would never forget that her father had loved her. Yet she mustn't cling to the past. What had she said to Ling about destiny? She frowned, trying to recall. *We choose, we always choose.*

She touched the centre of her chest. The secret wisdom would never leave her. All she had known and intuited, all she knew that was to come.

WESTERN MARKET,
WEST CENTRAL CHANG'AN

Two guards pasted up large posters on the public notice board. The posters bore the chop of the Imperial insignia. After they'd done their duty and had departed, the crowd moved in to study the announcements.

Old Chen had just finished loading supplies into the cart and secured the contents with a tarpaulin and ropes. Aside from the supplies of food for the nuns, he'd purchased ten more bottles of his favourite ale, Toad Tumulus. He chuckled with glee, thinking of the many evenings he would be enjoying the drink. He was so focused that he paid no mind to the murmuring throng until he looked up from his completed task, ready to leave. The cul-de-sac was packed. He made his way closer to the front of the crowd so he could read the announcement.

"By order of the Empress Wu Zhao, a reward of one thousand strings of cash will be offered to the person who has information about the whereabouts of a precious cultural treasure stolen from the Imperial collection. This treasure is an oracle bone of great antiquity. It bears an unusual inscription. It is believed that if this object falls into the wrong hands, there will be widespread chaos and danger to the populace."

A sallow-faced, slim youth stood on tiptoe, craning to read the announcement. "An oracle bone! So what? Rat's piss."

The middle-aged woman behind him, sporting a conch hairstyle tied at the base with purple ribbons, snarled at him. "Ignoramus! It's special. Only emperors get to have oracle bones. They use them to make big decisions."

Another woman piped up. "That cunning vixen. What's she up to next?"

A swarthy man pushed his way to the front, holding a hoe in one hand and a sack of sweet melons draped over his left shoulder. "Who cares about a stupid piece of bone? Are we paying tribute taxes so that these Imperial buggers waste our hard-earned money, searching for such a thing? Can this bone feed us, clothe us, keep us warm?"

A few people laughed nervously while others cheered.

The woman with the fashionable hairstyle replied in a whisper, "Hush! Soldiers still milling about."

The swarthy man was not dissuaded. "What about the mysterious deaths of late, the deaths of newborns in the Vice Hamlet? Why doesn't the court issue some edict to investigate what's happening there?"

"Who cares about those outcasts in the Vice Hamlet? And those born of outcasts?" shrieked the woman.

Old Chen had seen enough. He pushed past people and returned to his cart. He led his horse carefully through the thinning crowd, the cart rattling behind them. He'd better return to Da Fa Temple and tell Sister Orchid.

Fifteenth Day of Seventh Lunar Month,
盂蘭節 Feast of All Souls

THE VICE HAMLET,
EAST CENTRAL CHANG'AN

Xie lost track of time. It seemed only moments ago that he heard the drum sound the lifting of the curfew. He peered at the sundial in the courtyard outside his bedchamber and was jolted back to the present. There was only half an hour left before the Hour of the Dragon.

He changed into a light blue linen robe which did not betray his station or prestige and wrapped a dark brown sash around his waist. His cloth cap, a rather common kind, he wrapped around his head. Its tails hung down at the back of his head, without ostentatious flair. Once ready, he stepped out into the streets.

It was breakfast time, and there were already many people rushing about—not those who inhabited the shadows and floated through the darkness, ghostly and rejected, but those who sold tools, household wares, and food. He had a pang of envy for ordinary folk. He imagined that they did not possess the kind of darkness he felt—or did they? Perhaps he was mistaken, but for now, he would regard them as blessed beings, free of curses, scurrying with their carts and donkeys to the Eastern Market nearby, or perhaps to open up their eating establishments. He enjoyed observing the bustle. Today, he especially relished hearing the gossip about the notifications posted in the market. He smiled to hear someone exclaim, "The reward! If only I knew where this precious oracle bone was."

He strode quickly, feeling the extra lift and strength in his body. He circumvented the Eastern Market, turning down Ironmongers Lane instead. Although named for the trade, there weren't just ironmongers selling tools and implements; there were also pastry shops, each specializing in sweets from a specific region in the country. He headed toward his favourite.

The shop was tiny, with only three tables. Xie sat at one of the tables and ordered two bean cakes and a cup of hot barley tea. He reached into his pocket and pulled out a book. Flipping through the collection of poems, his eyes finally rested on one by Tao Yuanming, titled "Frolicking above the Graves."

This day, beautiful and clear,
Let's go fluting and play the strings.
The dead lay under the cypress,
Make merry when we still can!
Our singing fills the air with new sounds,
A young wine flushes our cheeks.
Can't predict tomorrow,
So I'll bare my soul today.

He bit into the deliciously sweet and smooth centre of the pastry. *Almost as sweet as a soul*, he mused.

After his meal, he took a walk. A cool breeze caressed Xie's face. Although his insides churned with a painful cold, his skin burned with fire, and his eyes glowed.

Xie passed by the face reader sitting on a stool on the street. He had a lineup of people waiting to get their fortunes read. Xie smirked, wondering what, if anything, the man could detect in him.

He headed southeast, toward the graveyard. As he walked farther and farther away from the hub, his body relaxed, and he smiled to himself without caring who noticed. It was gratifying to know that the potion worked on Li Zhi—thanks to the gu poison, the Emperor would be rendered completely helpless for at least a few more months. He might recover some speech but would have neither the strength nor the capacity to make important decisions. As Wu Zhao's powers increased, Xie felt sure that he too would stand to gain.

You'll become immortal. And I, along with you, will remain in the world, forever changing forms yet untouchable.

Li Zhi was such a weakling, too dependent on a woman. Even so, the Emperor served a purpose and was useful to keep alive until after the Feng and Shan rituals.

I like it when we think as one, whispered Gui.

The sky, sunny and clear earlier, now became crowded with clouds. A gust of wind stirred up the sand of the street and caused Xie's eyes to smart.

The graveyard was situated against the large city wall, several blocks south of the Chunming Gate. The area around the graveyard was quiet, with very few residences. There were mostly shops selling incense, altar papers, and ritual objects. Soon, many people would arrive at the graveyard to burn paper money and incense and to pray for the liberation of hungry ghosts. The world was an open field of possibilities. And he, a man possessed by a demon, now belonged to a world unseen by most. He, like one of those mysterious creatures in *The Classic of Mountains and Seas,* was a creature bound for immortality.

Here, at the corner of the ward, it seemed as if the wily wind gathered in eddies, trying to penetrate the walls. A few gingko leaves lay scattered on the ground around the roots of the parent tree at the far corner. He lightly touched the tombstones with his long, slender fingers as he walked between the rows, heading toward the tree.

When he reached the corner, he sat against the trunk of the tree. It soothed him to feel the tree against his back. He closed his eyes, thinking of nothing. But after some time, there was a noticeable change in the air. He opened his eyes quickly and looked up at the sky. He could see that there was some kind of disturbance in the air—invisible waves that were moving toward him. No, it was a single undulating wave, shimmering with edges of light gold and orange, changing to indigo.

Xie was about to get up, but the vortex of light got to him first and pinned him against the trunk of the tree. His body was paralyzed and the skin on his face prickled.

"Who are you?" he demanded.

The one who stole the plastron.

"What do you want?"

To do battle with you, in exactly four years' time.

Xie laughed. "Don't be absurd."

At the cursed temple, eleven years from that day you claimed this soul.

Xie stopped laughing.

Defeat me and you can have the oracle bone.

"How do I know you have the oracle bone?"

The branches overhead shook violently, throwing off a flurry of leaves. Then the ground beneath Xie shifted. An invisible force wrote out two lines on the ground in front of him.

夢要醒，天要光。

A dream wants waking, a sky needs light.

The vortex swirled higher and moved away, over the wall and out of the city. Gui, in a rage, left Xie's body as a cloudy blue column and also cleared the wall. It saw that the vortex had gone as far as an orchard and then disappeared.

Gui was sorely tempted to follow. But it hesitated—perhaps it was a ruse to draw it away from Xie. It turned around and returned to the graveyard, then re-entered Xie, who felt waves of cold pass through his body, down to his toes. He shivered awake, opened his eyes and began to weep.

"I remember how she used to make me feel," Xie said, between sobs.

What are you going on about?

"It's her," Xie said. "How could I ever forget?"

BOOK
TWO

Fu – Return

Toward the end of Longshuo 龍說 reign period
Xiaohan 小寒 Jieqi, Slight Cold,
Twelfth Lunar Month, New Moon

Da Fa Temple,
West Central Chang'an

Ling glanced up at the rooftop, which wore a thin blanket of snow from the day before. It was mid-afternoon, and the sky was overcast, portending more snow or perhaps rain.

She took one long deep breath, filling up her belly and bringing her energy right down to her toes. She took a few steps back then propelled herself forward so that her body was almost horizontal as her feet went up the wall. As her hands slapped the roof tiles, she leapt forward and curled into a ball in the air, landing on the roof.

"Well done!" exclaimed Qilan, having emerged from her study. "Next time, do it without making noise."

Ling jumped down and hunched her shoulders inward, looking crestfallen.

"Like this," said Qilan as she ran up the wall, gathering such speed that she shot up into the air and landed on the roof without a single sound, her body upright.

Ling looked down at the snow around Qilan's boots. It was as if she wasn't even standing on the snow.

"Now, keep up with me."

Qilan raced ahead, and the snow showed no trace of her path.

Ling pushed herself hard, but Qilan was always way ahead. Snow

now began to fall. Qilan wove her way from the southern wing, along the eastern edge of the temple, then sped along the northern roof. She leapt onto the roof of the stable and building where Old Chen and his family lived and completed the circle by proceeding along the western wing. Below them, in the outer courtyard, a few nuns were wrapping the bases of camellia bushes with hemp cloth and twine in preparation for the approach of colder weather. They were so engrossed in their tasks that they hadn't noticed the race overhead.

Qilan clambered up the height of the bell tower as if her hands and feet could stick to the walls. When she reached the top, she gently tapped her head against the bell, causing it to emit a low hum before she somersaulted back onto the roof. The nuns in the outer courtyard looked up, surprised to see Qilan. One of them exclaimed, "Oh, Sister Orchid! There you go doing your acrobatic tricks again!" The nuns giggled, enjoying the moment.

"How did you do that?" Ling pointed at the snow over which Qilan had run without leaving footprints.

"A spell. It changes the way my body moves so I can float." Qilan whispered the magic words into Ling's ear.

Ling mumbled the words under her breath. She felt her whole person grow lighter and her feet lift slightly off the roof. She smiled with pleasure.

"You reverse it by saying the words backwards."

Their practice completed, they jumped back down to the ground and walked leisurely to the kitchen, then to Qilan's study. They warmed their hands over the charcoal brazier before sitting down to hot tea and tiny steamed lotus-paste buns. Ling and Qilan ate the buns with relish and drank the tea noisily.

"You did well."

Ling blushed. One word of praise from Qilan meant the world

to her. She wanted to learn as much as she could, but it seemed to her that in the three-and-a-half years since she'd met Qilan, the nun had only taught her a handful of spells. To Ling, these were all minor spells, and it seemed that Qilan deliberately held back from teaching her the bigger spells.

"When you showed me the transformation of the caterpillar and the butterfly, when I first came to Da Fa ... that's a different kind of spell, isn't it?"

"I suppose you could separate spells into categories, but why do that?" Qilan smiled, a quizzical look on her face. "Mind you, not everyone can succeed in uttering spells. Even with the right words."

"Why—aren't the words enough?"

"Ah! Now we're getting to the heart of transformation."

"What makes the spell work?"

"A certain inclination of your mind ... how you focus your energy."

"I don't understand."

"Spells work only if uttered under two conditions. First, they must be invoked by someone who is an outsider to normal life. Distinct from others—"

"Distinct?"

"Not like others. Hard to explain. One just knows."

Ling nodded, picking up another lotus bun. "I know I'm different. What's the second condition?"

"For a spell to work, it needs a certain force. By 'force,' I mean strength. Sometimes those involved in the dark sorceries employ violent force. In our case, the spells I teach you have to be uttered with pure intent and clarity. That's good force."

"Pure intent?"

"Love and selflessness—not for personal gain."

"Just now, didn't you have a selfish motive in levitating?"

"I wanted to teach you. That, my dear, I would consider to be coming from a place of selflessness."

Ling laughed. Sister Orchid's mischievousness, her entertaining examples and generosity, made learning so much easier.

"Would you teach me the more serious spells?"

"There you go with your categories, again!" Qilan winked. But her expression changed abruptly, and she looked quite solemn. "Yes, I will. Some day soon, Ling."

"How about telling me more about yourself? I've been here almost four years, and I hardly know anything about you, I mean your past, that is."

Qilan poked Ling in ribs. "My, how bold and mouthy you've become." She was pleased by how talkative and expressive Ling was now, she had truly blossomed. She could even stomach tea.

"I'll tell you more soon. But before then, we must make preparations to return to Huazhou. I believe it's time for me to fulfill my promise to you."

Ling's eyes brightened.

That night, Qilan was shrouded in utter darkness as she stood alone in the courtyard outside her study. There was no moon. The water was slightly frozen on the surface of the magic urn. She whispered the spell into her cupped palms and dropped the radiant sphere toward the icy mirror. It cracked the ice and dissolved all of it until the surface once again became the portal through which she could view Xie at his mansion.

Xie lay on a couch in a drugged trance, the lit cannabis resin creating a thick, billowing smoke in the room. He coughed, shook his head, and mumbled.

Qilan reached into her sleeve and pulled out a paper doll. She dotted the eyes and drew a nose and mouth on it, then blew over it in her palm and sent it into the water.

The apparition entered the room and called out, "Father."

Xie slowly raised his head. The form was hazy, but the voice was unmistakeable. His voice trembled with emotion. "That was you who appeared at the graveyard, wasn't it, over three years ago?" He coughed and fell back against the pillow, his eyes rolling upwards. "It's too late. You mustn't ..."

The greenish-blue burn of the demon's gaze shot through Xie's eyes. Gui hissed, *How dare you take the oracle bone!*

"Remember, you must meet me at the temple on the fifteenth day of the seventh month in the new year," Qilan's apparition said.

Fool, what do you hope to accomplish?

"A chance to do battle with you. If you win, you will gain the oracle bone."

A cold mist stretched out tendrils but Qilan's apparition evaporated just in time, leaving behind the paper doll.

DA CI'EN MONASTERY, SOUTHEASTERN CHANG'AN

A rush of joy passed through Xuanzang.

His work was done. He and his disciples had completed the translation of all sixteen talks given by Shakyamuni Buddha on the perfection of wisdom. With the final rendition of the last line, Xuanzang breathed an audible sigh of relief and folded his hands together in his lap.

He shivered, partly from the cold, but mostly because he knew that his life's work was complete. He looked out at the rows of monks in the Translation Hall facing him, then nodded to his disciples around him.

The hall was silent, an awe descending on all present. Xuanzang reflected on the immense guidance he had received all these months.

A voice, a presence, always, whispering what ought to be uttered, whenever there was some struggle with a dubious passage or wording. He was filled with gratitude.

"Now my mission is fulfilled. The age of living is also finished. No reason to stay longer. After my passing, please make sure you wrap my corpse in a reed mat and bring it to some shady burial spot on a mountain."

His senior disciple Huili remarked, "Master, how could you say that, at such an auspicious moment?"

"Dying at the end of a life well-lived in the service of Dharma is to be celebrated. But make no mistake; I wish the funeral itself to be without fanfare." Xuanzang signalled for assistance to rise up from the dais. "Let us go to the Garden of the Buddhas and enjoy a stroll."

"It is cold today, Venerable Master," Huili said.

"Don't be silly. It has stopped snowing and there is a bit of sun. I need to see my Buddha statues."

A few monks helped Xuanzang bundle up with scarves and a fur hat and put boots on his feet. It took a while before he was ready. Supported on both sides by assistants, Xuanzang slowly walked to the Garden of Buddhas, which lay between the main building and the pagoda recently built to store the sutras.

It was peaceful in the garden. Only a few sparrows flitted between branches of the pines and junipers and the regal willow tree. The Buddha statues ranged in size, positioned in wooden shelters or alcoves, scattered throughout the garden.

Harelip caught sight of Xuanzang from his apothecary and rushed out to meet him. "Venerable Master ... you must not be out here—"

"I know, I know. You and everyone else," wheezed Xuanzang. He paused and leaned on Peerless's shoulder. "Look here." He pointed to the small Buddha figure in the fifth alcove. "This one. It was the first figure I got. After I entered the cave in Kapisa and wouldn't leave until I was given a vision of the Buddha there. I had to make over one hundred prostrations chanting and praying, before I was given the vision of Buddha, his body and robes of a yellowish red colour. I had this figure carved of sandalwood. How precious."

Xuanzang lightly caressed the figure and limped on to the next figure. Harelip silently went with the retinue of monks, witnessing the intimate farewell ritual.

"Oh look," murmured Xuanzang. He bent down to touch a figure. The sandalwood figure of the Buddha Turning the Wheel of the Law had a chip off the left thumb and a long furrowed line down the back of that hand. "How did that happen?"

Silence and shaking of heads.

"We can send for someone to come here to repair it, Venerable Master," replied Pu Guang.

"I know of an excellent sculptor," Huili said. "He usually works with his uncle at the Dunhuang caves, but he's back in Chang'an for the winter."

"Send for him quickly."

Xuanzang struggled on—he wanted to pay his respects to the remaining two Buddha figures. By the time he was led back to his private chambers, he was drained but waved away his hovering disciples. "Let me rest. Don't fuss!"

Later, when he was alone, except for a watchful Peerless lurking in the anteroom, Xuanzang sat at his desk and began a letter to the Emperor.

> *Most Wise and Supreme Ruler,*
> *I, your humble servant Xuanzang, write this from my private*
> *chambers at Da Ci'en Monastery to recount to you our progress in*

translations at this point. You have been generous in granting us your most brilliant monks from across the land to assist me in this difficult venture.

For the past few years, ill-health has prevented me from maintaining the relentless pace I was accustomed to, in my more robust years. I had been concerned I would not finish my most vital translation work.

But today, I am pleased to announce that our work on translating the Mahaprajnaparamita *is complete. Knowing that Your Majesty has made our work at Da Ci'en possible since my return from India, we are indebted for your patronage. You have accumulated merit from supporting this translation project, since this will lead to many being able to hear the Dharma and benefit.*

I will make sure that a contingent of monks delivers a copy to you. I regret that I am too weak to accompany them.

I hope Your Majesty is continuing to recover. I humbly request that Your Majesty ensure that this precious sutra will be copied and shared widely with people throughout this land and beyond.

Your Majesty will recall that, upon my return to Chang'an from India, I had asked if I might return to Mount Shaoshi to do the translation work at the monastery there. I felt a need to return to those hills of my youth. Your Majesty had deemed that it would be preferable that I remain in Chang'an, in the company of a team of qualified assistants and be publicly witnessed while conducting this important work. I am indebted to Your Majesty for that decision; it has allowed me to accomplish so much, and to gain from the team of assistants you had appointed.

I have devoted more than half of my life to this work, bringing the sutras back from India and translating as many of them as I could. The Buddhas and bodhisattvas have kept me alive so that

I may complete my work. In my final days, my deepest wish is to return to an important aspect of my Buddhist commitment that I have neglected all these years: the practice of meditation.

I long to free myself from the noise of the crowded city, roll up my shadow, and roam where elk and deer are my companions. May I dwell on a flat stone, to rest in the midst of nature.

My end is near. I feel it in my heart. I have left instructions with my senior disciple Huili for my burial. If I cannot fulfill my dream of living out my final days on Shaoshi Mountain, may I humbly request Your Majesty that my wishes for burial be honoured.

Your servant,

Xuanzang

Writing a formal, polite letter—one that showed sufficient obeisance to his Emperor—took a great deal of energy. It taxed him not just physically; it was a drain on his heart—bowing and scraping were tedious duties. This was far from who he really was, or had been—the rogue adventurer who disobeyed the previous Emperor and left for India without permission. Had he turned into a weaker version of his former self? He'd gone to India despite being forbidden to, driven by a greater force, a feeling deep in his being that he couldn't escape. Loyalty to that deep feeling had been far more critical than obedience to the Emperor.

Why did Li Zhi care about the translation project? Was it simply a political move? An unquestioned gesture, since his mother was Buddhist? He would never know. Regardless, he, Xuanzang, had had to rein in his rebellious energy and remain in the Emperor's favour for the sake of the Dharma. If not for that, why would he have consented to being imprisoned in this city?

He struggled up from his table and sealed the letter, then summoned Peerless and gave him instructions to have the letter delivered to the Emperor. Having completed his task, he picked up the drawing of the turtle and went to his daybed with it.

His public life had no secrets. *But this*, he fingered the silk drawing, *this had to be kept secret.* He thought back to how he had acquired it. That woman in Khotan. She had trusted him with it. This needs to be kept a secret, away from those in power, she had said. Certain ones will abuse their power, and if they possess this diagram along with a certain turtle plastron, they will be unstoppable.

"Why give it to me?" he had asked her.

"Because you are my successor."

Xuanzang shuddered at the memory. It was such an odd moment, and hence unforgettable. Was she truly a seer? Or had she been deranged? What had occurred between them completely challenged his notion of inheritance. He was raised to believe in inheriting from one's father and ancestors. When he became a Buddhist monk, he practiced renunciation, the conscious disinheriting of attachments, going against all those rules of inheritance he had been raised with. Now, when he thought about it, didn't renunciation require the existence of inheritance?

But what of that extraordinary encounter with the woman in Khotan? He sighed at the memory of her soft eyes and warm hands. Her breath smelled of honey and peach blossoms.

That encounter wasn't like anything he had experienced before, or since. It was a mystery fuelled by subtle meanings, one that defied words and explanation. Xuanzang had felt as if he *was* meant to receive the diagram, return to Zhongguo with it, and wait. Until the right successor came along.

When he first saw Harelip at the back of the Translation Hall, he had an overpowering feeling that he would be his successor, the next person who had to keep the drawing safe. He had to tell Harelip about it—all the things he'd been told. Yet there were still things no one knew, the woman had said, that none of the inheritors were allowed to know until the time came, many eons from now, when the final possessor of the diagram would know.

A mystery. "A five-sided mystery, to be exact," she had whispered.

FORBIDDEN PARK, NORTH OF TAIJIGONG

The landscape in Forbidden Park might have seemed barren in winter, but it held an appeal for Wu Zhao. *The willows were sadder*, she thought. The poplars to the west stood in a row, sentinels against the wind.

Wu Zhao could see the herds of horses as well as sheep in their separate penned areas, grazing and roaming, in the far distance. She gazed out at the scene, deserted and tranquil, from the second storey of the Purple Clouds Hall as dusk approached. The setting sun was a dark orange orb on the horizon. The Serpentine River to the northwest glimmered with the last rays of light. A few ducks and herons were barely visible in the marsh to the right, silhouetted in the dim light.

Twenty eunuch guards were stationed in a circle around the pavilion. Wu Zhao gathered the folds of her coat—made with fox furs and embroidered with gold thread—closer around her neck. The two braziers were filled with red-hot coals, keeping her warm.

She saw Xie ride toward the pavilion, dismount, and enter. Soon she heard the stomp of his boots on the stairs leading up to the second floor. He bowed deeply to her, clasping his hands in front of his face with gaze lowered. "Your Highness."

Of course it was all for show. The guards were below; their peripheral vision would take in the behaviours of the two, lit by the torches placed around the pavilion.

"More than three years have passed, and still no sign of the genuine oracle bone," began the Empress, turning her back to him. "All kinds of imposters have come forth with fake bones. Fools! I am most displeased."

"I have received recent news, Your Highness."

She turned around, her eyebrows arched.

"The scoundrel has sent me a vision. There will be a meeting on the Full Moon in the seventh month. I am sure I will obtain the bone then."

Wu Zhao shuddered. "Feast of All Souls, when there is no separation between the living and the dead." She reached out and placed her hand lightly on his chest. "How much do they want?"

"It's not money they're after. If the thief had wanted money, he would have come forward three years ago."

"Well, then, what's their motive?"

Xie's face darkened. "They want to destroy me, punish me first with all this waiting then ask me to meet on a date that they believe is auspicious for them, a day that they mistake for my most vulnerable time."

Wu Zhao grew quiet before she whispered, worry in her voice. "It could be a trap."

"There is no trap that could hold someone like me."

Wu Zhao laughed. "Are you so sure?"

"I am the wind. I do not belong to form. It belongs to me."

"You speak in riddles so much. I tire of it! Why are you so sure it's a genuine claim?"

"They know the inscription on the bone."

Her face flushed with impatience. "You exasperate me. You have yet to tell me what the point of that inscription is. I could decide to have you killed, have you tortured, exiled. Must I remind you?"

Xie pulled out a vial from the pouch hanging at his belt. The yellow cork was sealed with red wax. "For you. You know you like this. I always have your best interests at heart."

Wu Zhao smiled, her anger receding. His potions were indeed marvellous—they gave her an inordinate amount of energy and mental clarity.

"And this—" Xie brought out another vial, distinguished by its black coloured cork. "It will reverse some of those incapacitating symptoms so that His Majesty recovers slightly, at least enough to assist us when we need him."

Wu Zhao was pleased. Xie's gifts would advance her ambitions. He was immensely useful to her, despite his occasional foray into mysterious, vague pronouncements.

"When are you coming to see me again?"

Xie smiled slyly at her. "Tomorrow night," he whispered, moving a fraction closer to her.

She could feel the heat of his body. *It is a curious thing*, she thought, *how his body can radiate a heat even greater than that from the braziers.* She looked into his eyes and felt herself pulled into his gaze. It was more discomforting than seductive. This wasn't lust, yet it transfixed her. She couldn't understand it. There was nothing ordinary about this man. It troubled her slightly that she had become even more enchanted.

Dahan 大寒
Jieqi, Great Cold,
Middle of Twelfth Lunar Month

DA FA TEMPLE,
WEST CENTRAL CHANG'AN

"A re you ready?"

Ling nodded. She had no doubt that she was ready.

They left Da Fa Temple on two horses and rode out of Chang'an in the late afternoon. Their faces were covered, thick scarves wrapped around their heads. At the speed they travelled, they felt the icy air gnaw at the exposed parts of their faces, especially around the eyes.

At least the road was clear, with a compacted layer of snow over the rough ground, but it wasn't slippery. They rode without stopping, entering Huazhou just as the sun was close to disappearing behind the horizon, and made their way to Idle Tea inn.

"You must know," insisted Qilan, cornering Dried Reed in the kitchen area while his assistant tended to a room full of customers. She looked sternly at the old man who averted his eyes from the cloth with the drawing of a tattoo.

The innkeeper pursed his lips and shook his head. Ling noticed that his hair had definitely thinned since the last visit, and the skin under his neck was looking decidedly more wrinkled. *Less deference too*, noted Ling, *compared to last time when he couldn't stop fawning over Qilan.*

"Everyone who doesn't want to be noticed comes to your inn for food and drink and rest. This man ambushed Ling's parents' barge and killed them nearby, at the canals. It was in the summer, nearly three-and-a-half years ago. Now I'm repeating myself, aren't I?"

"Why didn't you ask me then?"

"Wasn't necessary at that time."

Dried Reed pursed his lips even more tightly.

Qilan pressed on. "You must remember what terrible shape she was in—couldn't even manage a cup of tea. She wasn't strong enough to match Shan Hu then. You see how different she is now."

"This young woman is now going to seek out Shan Hu and fight him?" Dried Reed gasped.

"We are *not* joking," replied Ling who glared at the innkeeper in anger.

Dried Reed leaned very close to Qilan and whispered, "What do you think this is going to do to me if the wrong people found out that I talked?"

Qilan whispered back, "Who's listening?"

Dried Reed threw a quick glance at the dining area before he continued, still in a whisper, "There are spies everywhere. The lout runs a large gang controlling the area. All I'm willing to say—head toward the market, and look for the symbol hidden between two bamboo posts." He nodded nervously, and flinging the mangy table rag over his left shoulder, scampered out to the dining area.

Qilan and Ling headed in the direction of the market, walking side by side. The shops were brightly lit from large outdoor lanterns. The shoppers' and stall keepers' breaths floated like dragon trails in the air as bargains were struck. The crunching sounds of boots on snow swirled around them, a chorus of varying rhythms. Both women were dressed in thick quilted robes, their heads and faces covered, so it would have been easy for others to mistake them for men.

"How on earth are we going to find that symbol if it's hidden?" mumbled Ling.

Still looking ahead, Qilan asked Ling, "Tell me—do you really want him dead?"

"I've been waiting all these years, training hard. Without a doubt, I want him to pay for my parents' deaths!"

Qilan stopped walking and turned to grasp Ling by the shoulders. Her gaze burned into Ling. "Then show him no mercy!"

"I ... uh ..."

"I'm sure you can do it," answered Qilan decisively as they resumed their walk down the street toward the market.

Snow began to fall more heavily. They found themselves wandering the alleys, listening and watching. It was Ling who spotted the sign. Just as Dried Reed had said, it was between two bamboo poles, a startlingly bright orange banner with the image of a tiger in the mountain. She touched Qilan on the arm and nodded in the direction of the sign.

Qilan entered the narrow alley next to the sign. Ling followed, walking behind her. At the end of the alley was an establishment that announced its business with a suggestive line drawing of a naked woman standing atop a male body, face down. Qilan exclaimed, "It looks like some kind of a massage parlour. Perfect place to get answers."

They stamped the snow off their boots and walked in. Off to the left was a waiting area, dimly lit. They saw a wisp of a man picking his nose at the front counter. The women brushed past him and headed down the hallway to the inner courtyard.

"Wait a minute! You can't go in there," shouted the man, but they kept walking. They crossed the inner courtyard, leaving imprints of their boots across the snow as they strode toward the heart of the main building. Qilan sniffed at the air before choosing to open the sliding doors of one of the rooms.

The room was suffused with a heady fragrance, musky and sickly sweet all at once. Two flickering candles burned in one corner. A man lay on a long, raised wooden table. A woman walked on his buttocks, which were covered by a cloth; another woman assiduously kneaded his shoulders. It was warm inside, heated by two sizeable coal braziers.

"Enjoying the massage?"

"What ... ?" The man raised his head slightly off the table and looked dazedly at Qilan.

"I have a message to pass on to Shan Hu. Tell him we're looking for him!"

The man pushed the woman off his back and scrambled off the table, holding on to the cloth covering his sensitive parts. "Just who do you think you are? How dare you barge in and ask for the Boss?"

"I can ask, can't I?" retorted Qilan.

"Just what kind of a whore are you? That dark face of yours ..." The man sneered at Qilan, staring her up and down.

Ling fidgeted and lifted her fists up to her chest. She wanted to punch the man for insulting Qilan, but the nun placed a restraining hand on her shoulder.

The man dropped the cloth and took advantage of that moment to lunge at Qilan, clamping his huge right hand around her throat. He raised his left fist, ready to punch her face.

Suddenly, the man's eyes widened in shock. Steam rose from his fingers and he yelped as he pulled his hand away from Qilan's neck. He stumbled backwards and smashed against the wall. The women screamed. He looked down at his hand; the tips of his fingers were all burnt black. More out of fear than modesty, he covered his privates with his other hand.

"Your boss murdered this girl's parents. It's time for her to seek him out and kill him!"

"Crazy bitches!" the man howled.

"I'm not crazed or bitching. You be careful with that dirty mouth of yours." Qilan's eyes flared up, lit by the candlelight. She growled and bared her teeth at him. "Just pass the message on. We'll be waiting at the Prosperity Tavern. He'd better show up there tonight. Or else rumours will fly that he's a coward who doesn't dare to face a nun and a young woman."

At the market, Qilan and Ling bought a small bamboo funnel of piping-hot roasted horse chestnuts and ate them as they made their way toward Prosperity Tavern.

Ling paused in the square, remembering the auction three-and-a-half years ago. It had been in the heat of summer, and the stench of greed soaked the air. She wasn't sure whom she was more afraid of now—Shan Hu or herself. Deep inside her, there still existed the tremor of that frightened, angry child she had been. But she was strong now. She made up her mind: She wasn't going to use any spells or magic but would rely on her wits and skills to fight Shan Hu. Ling shifted her weight left to right and back. She savoured the taste of chestnuts in her mouth, then took a few gulps of water from the gourd she carried on her belt. The water was cold, and it made her shiver.

Only steps away, ostentatious red lanterns bedecked the eaves of Prosperity Tavern, their candlelight flickering in the light breeze. It had stopped snowing. Overhead there was a half moon, and Venus hung close to it.

Qilan studied Ling's face. Sometimes, words were unnecessary; they simply understood each other implicitly. Qilan tilted her head in the direction of the tavern. "Let's have a proper meal before the scoundrel arrives."

The inn was impressively large and spacious, its three floors festooned with large red lanterns that hung from the eaves at every corner of the hexagonal space. All the windows were covered in yellow silk, reducing the draughts, and the coal braziers kept the place nicely heated. Customers were rowdily enjoying themselves, toasting one another, playing drinking games. The fragrance of various delectable foods wafted in the air, making Qilan's nose start to twitch with anticipation as she strode up the stairs to the top floor.

In contrast to the lower two floors, the dining area on the third floor was small and had only seven tables instead of thirty. Two of those were taken by customers; three at one and two at another. The tables were placed away from the staircase at the back of the room, and there was a door in one corner. *Private rooms*, thought Ling.

Qilan picked a table near the window. They took off their robes, hats, and scarves, and warmed themselves at the closest brazier. When the spritely, fresh-faced waiter arrived at their table, they could see he was unable to hide his surprise. He gawked at Qilan's elaborate hairstyle, so unlike that of peasant women yet not the style worn by a woman of the upper class. He eyed her up and down, took in the ordinary riding clothes, the exquisite glow of her dark-brown skin, the large eyes that were slightly drawn up at the edges.

Qilan ordered a flask of hot wine, chicken in hot sesame oil sauce, and eggs fried with preserved mustard roots. "Bring three cups for the wine," she instructed the waiter.

The food came quickly and they set to eating and drinking.

"Drink up," Qilan encouraged Ling.

The two customers at the next table pulled out musical instruments and started to play. Ling guessed they were in their middle years, husband and wife or maybe brother and sister. The woman played the erhu and the man the dizi.

Ling smiled wistfully. Old Chen would have enjoyed hearing this music. It made her think of the beautiful scenery of her childhood, the slopes on which the tea plants grew, and the rivers that wound their way through the region.

Qilan filled Ling's cup as soon as she had emptied it. Ling drank three small cups in quick succession. She felt the warmth of the wine suffuse and relax her whole body. Her reverie was interrupted by loud shouts from downstairs.

"Where are those filthy chickens?"

Ling shuddered. She could never forget that voice.

When Shan Hu reached the top floor, the three men at one table hurried away to the floor below, leaving only the musicians who seemed utterly unperturbed by the sight of the burly man; they continued to play.

Shan Hu sported a scabbard with a long sword slung across his back. He shouted down to the waiter, "Send up an order of pickled pig trotters! A large flask of wine. I'm going to be starving after I slaughter these two."

He took off his outer coat of heavy hide and his fur hat and flung them down on the table, narrowly missing the flask of wine.

"Started drinking without waiting for me?" He leered at Ling. "You! With the two different eyes. I remember you now. How dare you return?"

Against her will, Ling felt her legs start to shake and a thin film of sweat form at the back of her neck. She clutched the edges of the table. A low rumble of heat rose up from her belly to her face. She glared back at him, wild with desire to pounce at him. But she knew she had to hold back, had to wait for the right moment.

Shan Hu turned to look at Qilan who sat to the side, on his left. He recognized the pendant she wore. "The nun! First you purchase her, then you bring her back to me. What a pair you are!" His laughter echoed through the space, a grating contrast to the delicate music.

"Been attacking more innocent folks and killing them?" Qilan asked with a grin on her face.

"Your fucking Reverence. Why have you returned to Huazhou looking for me?"

"Don't ask me, I'm just accompanying my friend here," replied Qilan.

Ling's voice vibrated with restrained anger. "You are scum. Disgusting vermin. You deserve to die. So that others will no longer be terrorized."

Shan Hu ignored Ling, but continued to address Qilan. "How dare you bully my hireling at the massage parlour?"

"Because he is a worthless turd," Ling answered, her voice a barely audible growl.

Shan Hu eyed Ling again. "Why, you've certainly grown up, haven't you?" He eyed her breasts lasciviously.

Ling nodded, burping loudly once. "You noticed? So come on, have a drink on me before I slash your throat from ear to ear." She poured wine into the third cup and pushed it toward him. Shan Hu eyed the cup with suspicion.

"Don't you worry, I don't want to poison you. That would be too easy a death for you. Besides, I don't want to miss out on the pleasure of tormenting you."

Shan Hu surveyed the spread of food in front of him. He raised his right leg on the spare stool, leaned forward, and scooped up the third cup with his huge hand. He sniffed at the wine, then downed it and flung the cup at the floor, smashing it to pieces. "A mere mite on a buffalo's ass! You don't even have a weapon on you, so who are you kidding?"

Shan Hu moved back slightly to have more room. With his right hand, he reached over his left shoulder and withdrew his sword, which made a clear, swishing sound as it materialized from the scabbard. The blade was a beautiful beast, slim, well-fashioned, with a handle that was inlaid tastefully with three jade stones. He relished the thought that he would soon be slicing Ling up into chunks. The musicians stopped playing. No one moved.

"Maybe I should have a bit of fun with both of you before I waste you." He smirked suggestively. "You know, it's hard being a bandit. The more I pillage, the hornier I feel." With both hands on the handle, Shan Hu tilted the sword up and contemplated his strategy. Nobody at the inn would dare get in his way if he hauled these two off to a room behind that door.

He stared at Ling. She sat utterly still. Wasn't she afraid of him? He recalled the night when he'd ambushed the barge. She'd been terrified then; how she'd shivered with fear. Was this really the same girl?

He was about to make a straight thrust at her, aiming to mark the side of her face—just to scare her—when he was caught off guard as Ling headed straight for the sword for a brief moment before stepping off his direct line of attack. She ended up within a hair's breadth of his right ear and spewed out a sharp spray of hot wine at his face.

Shan Hu yelled as his eyes were stung by the hot wine. His left hand shot up to his eyes, and before he could regain his composure, Ling tucked her left arm very close to his armpit where she jabbed him once with pointed fingers. While gripping his right wrist with her right hand, she extended her left arm toward his neck, and dug her fingers into his throat. He yelped in pain.

Ling stretched out Shan Hu's right arm farther, pulling him forward until the sword clattered onto the table. She forced the back of his hand against the table. The sword trembled as she applied pressure to the back of his wrist, using her thumb and little finger to press on sensitive points.

Shan Hu howled and let go of the sword.

Qilan turned to the musicians and said, "How about some kind of ambush song?"

The erhu player whispered into her companion's ear. They launched into their performance. The bright, rhythmic notes imitated the charge of horses rampaging along a wide, expansive landscape.

Qilan approved and tapped her fingers on the table, keeping time.

Shan Hu's nostrils flared. He closed his left hand into a fist and swung it at Ling's head, but she managed to block it. He hit out with his right hand and struck her on the mouth then on the left side of her body. She staggered back and wiped her mouth with the back of her sleeve. Splotches of blood. The pain along her left side was sharp and shot down to her leg.

She crouched low, closed her hands into fists, and moved in close to him as she brought her arms up in arcs, hitting the sides of Shan Hu's head. She struck his ears with her fists then pummelled him vigorously on his chest and sides, followed by one side-swipe at his nose. She moved so fast that he had no chance to retaliate. He sputtered and gasped, staggering back. She stayed close to him, preventing him from being able to hit her. She ducked under his right arm and, forming the fingers of her left hand into a point, struck at the centre of his chest with the back of that hook. With an enormous amount of qi, she slammed both palms against his chest. The force of that energy travelled through him like a thunderbolt. As his head snapped back, Ling kneed him in the crotch. He buckled down and groaned, then reached out to grab her legs.

"Watch out!" shouted the erhu player, who intervened by smacking Shan Hu on the back of his neck with her fiddle.

He turned around and was about to grab the fiddle when he felt a series of stinging pains all across his back. When he turned around to face Ling, he saw that she had his sword in both her hands, the blade held horizontally at eye level, her legs in a wide stance. She angled her body and went at him. She wielded the sword with such skill that Shan Hu ended up with six bloodied diagonal slashes, three crosses down the front of his torso, just deep enough to slash his shirt.

Ling pointed the tip of the sword at his throat. "Hands behind your back," Ling commanded. She forced him to lean back even farther until he was precariously on the verge of falling over the edge of the railing.

"You have a very nice sword. It slices so well."

Sweat was pouring off Shan Hu. "Please ... please ... spare me!" His legs felt wobbly.

Ling wiped the sweat off her forehead with the back of her sleeve. "I bet you stole it from someone, didn't you? Can't fool me. You don't do justice to this beautiful weapon."

"Oh, how delicious!" sighed Qilan. "This moment reminds me of Zhuangzi's famous fable about Cook Ding. You know the story?"

The musicians nodded their heads enthusiastically, but Shan Hu was too terrified to respond.

"Cook Ding knew how to cut up oxen so well that his knife was sharp for nineteen years. Nineteen! As sharp as the day he bought it. Can you imagine?"

By this time, a crowd had gathered on the floor below, intently watching the scene unfold.

"As I was saying, this Cook Ding fellow. He was a good Daoist, you know. One of us. As Zhuangzi tells it—let me recall—it goes like this: Cook Ding said, when I first began cutting up oxen, all I could see was the ox itself. After three years, I no longer saw the whole ox. And now—now, I look at it according to my spirit and don't look with my eyes. Something like that. Then Zhuangzi goes on about the knife going through the big openings, missing the tendons. Nice and clean."

The crowd laughed and cheered. Someone shouted from below, "Kill him! We're tired of being bullied."

Someone else yelled, "He's stolen money from us and defiled our women. It's time to get rid of him!"

"Please don't. I beg you." Shan Hu quaked with fright.

Ling pressed the tip of the sword ever so slightly against his neck, causing a trickle of blood to appear.

The stink of urine permeated the air. *What a pathetic coward he is*, thought Ling. Her heart pounded hard in her chest. It took all her restraint not to finish him off. She could make him suffer long and hard before killing him. She was heaving from the exertion, but strangely enough, a sense of peace descended upon her. She pondered the fable about Cook Ding. She surmised that many onlookers at the tavern might understand the fable literally—it was about knives, cutting up oxen. Shan Hu was the ox up for slaughter.

Ling had heard the story from Qilan in the early days at Da Fa Temple. She knew it was a story that Zhuangzi used to demonstrate the secret of caring for life. It was about how to perceive the easiest way to move, how to wield one's weapons with ease. And then one no longer needed to be guided by the eyes, but according to one's spirit instead.

A vision came upon Ling. Shan Hu began to shrink, his torso growing smaller and smaller while his head stayed large. She saw the terror in his eyes—an image of herself reflected in them. How pitifully weak he was.

When the vision passed, she understood. Only a coward could commit heinous acts of violence. The thought came to her, *If I kill this scoundrel, I would be no better than him.*

"Turn around. Face the audience below."

With the sword aimed at the base of his neck, Ling used her free hand to press a few points on Shan Hu's back to immobilize him. His arms and legs twitched, then his whole body went limp.

She turned around and drove the sword firmly through Shan Hu's fur hat, impaling it on the table before she took the rope that hung on her belt and wound it around Shan Hu, trussing him up before the effects of the dian xue immobilization wore off.

She looked down the stairs to the floor below. "Hey, send up those pig trotters the man ordered, will you? Hurry up! And bring me ink and brush! Don't dally!"

The crowd below began to murmur among themselves.

Ling returned to the table. Her fists were bruised and her knuckles red. Qilan smiled at Ling who was still breathing hard from the fight. Sweat dripped down her forehead onto the table. The nun fished out a handkerchief from inside her sleeve and wiped Ling's face and neck. Next she poured some wine onto the cloth and wiped the blood from Ling's lip, which was starting to swell.

Ling picked up her chopsticks and resumed eating, even though her mouth hurt.

The tavern owner appeared with the tray of food and wine, and his assistant, now swooning with admiration for the young woman warrior, brought a tray with an inkstone, a small bowl of water, and an ink stick, along with a brush. Ling proceeded to create ink by rubbing the stick up and down against the stone while adding water slowly. Before long, she was ready.

She went over to Shan Hu and ripped off the shredded tatters of his shirt, exposing a broad writing surface, albeit a bit damp with sweat. She grabbed the towel that was slung over the innkeeper's shoulder and wiped Shan Hu's back dry.

She wrote on Shan Hu's back:

A scoundrel who failed to know
The value of others
His every slash and stab diminished him

Qilan watched and nodded approvingly. "Excellent."

Ling sat back down and sampled the pickled pork trotters. Dealing with Shan Hu caused her to feel quite famished.

By the time she was done with her meal, the effects of the dian xue were wearing off. Shan Hu started to move, but struggle as he might, he couldn't free himself from the ropes.

Qilan tilted her head in Shan Hu's direction. "Now what?"

Ling frowned and looked at the crowd of people gawking up at them. "We're going to parade him through Huazhou."

They paid for their food and drink, then dragged Shan Hu down-stairs and outside. A large crowd was waiting—men with lanterns and torches, women with their children, the elderly carried on the backs of donkeys or supported by younger men and women.

Ling addressed the crowd. "This man robbed my parents of their cargo of tea and precious stones. He then murdered my father and raped my mother. Overcome with shame, she killed herself. He threw their dead bodies into the canal. For almost four years, my need for revenge fuelled me. Some of you believe he deserves to die, don't you?"

The crowd cheered. Then Ling raised her arms to call for silence.

"I thought I wanted him dead. But then, when I fought him, something changed for me. I got close to feeling ... like him—murderous, treacherous, ugly. If I kill him, I will be no different. I don't want to become like him. So I'm going to take him to a special place so that he won't be able to harm anyone anymore."

"Are you going to lock him up?" asked an old woman up front in a shaky voice.

"Where we are taking him, he will be imprisoned by his own fears."

"Take him away from us!"

Ling and Qilan rode out, dragging Shan Hu behind them.

When they reached the edge of the Forest of Illusions, Ling and

Qilan dismounted. Qilan addressed Shan Hu. "There are caves in the forest. You'll find one without too much difficulty. You could forage for nuts and seeds."

Qilan cast a spell on Shan Hu before they untied him, put his coat and hat back on him, and gave him a pack with dried pork wrapped up in leaves and water in a gourd. He stumbled into the forest, locked in a trance.

Qilan raised her right hand and pointed the tips of her fingers in Shan Hu's direction. She mumbled some words, which Ling didn't understand. They watched him disappear into the darkness.

As they got back on their horses, Qilan explained. "I made sure he won't come to any harm. He'll always have enough food and water, but won't be able to find his way out of the forest for quite some time."

"How long? You're not going to prevent him from leaving?"

"No. He can leave once he's overcome his fears and he's no longer dangerous."

They rode hard, through a light snow. The road was dark, but the stars and moonlight were sufficient to guide them until they reached the city just before the drums signalled the beginning of the night curfew.

At the temple, Qilan put extra coals into the braziers in her private room. Ling winced from the sting of the tincture as Qilan cleaned the caked blood from the top of her lip. Ling rinsed her mouth several times with warm salt water. Qilan applied ointment to Ling's bruised hands and wrapped them with gauze.

"Did I make a mistake, Qilan?" asked Ling as the nun placed poultices on Ling's bruises.

"What mistake?"

"Should I have killed him? All these years of waiting for that moment. And yet ..."

"It takes courage and power not to kill someone, especially the very person you have reason to despise."

Of course she didn't regret not killing him. She just didn't understand her own confusion, the surge of emotions and the sudden onset of tremors. She began to weep without restraint. She hadn't wept like this since the first time she met Qilan. She lay her head against Qilan's chest and felt the warm, comforting embrace of her beloved benefactor.

It was all she needed. No words passed between them for a long time.

Start of new reign period
Linde 麟德
Lichun 立春 Jieqi,
Start of Spring, First Lunar Month of the New Year,
New Moon

GREAT ULTIMATE HALL AT TAIJIGONG, NORTH CENTRAL CHANG'AN

The Empress was dressed in a new robe that matched that of the Emperor's except that hers was emblazoned with phoenixes frolicking with qilin creatures and inlaid with gold threads and small precious stones. The Emperor's robe, although grand, was quite conventional, embroidered with agile dragons moving through clouds.

At the entrance to the Great Ultimate Hall, at the top of the stairs leading down to the ceremonial courtyard, the rulers sat on their thrones, side-by-side, on a raised dais. After years of making decisions on the Emperor's behalf during his bouts of illness, sitting behind a veil, Wu Zhao finally no longer had to defer to appearances.

In the ceremonial courtyard below were hundreds of guests— ministers, officials, and dignitaries from vassal states and far-flung kingdoms. Gloriously flowering plum blossom trees rimmed the circumference of the courtyard.

At the bellowing prompt of the Head of the Guards, the musicians raised the long trumpets made of rhinoceros horn and blew the anthem for ushering in spring. This was the cue for the ministers and officials to call out, "Wansui, wansui, wansui. Long live the Emperor! Long live the Empress!"

Since his setback almost four years before, Li Zhi had regained some function of his limbs, but he still required help to move from his throne and down the long flights of steps. He limped slowly ahead of Wu Zhao as they approached the incense urn in the immense courtyard.

Wu Zhao lit three sticks of incense then bowed to the four directions before planting them in the urn. Standing before the crowd gathered at the foot of the steps, Wu Zhao raised her arms to command silence.

When there was complete quiet, the Emperor leaned toward her and whispered into her ear. Wu Zhao nodded then spoke, as if simply relaying Li Zhi's words. "The Emperor wishes to decree this as the start of a new reign year, Linde. Throughout history, the qilin appears to signal the presence of sages and illustriousness. Heaven continues to sanction our rule. We proclaim that our reign of wisdom and moral uprightness will herald blessings for all."

After the Emperor and Empress ascended the steps and returned to their thrones, the guests in attendance also ascended the steps partway. The trumpets were raised and their fanfare announced the entry of the eight dancers dressed as the head, body, and tail of the chimerical qilin. The creature's body was covered with bright gold scales and ten thousand sequins, its head large, resembling in part that of a dragon's. The dancers whose legs represented the creatures' many limbs wore short boots that looked like cloven hooves.

As the sheng flute players began their refrain, the qilin prowled the courtyard, sniffing at the incense urn. Its enormous eyes blinked occasionally, its long lashes quivering with the movement of the dancer moving its head. A solitary musician played his set of bells, a tinkling melody that represented the voice of the qilin.

The creature performed a fast-paced dance, its body gleaming in the mid-morning sun. Toward the end of its performance, the creature reared upward, each dancer balancing himself on the thighs of the one below him, so that the qilin's head reached up to the top of a pole. A gem that swung from a string on the pole disappeared into the animal's mouth.

The qilin then exited the ceremonial courtyard, followed by the troupe of dancers and musicians.

Yushui 雨水 Jieqi,
Rain Water,
First Lunar Month, Full Moon

WESTERN MARKET,
WEST CENTRAL CHANG'AN

Ling was familiar with the Western Market, having followed either Old Chen or Qilan or one of the other nuns here once or twice a month to shop for supplies. She loved the bustle of the place, and it seemed to her that in the past four years she hadn't completely explored all the varieties of stalls in this enormous market.

It was toward the end of the Hour of the Snake when the sun drew close to its zenith. Despite the cold weather, the sky was an intense clear blue.

Qilan and Ling stopped at the stall that sold steamed dumplings. They each gobbled down six dumplings and a long stick of 油條 deep-fried pastry dipped in soy milk, making the requisite slurps of appreciation.

After their meal, they headed over to the Persian Bazaar, the section of the market that Ling loved the most, especially the stalls that sold gemstones, some tumbled, some rough. The first time Qilan brought her here, it was soon after Ling entered Da Fa Temple. At that time, they'd chosen a lovely black leather string that the merchant fashioned into a kind of web to enclose her turquoise stone. Now, they walked down the narrow aisle, between the shops on either side.

"What are you looking for, Missies?" cooed a seller standing next to the specimens of elephant tusks. As they passed the shops, the sellers called out their offerings. The bazaar was a maze of colours and possibilities. Qilan took them through several turns in the labyrinth until they arrived at one corner of the market, where an elderly merchant sat on a stool outside his stall, smoking his water pipe.

"Do you have it?" asked Qilan who bowed, palms together, to the man.

Without answering, the man got up and went to the back of the shop. He was gone for quite a while. His son and daughter-in-law tended to customers while their infant son slept soundly, tucked into a quilted basket next to the heat of the coal brazier. When he eventually returned, he handed a tiny box to Qilan. She in turn brought out two silver ingots from her pouch and dropped them into his open palm.

On the way out of the market, they passed a large crowd watching a magician. The young man—who could not have been much older than Ling—displayed a length of rope that stood upright, stiff and firm as a pole, and rose high in the air. He shimmied up the rope. The spectators craned their necks to keep the performer in their sights. When he was about twenty-five chi from the ground, the man stretched out his body at an angle, away from the rope, his arms strong and extended. He then released his hold on the rope, launched into air, and somersaulted repeatedly until he landed on the ground, his boots making a loud, slapping sound. He stretched his arms up in victory. There was a flurry of applause, then several people dropped copper coins into his tin on the ground.

By the time Qilan and Ling returned to the temple, the drums from the towers signalled the Hour of the Horse. After joining the last half of the morning meditation, they skipped the noon-day meal, Qilan indicating to Ling to follow her to her study.

"It's been a month since our return from Huazhou. You've recovered from your physical injuries. I think your invisible wounds are also mending quite well."

Ling nodded, then sighed. She supposed so, even though she felt a slight pang of sadness whenever she recalled her parents.

"So I think ..." Qilan paused, her brows drawing closer together. "this is a good time to tell you my story."

Ling's heart sped up slightly. This was the moment she had been patiently waiting for.

Qilan squeezed Ling's hand firmly while holding her gaze. "Promise me that you won't disclose my secret."

"I promise."

Qilan took a long, deep breath. "I'm sure you know from your time with me that I am different than other humans." She flashed a mischievous look at Ling, who returned it with a nod. "For one thing, my mother is a fox spirit. She crossed into the human realm and lived with my father on the outskirts of Chang'an. Would you say I am part human, part fox? I prefer to call myself a third kind of creature."

"A third kind ..." Ling cast her mind back to the first few days with Qilan, recalling various details she had noticed. She had never met a fox spirit before; it was unfathomable. All she knew was how she felt when she was close to Qilan—a feeling that words could never describe.

"Once my father achieved recognition as a scholar and official, he had to enter Chang'an to work in a government department. But my mother couldn't follow him."

"Why not?"

"Fox spirits cannot exist in the city. They are wild creatures. The political sphere of humans, even the life of the city, leads to quick death for them."

"Them? But what about you? You've been here in the city all these years."

"Since I'm the child of a human and a fox spirit, I have the capacity to exist in both realms."

"Did your father live with you?"

"He'd enter the city to work and return a few times a month to see us. Then, one day, everything changed. We lost Father, the man we knew as Xie."

Ling took a deep breath before she asked, "What happened to him?"

"He became possessed."

Hearing this from Qilan herself sent shudders through Ling.

"About a month before Father was possessed, I dreamt I was standing over a deep well, peering into the darkness from above. I heard the sound of water sloshing below. I felt a strong pull, as if some force wanted to suck me in, as if I could topple into the well at any moment. I smelled my father's scent. But he wasn't alone. There was another presence close to him, even though its scent was barely perceptible.

"I woke up with chills, shivering dramatically for half the night until dawn. I lost the ability to speak. The physician visited me a number of times, yet I could say nothing, not even make a sound. He looked progressively concerned with each visit. Sometimes he pursed his lips, other times he merely shook his head. My body felt heavy, as if submerged under some viscous liquid.

"In my delirious state, I saw my father cast anxious glances in my direction and talk to my mother in hushed tones. I had so much I wanted to say, but I remained unable to speak.

"I had no awareness of the weeks passing. I kept returning to the same dream, standing at the well and looking down. Until one day, the dream changed. I succumbed and fell for an eternity. I landed on my feet in the water. I extended my arms out, found the walls of the well, and walked the circumference. I had no sense of the size of the well. It puzzled me. Although my father wasn't there physically, I was able to detect his scent and, yet again, the scent of another presence, more powerful now that I was in the well.

"My mind called out to my father. There was no response. Was it only a few miao or even hours? Or years? Time became irrelevant. It seemed to me that I had entered a place outside of time.

"A flurry of heartbeat sounds thrummed at my ear. A heavy presence approached me from behind, then I felt a tight squeeze around my throat.

"My mother was shaking my shoulder when I screamed myself awake. I was drenched in cold sweat that smelled of rusty metal. I cried out—I was able to speak. All the details of my dream came pouring out of me."

Qilan's eyes misted over. She looked down at her hands.

Ling felt light-headed. She was frightened, yet she wanted to hear all that Qilan wanted to share. "What happened next?"

Qilan poured herself and Ling more barley tea before she resumed her tale. "My mother told me that I had spent many days in a delirium, about one hundred days. Most humans would have perished. The day before I emerged from this horrible illness, Father had gone in search of some kind of healer. He wouldn't tell my mother where he was going except to say that a trusted scholar had suggested a place where he would obtain help for me.

"Mother and I were suspicious. A person in so serious a delirium does not suddenly recover—unless there's some kind of exchange. What was the price Father had had to pay?

"As we spoke, Mother detected the rapid approach of some oppressive entity nearing our home. It would have been dangerous for us to remain. We changed into our fox selves and fled, rushing into the bushes in a corner of our front courtyard.

"Someone entered riding Father's horse. When we scanned the form of that person, we knew immediately that it was no longer the man called Xie, who had been my father."

"What do you mean, 'no longer the man'?"

"From the outside, this form vaguely resembled Xie, so that most ordinary people would be fooled because they wouldn't be able to penetrate past the appearance."

"You could see something else?"

"We saw the demon inside."

A shiver ran down Ling's spine. She clasped her arms at the elbows, holding herself in. These were terrifying things she was being told—a world of spirits and demons, a world of danger, of selling one's soul and body.

"Mother told me she would seek out her fox family. She instructed me to find my way to Chang'an."

"Why Chang'an?"

"Mother thought that Gui—the demon who possessed Xie—would want to be in Chang'an so that it could use Xie to infiltrate the Tang court."

Ling thought of Old Chen's words on that night after they'd emerged from the Forest of Illusions and were cooking at the fire. *Sister Orchid is not like the rest of us. She knows lots of things, but maybe she isn't sure it would be a good idea to tell us everything she knows.*

"Old Chen said you have gifts. Like your father."

Qilan's eyes flashed brightly and her mouth twisted into a half-grimace. "Not quite correct. My gifts, I have acquired from my mother. His powers are a result of being possessed by Gui."

"Your mother and you needed to flee this demon, so why do you need to be close to Gui?"

"To keep an eye on it."

Ling frowned, thinking hard about this. "How many years has it been since you and your mother escaped?"

"Almost eleven years ago."

"What are you keeping an eye on Gui for?"

"I am waiting for the eleventh anniversary of Xie's body being possessed."

"And then?" Ling's voice betrayed a nervous quiver.

"I must confront Gui at that time."

"Aren't you still afraid of that demon?"

"Of course."

"I don't understand. Why would you want to meet it? Could you still save your father—is that it?"

"Not his body. But his soul, perhaps. I'm not sure."

"Why eleven years?"

"The eleventh anniversary date is an auspicious time to halt Gui and immobilize it."

"Immobilize?" Ling thought of how they had released Shan Hu into the Forest of Illusions. "How?"

"I hope to capture the demon's soul. The constellations in the sky will assist me."

Ling shuddered. It was one thing to fight and conquer a human being, even one as repulsive as Shan Hu, but how does someone go about defeating a demon? "What has this demon been up to, all these years?"

"Gui wants to gain complete control of the Tang court by allying itself with Wu Zhao and installing her as the Emperor."

"Emperor? A female Emperor?"

"Yes, that's right."

"And then?"

"It wants to use its power at court to perpetuate more dark magic. Through Xie, it wishes to exercise control over the minds of the ministers and Wu Zhao and eventually cast a deep and lasting spell against this land and its people."

Ling stood up suddenly and spilled tea on her jacket. "That ... that is despicable!"

"It would only be the beginning of its scourge."

"The beginning?"

"It wants to destroy for destruction's sake—to destroy this city and then other parts of the country, and to possess many more humans. It wants to create havoc."

"Why?"

"Gui is motivated by sheer hatred of human beings."

Their conversation was punctuated by the sound of bamboo clappers. A man's plaintive voice called out the time. It was one xiaoshi, a small hour, past the Hour of the Horse. Ling's tummy rumbled. Maybe they shouldn't have skipped lunch.

"Sister Orchid, how will you go about immobilizing a demon?"

"It has something to do with freeing the demon from its attachment to hatred."

The colour drained from Ling's face.

Qilan reached out to take both of Ling's hands in hers. "Dear one, fear is the greatest obstacle. You and I—and anyone else who wishes to be liberated—must conquer fear, above all else."

"Is that more important than destroying a demon?"

"Fear is the demon. Eliminate fear and the demon cannot have power." Qilan's face reddened. She lowered her gaze and took a few slow breaths before speaking in a subdued tone. "All kinds of dark energies operate in our world and beyond. We can always choose how to respond, whether to join or resist. There are those, human and otherwise, who have decided to use their magic in the service of hate."

"In the service of hate," muttered Ling, mulling this over.

"I must capture Gui and free its soul."

"Isn't that a contradiction?"

"No. There are no contradictions and no separations in the realm of subtle realities. That is where I must travel to, bearing Gui's soul with me."

Qilan got up, went to the camphor cabinet, and brought out a cloth bundle. She unfolded the purple cloth slowly to reveal the object hidden within. She held it up gingerly.

Ling stared at the small plastron. There were squiggly symbols on the dorsal surface, but she couldn't decipher what they meant.

"A dream wants waking, a sky needs light," offered Qilan. "The demon is keen to possess this turtle plastron—it went missing a few years ago. Let's say I borrowed it. Just before I met you, actually. Gui believes the bone could be used to further gain power."

Qilan placed the plastron into Ling's hands. Ling looked at both sides of the shell. It was oddly warm. She closed her eyes. It was getting warmer in her hands. The heat spread from her hands and up her arms. It made her feel as if she wasn't simply confined in her body. She was expanding beyond the limits of her form and disappeared into the warmth completely.

When she eventually opened her eyes, she was surprised to discover that she was completely alone in the study. Where had Qilan gone? This was the same study, or was it? There were a few things on Qilan's desk that were unfamiliar. She looked out through the latticed doors to the courtyard and was astounded to notice the lush garden, the trees and plants in full leaf and bloom. There were other things in the room that weren't usually there—a few calligraphy scrolls that she had never seen before. What happened? It upset her. She closed her eyes and thought of Qilan. When she opened her eyes again, Qilan was there, sitting next to her, just the way she had been moments earlier.

Ling gasped. "Guess what happened?"

"What?"

"You ... you disappeared. Just for a few moments. I had to close my eyes and call up your image, and then you came back."

"I didn't go anywhere. But I suspect you did."

"Why would a turtle shell take me somewhere I didn't want to go?"

"Because it was showing you your destiny."

"But I don't want to make you disappear!"

"Or was it that you were travelling to some time ahead, when I am no longer here?"

That might be, thought Ling, but it was a deeply disquieting notion. "Qilan, what a mysterious plastron!"

There was a ferocious glint in Qilan's eyes. "There is a story behind this plastron," whispered Qilan. "Shall I share it with you soon?"

Ling blushed. "You know I love stories."

"But first we must go to the kitchen and find more food for you."

WU ZHAO'S STUDY, TAIJIGONG, NORTH CENTRAL CHANG'AN

In the early hours before dawn, Wu Zhao awakened, feeling restless and in a foul mood. Two of her maids washed and dressed her. Shortly afterward, she went to her study, which faced the Vermillion Phoenix Pavilion. It was still dark and cool; the oil lamps were lit early in anticipation of her arrival. The drum from the Sentinel Tower beat out the Hour of the Rabbit.

She sipped the smoky pine-flavoured tea, doing nothing else as she watched the sun peek above the trees, casting a slowly spreading yellow glow across the pond. The lotuses had not emerged yet, but there were signs of their roots below the water surface.

She thought of her father and how he'd ended up with the oracle bone. She'd been ten sui when he died. What could she have done at that time about holding on to any of his possessions? Her half-brothers disposed of as many treasures as they saw fit, taking some for themselves while other things were relegated to their uncle's care. She had known that the oracle bone was part of her father's collection stored at Hsu the

Elder's. She also knew the oracle bone was special, but she'd banished fanciful thoughts about it for the longest time.

And now—Xie seemed to know something about the oracle bone's power. Wu Zhao's heart rankled with unease. He was hiding something from her. Why was he so intent on recovering the oracle bone? Could she fully trust what he said? He had never completely revealed to her its purpose, although he had alluded to its usefulness for the Feng and Shan rituals.

She pushed her right sleeve up her arm, picked up one of her small calligraphy brushes, and dipped it in ink. She would write about how prophecy had first entered her life. "One day, I will fulfill the prophecy," she muttered to herself under her breath as she began to write.

> *As a young man, my father, Wu Shihuo, dealt in timber and fared reasonably well in his business. Our wealthy family came from the prestigious Taiyuan area. More importantly, our lineage is distinguished, going as far back as the first Zhou dynasty. My father had acquired a reputation for loyalty to his sovereign, impressing the last emperor of the Sui dynasty enough to merit being summoned to office. Yet my father refused because he had consulted a diviner who advised him to avoid such appointments. Years later, when my father met Gaozu, he recognized the man's greatness immediately and pledged allegiance to him. Not long after, he dreamed of Gaozu's overthrow of the Sui emperor.*
>
> *My father was a man of incredible sensitivity and intuition. In advising Gaozu on his military campaigns, he encouraged Gaozu to act decisively, saying to the future founder of the Tang dynasty that he was sure to be victorious. Gaozu valued him tremendously and rewarded him when*

he ascended the throne. My father was given a dukedom and promoted to the position of governor-general of two important prefectures, Lizhou and Qinzhou.

I was born during the time my father was governor-general of Lizhou. I was the second of three daughters born to a union sanctioned by Gaozu himself. It was my father's second marriage. He had two sons from his first wife, and then us three females. My mother, Lady Yang, was descended from royalty, having been a cousin of the last Sui emperor.

Father invited the renowned fortune teller Yuan to our house when I was barely a toddler. He did this because he was convinced that Yuan would prophesize that one of his two sons must have some propitious future.

Even my father, with his intuitive abilities, was mistaken. How could he entertain the possibility that one of his daughters, a child of his second wife, would evoke such a startlingly powerful response from the fortune teller? When Yuan first saw me—I'd been brought out by my wet nurse and was dressed in my half-brother's old clothes—he exclaimed, "The appearance of this boy is rare and remarkable. It is not easy to understand." Then the fortune teller told the nurse to put me down and let me walk. It was then, while watching me make my early clumsy steps, that Yuan detected the signs of greatness. "The semblance of the sun's rays! A dragon countenance with the neck of a phoenix, resembling Fu Xi!"

When my father revealed that I was female, Yuan realized that appearances—or rather, superficial interpretations of surfaces—were deceptive. A prophecy took hold of the fortune teller's mind, dismantling his biases, until he finally exclaimed, "Even though she's a girl, she will become ruler of the empire one day!"

Of course I don't remember the incident. I relied on my father's account of what had transpired. My father would describe to me what Yuan said, but I could tell how perturbed and puzzled he was by the prophecy. It upset his understanding of the order of things in the universe. I could tell from watching my father over the years that this whole notion of a female—his daughter—becoming ruler of the empire was a profound challenge to his beliefs about the rightful place of women in relation to men.

True enough, there had been other women who had risen to power and influence beside or behind their husbands, but a full-fledged female ruler sanctioned by Heaven? That was simply unheard of. Still, it is to my father's credit that he did not conceal the nature of the prophecy from me. He told me about Yuan's visit the way a parent would tell a fable to a child at night. To think that the reputable fortune teller and astrologer Yuan should be so bold as to make such an outrageous prophecy—that was the way my father relayed the tale. It was a good story, rather glamorous and delicious, but merely a story.

Despite my father's skepticism, some part of him took a childlike delight in the prophecy and proceeded to accord me special attention. As a young girl, I studied the classics, wrote poetry, and practiced calligraphy. My half-brothers, much to my father's chagrin, did not show as much interest in and aptitude for their studies. My father was sometimes startled by my degree of concentration. He was not used to children being as serious and intent as I was when it came to learning. I did not enjoy playing silly domestic games with my sisters. I often had wished my half-brothers would let me join in their war games, since I was sure I could have offered them some useful tips. I am certain they were jealous of me because our father took the time to teach me—yet whom could they blame but themselves? They were never as interested as I was in my father's library. Nor did they do any more than was required of them, whereas I was marked from a young age by an inordinate degree of curiosity. Really, my half-brothers' arrogant attitudes toward me were quite distasteful and always unfounded.

My father would tell my half-brothers and me many stories of his adventures with Gaozu. When he got to the story about the oracle bone he'd discovered in the pit at the base of Mount Li, my brothers were bored and could not wait to be allowed to go out to play. I asked if I could see the bone.

My father brought out a beautiful mahogany box that was two hands square and about four cun deep. Under the single lit candle, I stared at it, awestruck at the bone resting inside the yellow velvet-lined box. My father took the bone out of the box and let me hold it in my palms.

It had a mysterious inscription, yet it bore no signs of having been used for divination. What had happened? When I pressed my father to tell me more about the pit where the bone was found, he simply fell silent.

I was undeterred by his silence. I plied him with more questions. Is it really an oracle bone, when it has yet to be transformed by a divination ritual? Who had written that couplet onto the bone? Surely this was not a typical inscrip-

tion—that much I knew from having read into the history of oracle bones.

This was the only occasion when my father could not satisfy my curiosity to an adequate degree.

I am convinced my father died of disappointment at the age of fifty-nine, perhaps heartbroken over the loss of his benefactor Gaozu and the passing of an era. Disappointed in his sons, unwilling to place too much hope in his daughters. I wished he could have accepted the veracity of Yuan's prophecy. That might have caused him to live longer.

How strange we are, mortal beings, full of inconsistencies and contradictions.

"Your Highness." Ah Pu approached the entrance of the study and curtsied low.

Wu Zhao was annoyed at being interrupted. "What is it?"

"His Majesty would like you to compose some poems for the Lustration party this year."

"That is not for another month-and-a-half. Why would he trouble me this very moment with such a burdensome request?"

Wu Zhao sighed loudly and waved her hand at Ah Pu. "Just go away now. Don't bother me. Send a message to His Majesty that I am busy."

Ah Pu exited promptly.

Wu Zhao looked out the window and saw the white dove alight on the stone bridge. Its head was shaped slightly differently than other pigeons. It had a light sandy marking around one eye. She smiled with pleasure. She was still very much like that young girl whose mind was constantly curious, searching for answers. She picked up the brush again and continued to write.

Three years after my father's death, I was summoned to the Inner Palace. By this time, it was Gaozu's son Li Shihmin who reigned on the throne. One of my cousins had become the Emperor's favourite concubine. She was generous enough to persuade the Emperor to accept me. My heart rejoiced at such news, for I knew it marked the beginning of my rise to greatness.

When I entered the Inner Palace, I was called Zhaoyi, a diminutive of my actual name, Wu Zhao. I joined a retinue of concubines who had to tend to the Imperial wardrobe. This entailed learning about fabrics for covering furniture and for adorning rooms on various occasions and throughout the different seasons. Such boring work. But I did not lose heart.

I bided my time. Taizong's Empress Wende had died three years before. I never had too much to do with the man, except for the occasional visit from him. He was appreciative of my beauty, but even more than that, he was fond of my clever comments and my bold assertions. Of course, I must not fail to mention the famous—or should I say infamous—incident which all the records have already noted as an early example of my ferocity. I was standing watching him struggle to tame a very wild horse one day. I told him how I would handle it. This is what I said: "I need only three things: an iron whip, an iron mace, and a dagger. If the whip doesn't bring him to obedience, then I'll use the mace to pummel his head, and if that fails, I'll use the dagger to cut his throat."

Taizong understood my meaning very well. My words reminded him that I was the daughter of his father's military strategist. Even so, he never took me seriously enough as a challenge to his dynasty, did he? If he had, he would have recognized that I was the woman his court astrologers had prophesized about.

Venus was bold and visible in the daytime sky for several days in the seventh month of that year. The chief court astrologer told Taizong it signified that a female "Prince of Wu" would rule on the throne one day and that this woman was already in his palace. Taizong grew fearful and paranoid, yet his biases kept him from detecting who this future female emperor would be. The astrologer informed Taizong that there was nothing he could do to prevent this prophecy from being fulfilled. But the man acted foolishly, as if he could prevent the inevitable. At a feast, an official joked that, as a child, he had the nickname of Wuniang, Fifth Girl. He quickly became Taizong's prime suspect. Taizong exiled him to a provincial post. Poor wronged "Wu"! What a farce. Fear rendered Taizong unable to accept the literal meaning of the prophecy.

Why is it so hard for men to take women seriously? Does a woman have to become far better at being a man than most men to be taken seriously? In this world, relying on feminine wiles in the hopes of being rescued or protected by men is a risky and often futile strategy.

I was sad that my father died before I entered the palace as Taizong's concubine. He missed witnessing the beginnings of the prophecy's manifestations. I know I still harbour some bitterness toward my father for never having taken Yuan's prophecy seriously. What I would have given to see his reaction when I became Li Zhi's Empress Consort. He would have realized then that his willingness to instruct me in military and political strategies played a vital role in my success. He would have been exceedingly proud of me. Then it would not have mattered that I was merely a daughter. In truth, I was the true son he had wished for.

It would have brought me immeasurable satisfaction, to be

able to say to him, "You see how you could have accepted Yuan's
prophecy." It grieved me that I could not gain that ultimate
acceptance from my father.

What men like my father and Taizong failed to see was the
truth—that prophecy never occupies the realm of the logical or
convenient. Prophecy exists in its own right, withstanding even
the harshest disapproval.

Wu Zhao breathed a loud sigh and put her brush down. She looked up and saw a crow alight on the roof of the pavilion. The crow seemed to share her secret, watching her with knowing eyes. Of all the birds that flocked to the garden, it was the crow with whom she shared the most affinity. It seemed to her that crows were messengers of future events. Yes of course, the oracle bone was rightfully hers, just as the Throne was. Xie would fulfill his mission, and regain it for her. It would all come to pass. There was now no doubt in her mind.

DA CI'EN MONASTERY,
SOUTHEASTERN CHANG'AN

Snow had fallen several times over the past few days, but last night the rains came, and almost all of the snow melted. Xuanzang looked longingly at the scene outside. He would have liked to take a little stroll, even if it were just around the courtyard.

It was that part of the afternoon when most of the monks were doing their meditations while others cleaned and tidied the numerous rooms and halls of the large monastery. He cherished these moments of silence, but Xuanzang felt his whole body dragged down by the weariness of living.

He turned his attention back to the letter. It didn't sound like Li Zhi's style, not in the least. It congratulated the monk on completing the translation of the *Mahaprajnaparamita*. His eyes lingered over the last lines: *It is time for you to rest, Venerable Xuanzang. You have served the throne well.*

He understood the underlying meaning of the letter. There was a cruel innuendo to those lines, he was sure of it. Li Zhi would have not said such a thing. For all these years, the Emperor refused to grant Xuanzang permission to leave the city because he was intent on keeping the monk focused on his translation tasks. The Emperor never once encouraged Xuanzang to rest. These lines bore the tone of the Empress Wu Zhao who preferred to endorse Daoism, with its ornate, magical rituals that were not practiced in Buddhist monasteries.

Control. Power. That was what an Emperor was all about, thought Xuanzang. What was he about? Sometimes he had doubts about the direction his life had taken. Had he been purely motivated by a love of adventure? It might have been so, when he was young. At the outset of his trek to India, he was headstrong and impatient to explore the unknown. As he visited the various sites where Buddha was revered, he experienced a feeling that it all had been inevitable, as if the choices he'd made in his past lives had led him to this. He'd been driven; he had been meant to dedicate his life completely to the translation of sutras. Simply this, and nothing else.

Time passed slowly as he lay on the daybed, looking out at the scene outside his window. Now that he no longer needed to go to the Translation Hall every morning, he forced himself to rest.

Later that night, Xuanzang breathed in the sound of rain. He couldn't fall asleep. He thought of the damaged Buddha outside in the garden. Apparently, the sculptor had arrived earlier that day and had begun to work on the statue. It would take two or three visits to repair the damage. He wished he had enough strength left to make one more trip to see the repaired Buddha. At this thought, Xuanzang laughed gently at himself. In this life, he was terribly attached to his statues.

Peerless was moving around in the adjoining room, tidying and fussing about. That gave Xuanzang a warm feeling in his belly. Peerless was up because he was worried. With that thought, his eyes grew heavy. He descended into sleep quickly and entered the cave. There he was again, looking at the mural of Buddha surrounded by bodhisattvas. But this time Xuanzang was in the mural, standing to the left of Buddha, his hand almost touching the side of Buddha's robe. Rays of light emanated from Buddha and the bodhisattvas. A feeling of immense ease came over him. He thought to himself, *How did I become so blessed, to be here as one of his disciples?*

Xuanzang looked up at Buddha with adoration, yet it struck him how ordinary Buddha looked, like another human being. Why hadn't he noticed that before? The more Xuanzang stared, the more Buddha's face changed. It started to look more and more like his own. Yet there were other moments where Xuanzang once again had his own separate existence, standing next to Buddha.

The dream seemed to go on forever like this. Back and forth between being next to the Buddha, then being fused with him. Xuanzang was groggy when he woke up. He felt a chill pass through his body. His lungs seized up and he broke out into an episode of violent coughing. Peerless came rushing in just when Xuanzang coughed up blood into the palm of his right hand.

The young monk ran out to the main hallway and raised the alarm, shouting out, "Harelip! Call Harelip!"

When Harelip arrived, Xuanzang was being tended to by Peerless and Huili. His head propped up, Xuanzang was half-sitting, half-reclining.

Xuanzang turned his head to Huili. "That dream you told me you had last week?"

Huili's eyes reddened with tears. "Yes, Venerable Master?"

"It was about me, not you. A beautiful pagoda crashing down."

Harelip applied glass suction cups to Xuanzang's back and checked his pulses on both wrists.

"Leave me alone here with Harelip."

After Peerless and Huili left, Xuanzang said, "Now, so close to death, I have no regrets. Except one, which I cannot disclose publicly." He pulled Harelip close and whispered into his ear. Harelip nodded, eyebrows knitted together as he concentrated on listening to Xuanzang's comments and instructions.

Harelip proceeded to the apothecary. He lit a candle at the back of the room then returned the glass suction cups to their place on the shelf above his compounding table. Despite his confidence that he was utterly alone, he still looked nervously about.

It was hard to know where to put it. Piles of herbs on the table, jars on the shelves. On the floor below his table were several baskets. He took these with him on trips out to the forests and hills. The large ones would sit on either side of the donkey. Harelip would place any roots, bark, and leaves in separate hemp sacks, tie them at the mouth, then pack them carefully into the baskets.

He fished out two pieces of silk and laid the precious diagram that Xuanzang had entrusted to him between them and then rolled the layers up tightly. He secured the small roll with twine. Where could he hide it? He looked around.

His gaze finally came to rest on his altar. His Buddha statue, although carved from solid wood, had a small hollow opening at its base, just the right size and height for the rolled-up drawing. He inserted the precious roll without difficulty and then fashioned a piece of cork to fit exactly at the base, closing up the opening. Next, he dripped wax from the candle over the cork to seal it.

No one would think to look inside the Buddha, he reasoned, because this statue in particular was nothing spectacular as far as statues went. It was just ordinary, as if it had nothing to hide. He nodded, feeling reassured. *Something that needs to be hidden is best displayed without being seen.* Harelip rested his forehead against his hand on the table. He was so tired.

He was roused from his nap by the sound of a man's voice humming. He looked outside. It was already daylight. Where was the singing coming from? The tune was unfamiliar. The humming changed into singing. It didn't sound like any language he recognized. In all his years at the monastery, he hadn't heard any of the monks sing like this. Harelip listened to the soft, lilting voice and was charmed. He decided to go in search of the singer. He locked the door to the apothecary. *Which courtyard?* he wondered.

The voice grew louder as Harelip approached the Garden of the Buddhas. He saw the man from behind, kneeling before the damaged statue on a mat on the ground, his tools scattered about him. He was hewing out a piece of wood, fashioning a shape like the thumb that was missing.

Harelip cleared his throat, so as not to startle the man by coming upon him. The sculptor turned around. "You're looking for me?" He spoke Chinese with an unfamiliar lilt. The sculptor stood up. He was quite a bit taller than Harelip, lean and dark-skinned, with his head wrapped in a scarf. His jacket, somewhat worn and frayed, was not tightly drawn about him and revealed the smooth, hairless chest underneath.

"Oh, no. Well, yes—I followed the sound of your singing." Harelip was aware of an odd buzz in his body. He felt a bit dizzy. He wavered, unsteady on his feet.

The handsome man reached out for Harelip's shoulder to steady him. "Are you feeling ill?"

"Oh no, no. Just ... pins and needles ..." Harelip blushed. "You're the sculptor that Huili sent for."

"My name is Ardhanari."

Harelip bowed. "How is the repair going?"

"As you can see," Ardhanari said, bending down to pick up a piece of wood, "I am fashioning a small piece to fit with the rest of the hand. I can refine the piece at home. Then there's this crack to repair." The sculptor traced his forefinger along the back of Buddha's hand.

Harelip nodded, aware that his mouth was dry and his body hot.

"It won't take long. I have to come back tomorrow since I can't take this precious statue away. So another few hours, that's all."

Their conversation was interrupted by the meowing of the cat, who had arrived in time to slide her body across Ardhanari's leg. Harelip laughed nervously. "That's my cat, Maya. Well, she's the monastery cat, rather."

Ardhanari stroked the cat's ears, and in no time she lay on the ground and exposed her belly, which the sculptor dutifully rubbed.

Harelip bowed again. "Thank you for your work. My Master is grateful that you are here to tend to this."

"Ah, sorry that I couldn't come any sooner."

Harelip felt awkward. It fascinated him that a sculptor's work was to construct figures that were inanimate yet beautiful while, in contrast, he worked on living human bodies with all their idiosyncratic and fluctuating foibles.

"I must go." He bowed once again and hastened away, leaving Ardhanari with the cat.

Back in the apothecary, he tried to calm himself down. It was not the first time he had felt attraction to someone. In the past, it had either been a monk or someone he'd seen while on a visit out to the market or somewhere else in the city. It never crossed his mind that he was at risk of acting on his desires. Not until now, where his body felt strongly charged with a sudden hunger that had not existed, it seemed, until moments ago.

He turned his thoughts away from the encounter, back to Xuanzang's whispered request. He felt shaky. The monk he had revered all these years would soon be gone. It was a matter of days. He thought about his own devotion to the monastery.

What had kept him here for all these years? A sense of not belonging out in the world of normal-looking people? A need to hide from the taunts of others? At least, wearing the robes of a monk, he commanded some degree of hushed respect when he walked the streets of Chang'an. It was somehow more acceptable for a monk to be strange. A deformed mouth didn't add much more to what was already a sign of being separated from the populace.

But he had grown weary of the city too. Much like Xuanzang had. Helping the revered monk only intensified his own longing to leave Chang'an and do what Xuanzang couldn't. Unlike the great monk, what was he, Harelip, responsible for? Healing others. Or at least attempting to. He was not indispensable. If he left, they would find someone else to take on his duties.

There would be nothing to keep him here, once Xuanzang was gone.

Da Fa Temple, West Central Chang'an

In a formal tone of voice, Qilan began to tell Ling the tale. "During the period of the Warring States, the country was in chaos. Rulers no longer cared about the welfare of the people and became dissolute—uninterested in being virtuous and no longer in harmony with nature.

"Zou Yan was a philosopher who lived during that time. He was from the state of Qi and lived near the mouth of the Bohai Sea. He was driven by insatiable curiosity about the natural world. His senses were exceptionally attuned, and he possessed powers of great observation. Zou Yan examined everything down to the most minute of phenomena. He wrote essays on the increase and decrease of yin and yang energies, classified mountains, trees, animals, oceans—every living thing he could find—and then synthesized theories of yin and yang with the Five Elements. He called his system of thought the Yin-Yang School.

"Zou Yan rejected the rigidity of Confucianism because that system of thought ran counter to the occurrences of the natural world. He was not entirely comfortable with the sayings of Mencius either. He saw that violence inflicted by humans against one another was a result of being caught up in rigid adherence to rules—rules that didn't allow people to question the veracity of their ruler's decisions. To Zou Yan, what existed in nature followed complex patterns that were in harmony with one another; he wanted to cultivate theories that would mirror reality as opposed to theories and rules that went against nature.

"One balmy spring day, when he was not quite sixty-five sui, he sat down on a rock by the seashore and observed all that was around him, as was his habit—he loved to watch the subtle changes of colour and light in the sky and ocean and the movement of clouds. It didn't take long before he entered a trance.

"In the far distance, the ocean surface was ruptured by a slash deepening inward. Zou Yan could not make out what it was at first, but something emerged from the ocean's wound, shimmered, and moved toward him. As the vision drew closer, Zou Yan observed the shape of its extraordinarily large shell, its golden flippers, front and back, speckled with black markings, and a long protuberance that was its head and neck.

"The vision hovered close above him. Its mind spoke to Zou Yan's mind, using thought whispers.

"When Zou Yan emerged from his trance, there was a small turtle plastron at his feet. It bore an inscription that echoed the truths he had been observing in the natural world. He clutched the plastron to his chest and wept, overcome with the force of this encounter. Zou Yan sensed that this shell had been left as some kind of a pact between the turtle emanation and himself. He was convinced that the emanation had an intelligence, knew who he was, and spoke to him directly. It had told Zou Yan that it wanted him to seek an audience with King Zheng of the state of Qin.

"The philosopher resolved that he would do what the turtle emanation instructed, although it unnerved him that he had to journey far at great peril to his life and seek audience with King Zheng of Qin, the state that was at war with his home state.

"At that time, King Zheng was just nineteen sui. When Zou Yan reached the Qin court and gained an audience with the king, he recounted his vision with great trepidation. 'The turtle has foretold that, following protracted wars, King Zheng will succeed in unifying all the states under him.' Zou Yan uttered this prophecy, his whole body trembling, for he knew it meant that his own state of Qi would suffer great loss of lives as a result.

"Zou Yan entreated the king to follow the ways of nature by honouring the diversity that existed among the people he would be uniting. The turtle emanation had instructed him to say that if King Zheng did not heed the wisdom of the principles of yin and yang, his reign would be cut short.

"'Show me this plastron!' shouted the king. 'How can I believe you? How do I know that you are not some stark-raving madman?'

"Zou Yan felt torn. If he didn't show any proof, he might be executed. Reluctantly Zou Yan brought out the turtle plastron from his satchel and handed it to the young king, saying that he believed the inscription spoke about how yin and yang required each other.

"King Zheng was intrigued. He ordered the turtle plastron taken from the philosopher, then commanded, 'Now, be gone from here!' Zou Yan was chased from the great hall, deprived of the prized plastron. He was broken-hearted, for he deeply valued that gift from the magical turtle.

"King Zheng contemplated all that Zou Yan shared with him. The ideas of the Yin-Yang School fascinated him. He wondered how such ideas could serve him. The king sought the help of various alchemists and diviners and became obsessed with acquiring immortality.

"Twenty years later, when King Zheng succeeded in conquering all the other states, he crowned himself the first Emperor of the country, calling himself Qin Shi Huangdi. Afraid of losing control, Shi Huangdi went against all that Zou Yan had said. He had thousands of books burned so that all evidence of views at variance with his were destroyed.

"Shi Huangdi, like his forebears, was a Legalist. He had been raised with the belief that rulers had to instill fear in their subjects. A certain Lord Shang had been the adviser to previous kings of Qin, and this adviser had said, 'If you rule the people by punishment, the people will fear. Being fearful, they will not commit villainies.'

"The Emperor forbade his subjects from owning the *Book of Songs* and the *Classic of History*, banning these books and many more. Language was powerful, hence dangerous. All traces of inspiration—anything that was an observation of the universe or of the mind, anything that might lead others to think for themselves or to imagine other realities—had to be eliminated.

"Shi Huangdi wondered what would happen if the plastron was used for divination. After all, plastrons had been employed by rulers during the Shang and Zhou dynasties. He went to the summit of Mount Li with his retinue of diviners.

The Emperor felt emboldened by his power and told his diviners to ask the bone how long his reign would last. They tried to carve the bone, but however hard they tried, the bone remained intact. In order to save themselves from the Emperor's wrath, they cast the plastron into a pit at the foot of the mountain and told the Emperor that the prognostication was for a long and prosperous reign."

At this point, Qilan paused.

Ling was wide-eyed. She touched the turquoise pendant at her neck and rolled it between her index finger and the thumb of her left hand. She looked outside at the courtyard. It was raining heavily, and the wind tossed the trees and bushes about. Ling turned back to look at Qilan. "Sounds like Shi Huangdi was a big bully. Like Shan Hu."

"Except, of course, Shi Huangdi had much more power than that small-town villain."

Ling recalled seeing the frightened coward inside the big villain. "Shi Huangdi was really quite weak, wasn't he?"

"Many rulers are weak. That's what makes them so dangerous. This will not change in our lifetime or for many lifetimes. Remember what the inscription on the turtle plastron said?"

"'A dream wants waking, a sky needs light.'"

"So simple, yet one can interpret it so many ways."

"One thing interpreted many ways," echoed Ling, letting this profound idea sink into her mind.

"Did Shi Huangdi grasp the preciousness of the turtle plastron?" asked Qilan.

"I think that if he had, he wouldn't have tried to use it as an oracle bone." Ling was silent for a moment, then said, "I wonder, why was Shi Huangdi unable to cherish the plastron?" She narrowed her eyes and stared at the red coals in the brazier. People did the most awful things. She blinked. "He judged the plastron according to his own selfish needs and failed to investigate its true nature."

"Precisely," Qilan said.

"He was impatient and greedy," Ling continued. "That rendered him blind to the true gift of the plastron. Then, when he had been 'satisfied' by a lie presented to him by his diviners, he no longer needed the plastron. It had served his purpose." She continued to think aloud. "In the first place, he refused to acknowledge the truth of the message from the turtle emanation. Next, he failed to respect the relationship between the philosopher and the gift entrusted to him and he greedily stole it, after which he tried to force the precious plastron to function like an oracle bone! Travesty upon travesty!"

"Remember Zou Yan's warning from the turtle emanation?"

"If the Emperor didn't follow the ways of harmony, his reign would be short." Ling narrowed her eyes to ponder this. "Are you saying it was already predestined that he would have a short reign?"

"The prophecy was stated as a set of conditions. It said, if you do such-and-such, then certain consequences will occur. That's what true prophecy is; it doesn't eliminate one's capacity to choose. But it might suggest knowledge of a person's tendencies. What they do is still up to them."

"So, how long did he reign?"

"Ten years. Before his death, he was obsessed with achieving immortality and had various magicians make up elixirs for him. He even had a massive army of terracotta soldiers built to guard what would be his tomb. He truly believed he would reign even in the after-life.

"One night, the Emperor had a dream in which he stood on the very spot where Zou Yan had had the vision of the turtle. In the dream, Shi Huangdi looked out anxiously to the far horizon. He was waiting for the turtle to come to him at the ocean's edge. When he woke up, he was delirious and mumbled that he would become immortal if only he could possess the turtle. The Emperor died shortly after."

The rain had stopped. Sunlight streamed into the study from the windows. Both Qilan and Ling spent a few moments in silence watching the sky. The bells from the Western tower sounded the Hour of the Snake.

Ling exclaimed, "I think the turtle possessed him first."

Qilan laughed. "Maybe."

"How do you know the story, Qilan? Does this turtle have a name?"

Qilan shrugged her shoulders. "The story came to me by spending time with the plastron. Now I share it with you. You could repeat this story to whomever you trust. In this fashion, the story, and other ones like it, will get passed down to future generations of outcasts."

Ling nodded thoughtfully, then looked up at Qilan. "Are we outcasts because others reject us? Or because we reject them?"

"We must not reject others. But as to whether we become outcasts only because of rejection, or for some other reason ... well, my dear, I leave it up to you to contemplate."

"What are you going to do with the turtle plastron, Qilan?"

"Some day, I will need to return it to its rightful owner."

"Zou Yan?"

"No. Ao, the turtle."

"Ao?"

"That is the name of that turtle emanation."

"Where does it live?"

"At the edge, where land no longer exists. In the Great Ocean, beyond earth. Beyond."

"When will you do that? Didn't you say you were going to meet Gui? Would you take the plastron with you?"

"Yes, I will bring the plastron with me when I meet Gui. Then, much later, many years from now perhaps—I don't know when—I will return the plastron to Ao."

"When you are much older?"

Qilan smiled at Ling. "Age and time in years—these are not necessary for someone like me, Ling."

"But you wouldn't ... disappear—or die, would you? I would be so sad."

Qilan took Ling's hands into her own and squeezed them tightly. "We will meet many times over several lives."

These notions both excited and puzzled Ling, who could only say in response, "I hope so."

Jingzhe 驚蟄 Jieqi,
Waking of Insects,
fifth day of Second Lunar Month

DA CI'EN MONASTERY,
SOUTHEASTERN CHANG'AN

At dawn, Peerless looked in on Xuanzang.
"Come close and write my words down."

The revered monk's voice was faint, and he was too weak now to get up. Peerless barely kept himself from shedding tears as he pulled a stool close to the bed.

"I, Xuanzang, when I was twenty-six sui, in the year of the Ox, went to India. At the age of forty-two sui, in the year of the Snake, I returned to Zhongguo. From that time until the present, my sixty-third, in this year of the Tiger, the record of scriptures translated from Sanskrit to Chinese is as follows: sutras and shastras numbering seventy-four; one thousand, three hundred and thirty-eight chapters. I have given alms and offerings to ten thousand people, I have lit candles at thousands of rituals.

"My work has been accomplished. Sixteen years of arduous journeying followed by nineteen years of staying tethered to the city, undertaking the rigours of translation work. My physical body is soon to die. I wish to offer all the merits of my good deeds to all sentient beings so that we may all be reborn in the Tushita Heaven to serve Maitreya Buddha. When the future Buddha appears in this realm, may we also appear again to perform the tasks of compassion, so that all sentient beings may attain enlightenment."

Peerless placed the brush carefully on the rest after dipping it into the jar of water and wiping it dry. Now his tears fell freely.

"Don't get carried away by these feelings of grief, Peerless. Replace your grief with compassion for all sentient beings."

Xuanzang closed his eyes and went into a deep state of meditation. He recited the Heart Sutra, his voice a wisp of sound.

> *The noble Avalokiteshvara Bodhisattva,*
> *while practicing the deep practice of Prajnaparamita,*
> *looked upon the Five Skandhas*
> *and seeing they were empty of self-existence*
> *said, "Here, Shariputra,*
> *form is emptiness, emptiness is form;*
> *emptiness is not separate from form ...*

Throughout that day and into the night, he continued to recite the sutra, albeit in a diminishing voice. By the time the Hour of the Rat arrived, his voice was barely a whisper. His closest disciples as well as Harelip and Peerless surrounded the dying monk. At close to 夜半 midnight, Pu Guang asked Xuanzang, "Are you sure, Master, that you will return in the future to the inner courtyard of Maitreya Buddha?"

The monk, eyes closed, smiled knowingly and nodded. His breathing was so faint that Harelip had to lean close to Xuanzang's face, to sense each breath. When he could no longer feel that caress of air on his cheek, he straightened up and looked with reddened eyes around him.

The hallway outside was crowded by monks with heads bowed, so numerous that they formed a thick chain of bodies that wound around the corner and beyond.

Rogues' Mansion, The Vice Hamlet, East Central Chang'an

Xie was awakened by the sound of weeping in the streets. Clanging ensued, as if a host of people had found all kinds of metal to bang, the rough sounds of many timbres shattering the air. He lay in bed and listened. The voices grew louder. His right eye twitched with annoyance. Xie got out of bed and summoned his manservant.

"What is happening?"

"Master, the great monk Xuanzang has died."

"Oh." *What a fuss made over a monk*, he thought. *People are ridiculous.*

He ignored the noise, now that he knew it had no relevance for him, and fell into a deep sleep. Soon he found himself in a well. Gui was no longer inside him but was outside of his body, close by. *Why?* he had asked the demon. There was no reply. Instead, he heard the voice of his daughter calling out to him. Suddenly she was there, a movement, a fleeting presence. Try as he might, he couldn't touch her. He stood in the well, helpless, as she passed through him.

Xie woke up covered in sweat, shivering furiously. Surely only humans had nightmares, not demons. Why would Gui be outside of him, and his former daughter pass through him, like a being that no longer could be confined to a body?

There was power in not being confined—this he had understood only too well, thanks to Gui. But the truth remained that the demon had needed to use his physical form, to advance its ambitions in the human realm.

He wrapped himself in a blanket and got up. Peering through the latticed window into the courtyard, he wondered how his snake was faring in the jar. He needed to extract more venom, just in case he might need it. Xie lit the cannabis pellet, and the smoke relaxed him.

He felt much less like the former human he had been. There were now far fewer conflicts between him and Gui. He was no longer so sure they were two separate entities. But the nightmare—what was that about? A trace of his former self? A fear of his own helplessness?

Li Zhi's Chambers, Taijigong, North Central Chang'an

"Most certainly, a large ceremony to commemorate the great man," Wu Zhao said, with an air of solemnity suitable for the occasion.

Li Zhi raised an eyebrow. His Empress never failed to surprise him. "But of course. What do you suggest?"

"It has to be grand, whatever it is. A parade through the streets and a grand burial befitting a dignitary. We must show our people that we care about Xuanzang and what he has done."

"But you were complaining not too long ago, my dear, how much attention I'd paid to his work."

"Things have changed. Once a great man dies, we need to make use of his reputation and let people know we haven't forgotten him. This will cast us in even more of a favourable light."

Li Zhi smiled, nodded, and stroked his beard. He approved of the astute strategist in her. The people of Chang'an were already responding to the famous monk's death with a noticeable degree of grief. Surely they would be pleased to see that their Emperor also shared their feelings. He closed his eyes to imagine the scene. A massive show of riotous colours. Banners made by the people to honour the man. Yes, of course, a spectacle. Thanks to the generosity of the Tang emperor.

With some effort, he lifted the small bell and rang it. The maid entered. "Help me to my study." Once there, he was carefully lowered into the wide-armed scholar's chair. His eunuch servant prepared the ink for him.

Li Zhi struggled, but he wanted to write the letter himself and, with effort, he succeeded. He sent for his scribe to copy it out for him. Copies were sent to merchants in the city, asking for speedy proposals to be made for various aspects of a parade and funeral for Xuanzang.

Exhausted from his exertion, Li Zhi slumped back into the chair and took a few sips of tea. He was proud of himself. After all, wasn't he the son of Li Shihmin? That dignity and fierce warrior spirit ran through his veins. He'd recognized Xuanzang's greatness from the very beginning, and he'd ensured that the monk dedicated his remaining years to translation work. The Tang dynasty would forever be remembered as one that honoured its heroic sons and servants.

Da Ci'en Monastery, Southeastern Chang'an

All activities were thrown into disarray. The monks became distracted and dispirited.

Harelip was also listless. He had grown so used to the great monk's presence. Even fond of him. He was upset, of course, like everyone else. But in the past week since Xuanzang's passing, he was also angry because the Emperor wanted to put on a fanciful funeral service for Xuanzang.

He ventured out to the Garden of Buddhas to sit for a while. The weather was unseasonably mild. There were signs of the approaching spring—small buds on the two peach trees, a sparrow singing, the camellia bushes already full of buds about to burst. The sky was a mauve colour with a few clouds moving across the horizon quickly. It was going to be a lovely day.

Da Ci'en Monastery was being subjected to immense pressures to conform to the Emperor's dictates. Yet all of them at the monastery knew what Xuanzang had wanted—a peaceful, modest burial on a mountain. Would Huili and the others manage to convince the Emperor to change his mind? He couldn't bear to watch Xuanzang's wishes be ignored and undermined. Harelip's face flushed to think of this.

Why was it that ever since Xuanzang's passing, no one had been coming to him with health complaints, even though he could tell that some of them were not well? For instance, he had observed the pale, wan look on Huili's face, the sharp and shallow breathing, and the dry, cracked lips—Huili was definitely in need of treatment; but the monk who had been Xuanzang's main assistant had no time to think of himself. He was now one of the senior monks who had to deal with the Emperor's wishes. Harelip wished to help Huili. Perhaps he would brew the herbs, bring the bowl to him, and insist. Perhaps.

He groaned, and looked up at the buds on the peach tree. The sparrow was now on one of the branches. He would go talk to Huili—say that if he wasn't needed, he would venture out to the market to buy some supplies for the apothecary. His thoughts turned to the Indian sculptor Ardhanari. He'd overheard Huili mention where to find the sculptor. Harelip decided to go to the Western Market.

Harelip felt a growing sense of lightness as his steps took him further away from the monastery. Today, he wanted to be on his own. It took him more than one double hour of brisk walking to reach the Western Market. The Turkish teashop was at the southwestern corner. When he got there, he sat down at the communal table and ordered some tea.

"Does the sculptor Ardhanari live nearby?" Harelip asked Hamed, the tea seller.

"He comes here in the afternoons. Ask him yourself."

Harelip tried to suppress his joy at hearing this. He patiently sipped tea and observed the other customers. Hamed sometimes served up renditions of Sufi poetry alongside the tea—as he raised his teapot high in the air and allowed the milky tea to descend in an arc aimed precisely into each small glass, he intoned with a rapturous air,

You have infused my being through and through
As an intimate must do
When I speak, it is always of you
Even in silence, I yearn for you

Hamed, aware that one of his customers didn't know Arabic, translated the poem into Chinese for Harelip. Occasionally, a customer would pipe up and recite other lines of poetry. There were languages spoken in that tea shop that Harelip didn't recognize. What he understood was the spirit of each shared poem, its energetic recitation and the reverential, almost ecstatic tone. It struck Harelip that sacredness and passion co-existed in these spontaneous recitations. The tone was pure, yet there was heat. He was intrigued.

Soon after the next drum call, he detected a lovely light fragrance in the air. He turned and saw Ardhanari walking toward the tea stall. Harelip drew in a sharp breath.

"Ardhanari." Harelip stood up awkwardly and bowed slightly.

"You!" There was a sly glimmer of insight in the man's eyes. "Taking a break from the monastery?"

"On an errand to buy supplies," answered Harelip quickly. "Thought I'd pause here for tea."

Ardhanari sat at the table across from Harelip and ordered food.

"Have some," Ardhanari offered when the flatbreads were served alongside some kind of paste or dip in a bowl. "Very delicious. Try."

Harelip liked it. Some kind of beans or peas, perhaps, ground up and blended with oil and a hint of lemon.

Ardhanari once again comfortably spoke to Harelip in Chinese while speaking to the tea seller in a different language.

"How many languages do you speak?"

Ardhanari grinned at him as he continued to eat and answered with his mouth full. "It depends on what level of skill you want. I am most fluent in Hindi. Speak a bit of Turkish, quite a lot of Chinese. A few Mongolian phrases."

Harelip beamed at him, impressed.

After they finished eating and drinking, Ardhanari suggested that they walk over to where he lived. They went a short distance west of the market, and soon passed through the gate into another ward. They went through a maze of alleys until they reached a quaint fountain in front of a small house with a set of terracotta-coloured doors. Harelip followed Ardhanari down a narrow walkway next to those doors to a winding staircase at the back. Ardhanari's room was on the top floor. A low table sat beneath the tiny window overlooking the street; the table was crowded with small clay figures of animals, pottery shards, and wooden carvings. A pile of sketches on parchment lay in the far corner.

"Nowhere to sit, except on the bed. Please, don't stand on ceremony." Ardhanari stretched his arm out and pointed to the bed. Then, his back turned to Harelip, he lit the coals in the brazier. He stood and looked directly into Harelip's eyes. "I'm sorry to hear about the death of your Abbot."

Harelip lowered his eyes. He suddenly felt tearful and very uncomfortable. He didn't want to talk about Xuanzang. "Thank you," he mumbled. "So... do you work at various sites, doing sculptures?"

"In the summer and spring, I help my uncle at the Dunhuang caves. In winter, I return to the city. Sometimes I travel to other places in the autumn."

Ardhanari sat down next to Harelip. "Why have you come looking for me?"

"I ... I ... don't know."

Harelip looked down at his boots. He should have taken them off, he thought to himself. There were patches of water on the floor. He looked back up at Ardhanari and blushed. He'd never felt such a powerful attraction before. He felt exposed.

"Don't know, huh? That's a very interesting reason." Ardhanari smiled and took the monk's left hand in both of his. He caressed it, intently studying its shape and size, marvelling at the softness, the veins that were visible. He marvelled at the clean fingernails. His were often dirty.

"Have you ever been with a man?"

Tears now came to Harelip's eyes unbidden. He gasped, trying hard to choke back tears. "I have never been with anyone."

"Whereas I've slept with many men. And some who feel like women inside."

Ardhanari's candour startled Harelip. He had never spoken with anyone who was so forthright and matter-of-fact about carnal desires. He pulled his hand away.

"I was deemed too ugly for anyone to like me."

"Not ugly. Just noticeably different."

"How could you say that? You sculpt beautiful statues, figures with refined proportions."

"I appreciate other kinds of beauty as well."

Harelip stared at Ardhanari, thinking that the man himself was the embodiment of immense physical beauty. "I don't understand."

"Shall I be blunt? There's beauty within physical deformity. Under the surface. One must look deeper to see beyond the conventions of the mind. That's what I like about this part of the Foreign Quarter.

It has all kinds of unusual types. But unlike the Vice Hamlet in the Eastern Sector. How shall I put it? Here we have men and women who haven't sold their souls to please others."

Harelip felt his body start to tremble. This man possessed wisdom that rendered him fearless and allowed him to be undeterred by Harelip's deformity. He stared into the embers in the brazier, his face as hot as those lit coals. "I want to break my vow of celibacy," he said softly. "I don't want to be so lonely anymore."

"Is that why you are here?"

"No, it's not, not as if I think of you as my, my ..." He was at a loss for words.

Ardhanari frowned, his beautifully arched eyebrows coming slightly closer together. "Never mind. Let's not talk anymore." Ardhanari gently cupped Harelip's face with both his hands and drew it closer to his own.

DA CI'EN MONASTERY, SOUTHEASTERN CHANG'AN

Huili stared at the bolts of colourful cloth stacked up along one side of the candle-lit Translation Hall. "Enough, enough of this! Take these away from here!" he shouted at the top of his voice, shocking the delegation of artisans. "Venerable Master's dying wish was to have his body wrapped in a bamboo mat and buried on a mountain. Do you think any of us at the monastery could be at peace if we didn't carry out his wishes?"

"But—but—what about the Emperor?"

"Let the Emperor punish me. The Emperor can no longer override Xuanzang. He might have prevented our Venerable Master from leaving the city, but no, not anymore!"

Many of the monks smiled and some even shed a tear. The artisans were politely ushered out of the hall, along with all the beautiful tapestries they had brought.

Xuanzang's body was bound in muslin and preserved with herbs and oils. It lay in a reed cradle raised on stilts in the hall. Six monks, three on either side of the body, bore it to the back entrance, where they placed it in an enclosed carriage.

Harelip went up to Huili and whispered into his ear, "Let me go with them. I have some herbs to place alongside the body when it is buried."

Huili nodded his consent. Harelip rushed into the apothecary, selected some herbs, and placed them into his satchel. He joined Peerless on horseback while Huili rode his own horse. Two other monks drove the carriage. The remaining monks, totalling close to five hundred, walked behind the carriage in two lines.

Outside the monastery, people waited for the body to pass by. They lined the main east-west avenue. Many spectators carried branches of peach blossoms or offerings of lit incense sticks clasped between their palms. In the early dawn light, the cold air was suffused with the fragrance of incense. The crowds were silent, their heads bowed low.

Harelip's tears rolled down his face. He didn't bother to wipe them away.

At the Chunming Gate, Huili halted and raised his hand. The walking monks stopped. Only Harelip and Peerless followed the carriage heading toward Mount Hua.

Chunfen 春分 Jieqi,
Spring Equinox,
Second Lunar Month,
Full Moon

DA FA TEMPLE,
WEST CENTRAL CHANG'AN

Qilan brought the back of her right hand up to her face and licked it, then wiped her face the way a cat might do. She did this several times, then repeated the motions using her other hand. It was comforting to do this for herself in her private moments.

It was very late. The drums had sounded the last night watch, but she was still awake on the daybed in her study, after spending many hours reading. Being a third kind of creature—a third thing—was lonely. Other than Abbess Si and now Ling, the other nuns didn't know that about her.

When she'd arrived, she was chilled from travelling too long through the woods out in the open, fleeing from their family home. By the time she'd transformed herself back to human form just outside Da Fa Temple, she was drained. She remembered how Old Chen had opened the side door and brought her in to see the Abbess.

In the infirmary, in her weakened state, she had lost control of herself and changed back into a fox. The Abbess had drawn back in surprise and exclaimed, "Who are you?"

"I ... I ... am the daughter of a fox-spirit and a human. I had to escape—a demon threatened our lives." She didn't remember what happened right after that, because she must have fainted.

The Abbess had helped her all these years to cultivate the best of her nature, letting her develop both aspects of herself, granting her access to the rare books and ancient scrolls in the library, which contained mysterious diagrams, and her favourite fables, passed down in apocrypha.

From that very first day, the Abbess had partitioned off a corner of the temple just for Qilan so that she had her privacy and didn't have to maintain her human form at all times. It had a bedchamber with an adjoining study that opened to a small courtyard from which she could jump onto the roof and escape to the outside, cross a street, and quickly wind her way through parkland to reach the woods. Qilan needed to travel frequently outside the city walls on her own, in the form of a fox, to hunt small rodents and other prey. She had to eat raw meat whenever she had the chance.

To her relief, the other nuns had completely accepted the special treatment the Abbess accorded her. Gossip served its purposes. When it became known that Qilan's father had become possessed by a demon and this had required her to flee her childhood home, there was, of course, a natural sympathy aroused in the others. The nuns soon also appreciated how skilful Qilan was in martial arts. She began to assume responsibilities for teaching them various fighting skills. Many of the nuns weren't physically strong, but Qilan devised techniques that were suited to their bodies. Over the past eleven years, she had taught the nuns close-hand techniques and immobilization tricks no one had seen before; she showed them ways to use ordinary kitchen utensils as well as their malas and other objects as weapons for defence. Recalling the delight and surprise of the nuns when they succeeded in using their malas as weapons, Qilan snorted loudly.

She, in turn, benefitted from learning Daoist meditation techniques from the nuns at the temple, and over the past decade, she had been consistently cultivating her inner elixir. She was further indebted to the Abbess for teaching her how to use needles and moxa and how to set broken bones.

Ling was the first human she had trained who possessed physical abilities as well as refined analytic and intuitive capacities. She was also the only human to whom she taught spells. Qilan felt a passing sensation of emotion—what was this called by humans? Affection? Love?

She jumped down onto the floor, stretched her whole torso, and yawned, her mouth revealing her sharp fox teeth. She jumped back up onto the daybed.

Not all fox-spirits were bad. Why did so many humans misunderstand and pull away, failing to distinguish between those who were good and those who had ill intent? The majority of humans relied on hearsay, after all, and didn't trust their own experience.

She picked up the scroll she had been reading. It was a copy of Zhuangzi's *Autumn Floods*, section 17: "The Way is without beginning or end. Mundane things of this world have their life and death—you cannot rely upon them for fulfillment. One moment empty, the next moment full—you cannot depend upon their form. The years cannot be held off, time cannot be stopped. Time moves beyond the human. Decay, growth, fullness, and emptiness end and then begin again."

She yawned again and grunted with pleasure at the warm feeling of relaxation spreading through her whole body.

Zhuangzi was her favourite human philosopher. He understood that a being had to be free from fears in order to live wisely; a being was constantly evolving. Zhuangzi was mischievous too, which endeared him to her, thoroughly unsentimental and yet compassionate. The fox in her disliked sentimentality—too many humans could be sentimental one moment, and callous the next.

The realms were rich with mysteries—the most important thing to do was to listen well and conduct oneself with wisdom and virtue. Her eyelids were heavy, and she let herself surrender to sleep.

She soon travelled to a place that was neither land nor sea. There were many caves on the side of a mountain. She had wings, or at least possessed the power of flight. Swiftly, Qilan entered a cave and once inside followed the familiar scent.

"Mother," Qilan cried out.

"My heart, you have been so patient." There stood her beloved mother in human form, her fox eyes gleaming, her skin shimmering with golden flecks.

As they embraced, Qilan's body was infused with a blissful warmth.

"Where are we?"

"Dunhuang. This is the cave where women come to pray to the White Fox goddess for their wombs to be fertile and offspring given to them."

"You pick the most interesting places to meet, Mother."

"In a few months, on the anniversary of Gui's possession of your father's body, you will meet the demon at its lair. Quite unlike the lairs of we fox spirits, that place has energy that saps one's life force. To enter it is to enter into a realm of absolute cold stagnation and to risk being drained of vitality."

"What advice do you have for me, Mother?"

"You must travel there riding your horse, rather than by extraordinary means. Save your energy for the encounter with Gui. Remember, it is not a question of being conquered or of conquering. The plastron will direct you. Above all, do not fear. There is nothing to fear."

Qilan was startled awake. She sped down the hallway to the library.

It was chilly inside. The dust in the room made her sneeze. She began to light the coals in the brazier, then realized it would be too slow, so she cast a spell that sent an intense blast of warmth through the room. Satisfied, she went down one of the aisles and looked for the text. She found the manuscript and blew on the palm leaves. They turned themselves, stopping when the section she was looking for was revealed.

Be like a virgin,
The enemy opens the door.
Be like an escaped rabbit,
The enemy will be unable to resist.

BOOK THREE

Ji Ji - Completion

Liqiu 立秋 Jieqi, Start of Autumn,
Beginning of the Seventh Lunar Month,
New Moon

THE IMPERIAL COURT AT THE ADMINISTRATIVE CITY, NORTH CENTRAL CHANG'AN

The official knelt in front of Emperor Li Zhi. His Empress sat next to him, no longer behind the veil since the Lichun Jieqi celebrations.

"Your Majesty," began the official, clasping his hands in front of his face. "I have come with a petition from residents of the Vice Hamlet that you send someone there to investigate a series of strange deaths."

The Emperor blinked several times. "Wh ... what kinds of deaths?" he stuttered.

The official kept his gaze lowered to the ground. "We have reports that some women in the North Alley area were attacked during the process of giving birth. Their babies were alive one moment and then suddenly, mysteriously, were ..." His voice trailed off and he drew in a sharp breath.

Wu Zhao leaned forward, intrigued. "Speak up, man!"

The official began to tremble now, his topknot shaking visibly. "Your Highness, as soon as they were born, their bodies became limp and they turned blue. They were dead."

"How many of them?"

"Ten deaths last year. I was told there were others in previous years, but—"

"Prevarication is not a useful trait in our court!" The muscles in Wu

Zhao's neck were tensed as she glared at the official who held a minor post in the Department of Justice.

The Emperor's hand was shaking as he pointed at the official. "You, why do you hesitate to report this piece of alarming news? Do you not understand that I am a benevolent ruler? That my consort and I have the country's welfare at heart?"

"Your Majesty, Your Highness! I beg your forgiveness! I've been stunned by the recent revelations. I was not informed of the extent of the crimes until last week. I am shocked that such crimes have been perpetuated in the Vice Hamlet!"

"What has been the delay? Please explain yourself fully. Do not waste our time," Wu Zhao said sternly.

"There were several crimes committed over the past few years, but for some reason I have yet to discover, the news has not reached the authorities," the official said. "It was only because I myself was, uh, visiting the Vice Hamlet last week, on a, a personal matter, and I was told ... by one of the courtesans about the infant deaths. Her sister is one of the midwives who has attended many of the pregnant women over this past decade."

"What have you discovered about the crimes?"

"That no one else was present other than the woman giving birth and the midwife. Some midwives reported they saw a blue mist and some even swore they perceived a creature. They said that it had deep-set eyes and long limbs with claws. Oh, the word they used often—ugly. Yes, ugly."

The hairs on the back of Wu Zhao's neck stood on end. "What does your courtesan friend say? Did you speak to her sister?"

"Yes, Your Highness. I took it upon myself to speak with the midwife the next morning. She was the one who told me those details, and then I spoke to another midwife who reported the same thing."

"But why wasn't this made known to us?"

The official shook his head. "They said they were afraid that this demon would kill them if they reported its presence. They felt that the demon was only interested in the young babies' souls, so they went to temples to pray and use talismans, but the midwives aren't certain if their attempts to protect future babies have helped, since such deaths are still occurring."

"Sorcery! There must be a sorcerer doing such things in our midst," exclaimed Emperor Li Zhi, his right hand still shaking vigorously.

The official looked down nervously. Would the Emperor and Empress punish him?

Wu Zhao whispered to Li Zhi, whose face turned red immediately. He dismissed the official as he continued to listen to the Empress. After Wu Zhao finished, the Emperor announced to their retinue: "We will postpone making a decision about this matter."

Later that afternoon, in the Emperor's private chambers, the Chancellor's arrival was announced by the eunuch guard. Shangguan Yi knelt in front of the Emperor, touching his forehead to the floor.

"I have sent for you because I am ... not happy with Wu Zhao," Li Zhi said. "You know she can be quite—how shall I say it—imposing?"

"I understand, Your Majesty." The Chancellor remained bowed, not yet lifting his head.

"That is why I have summoned you. You may sit up."

The Chancellor watched the Emperor motion to the scribe, who passed a scroll to Shangguan Yi.

"My spies inform me that it is very likely Wu Zhao's lover Xie who has been behind the acts of sorcery leading to the deaths of the infants in the Vice Hamlet," Li Zhi said.

Shangguan Yi raised an eyebrow but kept his gaze lowered. *What an interesting development.* His mind raced ahead to the possible scenarios.

It was the chance he had been waiting for, all these years, a chance to rid the court of that meddling vixen. "Your Majesty, what is your wish?"

"I have drafted an edict. I want you to be in Court with me tomorrow, and I want you to suggest that I remove Wu Zhao as Empress because of suspected alliances with a sorcerer."

"Your Majesty ... Are you saying you are now ready to demote the Empress?"

"I'm tired of her complaints. Her excessive needs. Ridiculous things like establishing Luoyang as a second capital. How could we keep running between two capitals?" He sighed and consoled himself with a loud inhalation of snuff.

"Most expedient of you, Your Majesty." Shangguan Yi bowed again and, raising himself up, bent at the waist as he continued to walk backward until he was close to the door.

After the Chancellor left, Li Zhi's maid brought him some tea. He whiled the afternoon away reading poetry and paid especial attention to Shangguan Yi's poems. The elder statesman was a loyal subject, someone who had served his father, and now him. *An Emperor must remember the partialities of his Ministers*, he thought. *Shangguan Yi had preferred the former Empress Wang. Such things couldn't be helped. The whims of women.* He had thought Wu Zhao was devoted to him. He would have done anything for her. But why would she become so besotted with the sorcerer Xie?

He looked back down at one of Shangguan Yi's poems, "Early Spring in Guilin Hall."

The pacing palanquin emerges from Bixiang Palace
Clear singing regards the pool at Daiye
Morning trees filled with warbling orioles
Spring slopes swell with fragrance

.Li Zhi's reverie was interrupted by a guard announcing the arrival of the Empress. He was conscious that the poem lay exposed and quickly flung a cushion over it. He was overcome with an intense dizziness.

Wu Zhao strode in and sat beside him. She stroked his left ear, causing him to feel slightly aroused.

"I've heard a rumour," she said.

"Rumour?" Li Zhi tried to suppress his anxiety.

"That you're trying to get rid of me!" Without delay, she felt for his testicles with both hands and squeezed hard. The pain was exquisite. He moaned, thinking of all the times she'd had him at her mercy.

"Oh, no, no! That isn't true at all!"

"Well, then, why would this rumour be circulating?"

Li Zhi cast a quick glance down at the cushion. An idea came to him.

"My dear, you're absolutely brilliant. Why, in fact ..." He moved closer to whisper into her ear. "In fact, there is someone suggesting I get rid of you."

"I thought so!"

"We mustn't pay any attention to him."

Wu Zhao was livid. "Are you going to just ignore him? How absurd! My reputation is at stake. I could lose my position. And where would you be, if that were to happen? What if he put forth an edict and the other ministers were in support of it?"

Li Zhi broke out in a cold sweat. A sour smell rose from his body. "Of course, you're right. You think many steps ahead. All right, if the man is foolish enough to present an edict, I will make sure to punish him."

"Squash the man before he even gets a chance to present an edict!" said, her voice raised.

"Yes, yes," Li Zhi whimpered.

Shangguan Yi was sound asleep when the guards came to the door of the outer courtyard. He didn't even hear the loud banging and the shouts of the guards ordering the servants to open the door. By the time the maidservant shook him awake, the guards had already entered his bedchamber and loomed over him.

One of the guards unrolled a scroll and read aloud: "By the order of His Majesty, Emperor Li Zhi, you have been found guilty of sedition, of plotting to overthrow the Empress Wu Zhao as part of a plot to restore honour to the relatives of the former Empress Wang. You are thus to be apprehended and executed. Your son, your only male heir, will also be executed, as punishment for treason."

Shangguan Yi gasped. He couldn't believe it. Had this been a plot on the Emperor's part all along? He thought of the edict lying on the side table and panicked. As the guard roughly yanked him out of bed and shackled him with irons at his wrists and ankles, he trembled. The other guard found the edict. "What have we here?"

Shangguan Yi had lost control and wet himself. The guards snickered. The Chancellor hung his head in shame as they dragged him through the main hall, across the courtyard, and out the front door, watched by all the servants. He was forced into a carriage and taken away to be executed.

The Inner Palace at Taijigong,
North Central Chang'an

By the light of a single candle, she marvelled at the luminescent quality of his skin. Could she be imagining that his whole body had become more supple and younger? His skin was like that of a young woman's or a boy's.

"What is your secret?" She placed a hand against his sternum as he moved inside her, moving through her, as if he existed elsewhere and she too was being transported to some mysterious place.

She closed her eyes and wished he would show her where he had gone. Although he didn't answer her, the visions arrived slowly, as if she were being taken through a tunnel, a long burrow through the forest. She heard a low, not unpleasant humming. When she opened her eyes, she wasn't sure what she was seeing. His eyes gleamed with a greenish glow, and he seemed not as solid. She became even more excited. When she closed her eyes again and climaxed, she felt that wild careening spiral into nothingness. An utter relief. Nothing mattered for a few moments, except this free-floating pleasure.

He rolled off her, still erect, and she, too tired to help him, looked at him as he made himself come. A sweet fragrance exuded from him. *What was that scent?* she wondered as she inhaled deeply. It smelled fresh. Like skin that had never been sullied by the dross of this world. The word that came to mind was "pure," yet she didn't understand why that would be the association. It was a familiar scent, but she wasn't sure where she'd encountered it before.

He lay on his back and fell asleep, or she thought so. But suddenly he turned toward her, eyes wide open. "The time is fast approaching when I will encounter our enemy and gain possession of the oracle bone." He reached out and grasped her chin firmly. "Promise me that you will reward me for my efforts."

"My sweet, of course you will be rewarded."

"My Empress, we will conquer all those who hate us," he said, still holding tightly onto her chin.

She shook on hearing his words. There was such a resolute force behind them.

OUTSIDE DA FA TEMPLE,
WEST CENTRAL CHANG'AN,
THREE DAYS BEFORE FEAST OF ALL SOULS

It was a lovely late afternoon, the sunlight beaming down on them as they skirted through the woods, heading down a slope to the stream. They picked their favourite rocks to sit on quietly with eyes closed, their hands clasped in mudras in front of their bellies as they listened to the trickling sounds of the stream.

After half an hour, Qilan opened her eyes and Ling, sensing this, followed suit.

"This is a special day for us, Ling. I am going to teach you a powerful spell. You are only to invoke this spell under rare circumstances. Perhaps only once."

"What is this spell?"

"It is the spell for ending life."

Ling was startled. "Why would I want or need this spell?"

"As I said, under very rare circumstances."

Qilan leaned over, cupped her hands over Ling's right ear, and whispered the spell.

"When I whisper it like that, it is not being invoked. The important thing with this spell is, as with other spells, the intent and force with which it is uttered. The purity of the person—the being—casting this spell is critical."

"Do you mean it cannot work if it's whispered?"

"It can be invoked that way. But again, it's the combination of the intent and the energy behind the spell that activates it. So one could whisper, and with focused intent, it would work."

"But why would I ever need to use it?"

"When I say it is for ending life, what I mean is that it ends the physical form of that existence. One only uses it when there is tremendous suffering and the afflicted being asks for it so that there is release." Ling listened to Qilan's voice, resolute but without tension. "This spell is for when a being needs to be sent into its spirit form; to linger any longer in its physical body would prolong its suffering." She paused. "Do you remember the spell?"

"Yes."

"Repeat it to me. Whisper it, so that no creatures around us can hear."

Ling repeated it to Qilan. When Qilan was satisfied that Ling had learned the spell, she stood up and led the way through the woods as they ran back to the temple. When they reached the street, they crossed it in three breaths and, when no one was looking, scaled up to the roof, then down into the courtyard outside Qilan's study.

Qilan closed the doors to her study. "The time has come for me to leave."

Ling's heart gave a lurch. "When?"

"Tomorrow morning."

"Where will you go?"

"I must travel to the place where my father had been possessed."

"But ... for how long?" stammered Ling.

"Not sure."

"What if—" She didn't dare say it.

"If I don't succeed?"

Ling nodded. Her heart pounded furiously.

Qilan smiled. "I don't know, my dear."

Ling curled her hands into fists. "I want to go with you."

"No. You can't."

"Why not? You went with me to Huazhou!"

"That was different."

Ling looked directly into Qilan's eyes. She needed to speak her mind. Even though Qilan was her benefactor, she wasn't going to stay silent on such an important matter. In Qilan's eyes, she saw her own face partially reflected back to her.

"You said I have a close connection with the plastron," Ling said. "Couldn't that come in handy? You've always taught me not to let preconceived ideas get in the way of what wisdom offers. When I faced Shan Hu and fought him, I let go of my old ideas. Up until that moment, and for all the years before that, I always believed I had to face the villain and kill him. But I didn't. I couldn't."

"Are you saying I might be mistaken about going to face Gui alone?"

"Yes." Ling's tone was firm, but she was far from feeling confident.

After what seemed like a long pause, Qilan took hold of Ling by her shoulders. "No, you can't go. This is my journey. Mine alone. My father lost himself for my sake, so now I must fulfill my karma—not so much to save his life, but to liberate his soul."

"Let's ask the oracle bone!"

Qilan sighed and shook her head. "It would be dangerous. And you are needed here."

"What do you mean?"

"You ... are to succeed Abbess Si one day, if you wish to."

"Who decided that?" She felt a rush of heat through her face. "I mean, no one asked me. Now you're insisting I can't follow you. You saved my life, and you want me to repay you by staying here? Shouldn't I be loyal to you?"

Qilan turned her face away and stepped out through the doors into the courtyard. "You mustn't fall prey to such rigid ideas of loyalty," Qilan said, her back to Ling. "Remember that vision you had of being in the study here, but I wasn't present?"

Ling nodded.

"It was a vision of you carrying on my legacy of teaching and serving here."

"I can't imagine that—I just can't believe it."

"Trust me. Trust the vision. The Abbess recognized the greatness in you."

"Greatness?" Ling laughed.

"There are times when one must accept that to repay a debt is not straightforward; instead, consider that you can share the benefit of your gifts with many others by assuming the role of Abbess one day."

"I thought you said we have choices—that we always get to choose."

"Yes, it's true. Completely. Consider then what other choices you would want to make and why."

Ling's body began to tremble. This felt familiar. It was exactly how she'd felt when her parents had been killed. How her body shook then—for days, for weeks. She was afraid once again in a way she hadn't felt for four years. She took a deep breath. "How will you defeat Gui?"

"I won't need to defeat the demon. I believe I've told you, I'll be going to save it."

"What?" She didn't remember Qilan saying that.

"I'm going to follow an intuition based on what I've learned these past four years spent with you and the turtle plastron. Why—I've known you as long as I've known the plastron!" Qilan smiled and her eyes shone as they filled with tears. It made her uncomfortable to cry; she never quite understood where all the human emotions came from. "The turtle plastron is a different kind of oracle than what people have expected it to be," she continued. "It certainly hasn't behaved in the way it was expected to. Humans have vast, ambitious notions of how to harness the universe for their own purposes. But what if the bones of other creatures have lives that assert themselves in extraordinary ways? What if they carry wisdom beyond human beings' narrow conceptions of what is acceptable?"

Ling, stunned by Qilan's words, walked over to her benefactor and tentatively reached out her hands to grasp Qilan's. "Please come back, Qilan."

"We will meet again, in this life or the next. Don't be afraid." Qilan drew Ling to her and held her tight. She had passed on all that could be imparted to this dear one.

They closed their eyes and were silent as they held onto each other. They listened to the sounds that filtered to them from beyond the walls of the temple. Occasional vendors shouted out what they were selling. Children squealed in delight as they played their games, unfettered by cares.

Later that night, Qilan went to the stables to look for Old Chen. He was cleaning out the stalls. It was a messy task. "Our young girl is grown up now," she said.

Old Chen chuckled and continued to scrub down the sides of a stall. He was used to the stench but had been impressed from the beginning that she'd never minded the smell. "You've come out of your way to the stables to tell me this, did you?"

Qilan went to her stallion, patting and speaking softly to him.

He wasn't at all surprised that Qilan ignored his question. Sister Orchid never felt obliged to answer questions just because she was asked. He stopped what he was doing and, placing his hands on his hips, watched Qilan as she continued to talk to her horse. He could never understand what she said to the creature. Old Chen sensed there was something important she wanted to say, but there was no way he could prompt her to say it any sooner than when she was ready to.

He turned his attention to raking in some new hay, then he started to brush down the horses, going from one stall to the next. Qilan took over when it came time to brush down her horse. He stood just outside the stall and watched her.

"Yes—you know, I am proud of her, of how she's grown up into a strong and sensitive person," Qilan said. "She may be young, but she's gained a lot of wisdom."

"Indeed."

"I want you to keep an eye out for her."

"What could you possibly mean? She's there in the temple under your guidance and looked after by the Abbess and all the other nuns."

"Yes, of course. But you have a special place in her heart. She knows she can talk to you if she needs to. Your own children are grown up now, but could you find it in yourself to look out for this one ...?"

It dawned on Old Chen why they were having this conversation. "You're ... going away?"

She nodded, not breaking the rhythm of her brushing routine.

"For how long?"

Qilan shook her head. "Don't know, can't say yet."

"Another one of your secret missions."

"You could say that ..." She turned to him. "Please prepare my saddle and equip me with my usual weapons. I'll be heading out very early tomorrow." Qilan put down the brush and nuzzled up to her horse.

Old Chen felt disturbed. It was the way she didn't say things, how she was silent between the few words she uttered, that told him that what she was about to do was quite serious. "It's about your father, isn't it?"

"You've been listening to the gossip."

He wished he could protest but he dared not, so he remained silent, remembering his own counsel to Ling years ago. He too had to accept what Qilan was about to do. "I respect that you have your reasons, Sister Orchid." He bowed deeply to her.

"Thank you, Old Chen," she said, bowing back to him.

She placed one hand firmly on his shoulder. Such a powerful grip; it sent shivers through him. Tears came to his eyes. He wanted to say, *Don't go, you're like a daughter to me.* But he refrained from speaking further—it would only make the parting that much harder.

Very early the next morning, while it was still dark, Qilan went to the Abbess to say goodbye. Next she crept into the nuns' shared sleeping quarters and slipped a note under Ling's pillow.

It was raining outside when Qilan left the temple. She had a large conical straw hat on, worn at a forward tilt to conceal her face, though there was hardly anyone on the streets outside to see her. The air was damp, and a thin film of sweat formed on her upper lip. She curled her tongue up to taste it. Salty.

Qilan reached the Yanxing Gate just as the drums sounded the ending of the curfew. She was the first to leave the city when the guards opened the gate.

Even travelling at top speed, the journey would take about a day and a half. She estimated that she would arrive at the full moon, on the Feast of All Souls. After riding hard and fast past sunset, she stopped at a small inn off the main route and asked that she be allowed to sleep in the stable. Her stallion needed hay and water and she wanted a large meal. Qilan paid the innkeeper generously with some silver. She was tired and fell asleep quickly, the oracle bone in a hemp pouch tucked inside her tunic jacket. Many images visited her that night.

Waking up in the half-light before dawn, she had a vision of her mother, an apparition sent from a remote distance. "Dear heart, I am safe. I will guide you to the temple."

She quickly departed to resume her journey.

Ling sneaked out to the stable instead of attending the morning prayers.

Old Chen was snoring, lying in the hay with a bottle of ale next to him.

She poked at his belly. "Did she just leave? Where did she go?"

He opened his eyes and looked dazed. "How would I know?"

"I need to find her."

"Don't be silly. She doesn't want you to do that."

"Stop sounding like her!"

"No one knows where she's gone," Old Chen replied.

"Do we simply just wait here? I mean, she's gone on a dangerous mission. How can we do nothing?"

Old Chen cleared his throat by spitting into the corner. He took up his empty bottle of ale and looked down into it. "Huh, I didn't think I drank it all already. Bah, that was a short night of sleep. I need to get more ale."

"How can you be thinking of ale at this time?" Ling felt a flush of impatience and anger. "I'm going to take a horse and ride out."

"Where would you go? Tell me."

"I ... uh ..."

"If you had really wanted to follow her, you would have shadowed her the moment she left the temple. But then, how could you know when she was heading out, short of sleeping in the stable with me all night? Besides, she would have stopped you dead in your tracks with a spell!"

Ling kicked at a bale of hay. "I didn't suspect she would leave before dawn."

"She left so early you were probably still snoring away, along with all those other nuns."

"All right. I'm a fool."

"Come now. Don't give me that ugly scowl. We can't always follow the ones we love, Ling. You're supposed to be here, at the temple, now." Old Chen yawned and got up. He stretched and tucked in his shirt. "Listen, I need to go into the market later. Why don't you come with me and give me a hand? You're the strongest one in the lot, after all."

Ling knew this was Old Chen's ploy to distract her. She nodded reluctantly.

Chushu 處署 Jieqi,
Limit of Heat,
Fifteenth Day of the Seventh Lunar Month,
Feast of All Souls

En route to Demon Star Temple

Before dawn, Qilan was already awake when the vision of her mother appeared.

"I will meet you outside the temple. Ride for another forty-three li and you will come to a fork in the road. You will recognize that one of the forks eventually leads to our former home. Take the other fork and ride until you see a rock marked with the characters, 鬼星寺. The rock is well hidden, so it means you must use your fox vision to find it. Dismount there at the rock. Take the narrow trail leading up to the temple on foot."

Qilan reached the fork in the road by the early afternoon. A fleeting image of their former home came to mind, but she didn't dwell on it. The other fork was the one she needed to take. As she rode up the path, her face prickled as if poked by needles. Her horse had to be goaded to travel that way, almost bolting a few times. The sky went from clear to cloudy in an instant.

The sun was halfway past its apex when she spotted the stone marker with her fox vision. Indeed, it was far back from the path and concealed by grass and moss. She alighted from her horse and spoke softly into his ear, reassuring him with a few firm pats on his side. She removed the oracle bone from the saddlebag and tucked it into her jacket. She carried a cloth bundle filled with offerings. She removed her hat and let it fall on her back, held in place by the string against her neck. She took a deep breath before she made her way on foot.

It was a hot, sweltering afternoon. There was no sound other than her boots on the hard ground. The air was still. There wasn't even the sound of cicadas. No sign of birds.

The distance felt interminable. It must have taken more than a small hour before she spied signs of the temple ahead. The stillness was broken when she saw, just ahead of her, a raven hopping around on the ground at the entrance to the temple. She paused. She and the raven stared at each other for a few minutes before it flew off.

The closer she got to the temple entrance, the heavier her body grew. It was all she could do to move one foot in front of the other. Near the entrance, the vision of her mother appeared. "Dearest, I have guided you here, but I cannot enter. I will help you from a distance. Courage, my daughter."

Qilan looked back and scanned the landscape around the temple. There were a few bundles of twigs in one corner of a garden long neglected. A few dead shrubs. No sign of life. Then her eyes caught the quick gleam of an animal scurrying away.

Da Fa Temple,
West Central Chang'an

The chanting of the nuns soothed Ling. It was going to take her a long time to digest what Qilan had shared with her.

Today, the boundaries between all worlds disappeared. Heaven and Hell and the realm of the living were open to crossings and visitations. It was important to honour the ancestors and offer incense and food to the hungry ghosts roaming about.

Sister Lizi was the one leading the chant today. She struck the wooden frog with eyes closed, the short stick never missing a beat. Ling half-listened to Sister Lizi's voice, her mind riddled with many questions.

For the first time since she had lost her parents, she felt utterly terrified and unmoored. The fear she felt when she'd confronted Shan Hu was nothing compared to how she felt now. Didn't Qilan care about dying? Wasn't *she* afraid? After all these years, Qilan remained a mystery to Ling, though Ling felt as though Qilan knew her through and through. Why had Qilan been so calm when she announced she would leave Da Fa? Had she put on a show of courage for Ling's benefit? Or did being part fox spirit somehow grant her an extraordinary capacity to be calm?

Ling's eyes filled with tears as she recalled the note that she'd found under her pillow yesterday morning: "To the soul that is still, the whole universe surrenders." She thought to herself, *She has commanded me to be still. Not to rush ahead to follow her.* Ling looked around the room at the nuns. For the past four years, they had all been kind to her, and she'd appreciated the respect they showed toward one another. She didn't know how any of them had ended up here at the temple. Did their parents die, like hers? Had they been escaping danger, like Qilan? Did some of them feel a calling to become a nun? She had never dared ask any of them about their histories. Only Qilan volunteered her story. Did donning a nun's robe somehow change a woman or girl? Was one's history erased in some way by such a ritual? If she ever did decide to become a nun and remain at Da Fa, she would never forget her former life. But would her commitment to the temple somehow change her relationship to her past?

She brought her mind back to the chanting and looked up at Abbess Si who sat facing them. The elderly nun looked frail. Her lungs were more congested lately, and she coughed often. Sister Lizi was leading most of the rituals and chanting these days.

Ling hadn't even turned the pages. She realized finally that they were close to the end of the scriptures. She sighed quietly to herself.

DEMON STAR TEMPLE

The sign over the entrance read, 鬼星寺.

Qilan maintained the protective spell over her entire person and stepped over the threshold. All at once, a chilling presence descended from above. She felt its force, pressing hard, attempting to force her down to the ground.

She stretched her arms upward and met the chill with a hot, glowing stream of energy that shot out from her open palms. The chill receded enough for her to look around. There was little to be seen with the naked eye except ruins—cobwebs, toppled ritual objects, a broken altar table, some stone stools overturned.

She thought for a few moments about what she needed to do. She brushed the cobwebs off a stool, righted it, and placed her cloth bag carefully on top of it. Then she picked her way through the rubble, sniffing the air as she went. There was a strong smell of stagnation. Energy had become static and sunk downward. After walking around the main hall, she spotted the blocked passageway. What looked like broken parts of chairs and tables formed a web-like obstruction. On studying it more closely, it reminded her of some other pattern, but she couldn't recall what it was. *Is the obstruction really an obstruction? Perhaps not,* she thought.

She turned her attention back to the main hall. She placed her right index and middle fingers up against her lips and whispered. Then she aimed those fingers at the cobwebs. They disappeared instantly. She waved her hand toward the broken table, causing it to be mended and the ritual objects to be righted. Next, she directed her fingers at the candles left in the burners, and they became lit.

Qilan glanced outside. It would soon be dusk. She retrieved her cloth bundle, unwrapped it, and placed the dried fruit on a green ceramic dish. On another small plate she poured the melon seeds and pine nuts. Then she brought out the small box which she had obtained months earlier at the Persian bazaar. Opening it, she lifted out a single rod of cannabis resin, the length of her middle finger. It was embossed with the figure of a snake. She placed it in the urn on the altar table.

She took off her outer jacket and placed it on the stone floor, forming a makeshift cushion. She then sat down, legs crossed, and proceeded to recite out loud. "I, Qilan, nun at Da Fa Temple, begin this petition by addressing the divine presences, male and female, in the Heavenly Realm.

"As daughter of the man named Xie, now sorcerer in service to the Empress Wu Zhao, I recognize that his soul has been captured and his body occupied by Gui, the one who originated in the Underworld and that came to occupy this temple for several years before it took possession of my father.

"I invite the Ones Who Dwell in the Stars, the Ones Who Execute Harmers, and the Illuminated Ones of Venus's Central Phalanx to join with me. Together, on behalf of the seven generations of deceased ancestors of Xie's household, may you assist me in dispersing the infectious and stale vapours associated with the demonic, forcing Gui to come forth and depart from the family gate. Cut off infectious infusions. Cause Gui to be brought under the control of the Demon Statutes.

"I invite the Divine One of Vermilion Cinnabar to apprehend the five Gu-Poisons, the Six Goblins, and the demons of malignant disasters and impoverishments that are causing decrement and loss. Annihilate them all.

"I pray to the Most High Beings on behalf of the man Xie and his soul. In order to disperse the inquisitorial pneumas, your servant respectfully offers up this Great Petition."

After Qilan finished chanting, she bowed and rose up slowly. Her mother's voice entered her mind. *Gui had arrived.*

She heard the growling presence approach from behind. Turning around, she saw Xie who smiled coldly at her.

Qilan brought one hand up to the centre of her forehead. She looked beneath Xie's form and saw the demon crouched inside his guts. It extended its front limbs up and wrapped its claws around the inside of Xie's throat. Its tongue flicked up and down sporadically.

"You were once my father," she said.

"I chose the demon," Xie responded in a tight, raspy voice.

"Xie came to this temple eleven years ago, wishing to save my life."

"I suppose a father has to do that, doesn't he?"

"But you are no longer my father."

"Oh? How unfilial of you!"

Two rays of green light shot out from Xie's eyes. Qilan evaded them; they struck the stone floor, causing it to crack. An acrid smell rose up from the fissure, like the smell of burning flesh.

"How dare you steal the oracle bone!"

"I only borrowed it. I'm going to return it to Ao."

The walls of the temple shook and the ground vibrated. A blue mist issued from the top of Xie's head. His form slumped down to the floor.

"You won't get your father back," Gui sneered.

"I'm not here to rescue his body."

"Oh? Well then, what are you here for?"

"Why explain? You wouldn't understand."

"Where is the oracle bone?" The demon uncoiled its body and stretched its front limbs out. It reared up, standing almost twice tall as Qilan.

"Here," Qilan whispered, tapping her sternum.

"You expect me to fight you for the bone, is that it?"

"Look at the offerings I have laid out for you here. I'm doing this for your benefit."

"Absurd nonsense!" Gui screeched. "But allow me to commend you for being ingenious enough to have evaded me all these years. Before I annihilate you, I'd like to entertain you with the story of how I came to be a demon."

Gui blew out a steady stream of blue mist that sank to the ground between it and Qilan. "In my previous life as a human, I was a man of great learning and wisdom. I had a lot to offer the ruler and his people. Yet I was reviled because of my physical deformity. Women mocked me and avoided me. Even though I should have been awarded the top prize in the Imperial examinations, the Emperor refused to do so because he succumbed to popular opinion. All the knowledge and wisdom I possessed was completely ignored, simply because I looked ugly!"

Gui sank down on all fours and began to move in an arc, and Qilan immediately followed suit by walking in the opposite direction. She sensed the demon had a lot more to say before it decided to attack her.

"I was supposed to receive accolades. To stand alone on Ao's head, the victor in the examinations. Instead, I was robbed of glory. So I hate, I *hate* the craving of humans for beauty and goodness."

"And in hating, you've become cruel."

Gui stopped and reared up. "I am justified. Justified."

A wave of cold radiated toward Qilan and instead of sinking to the ground came within a few cun of her. She shivered, her teeth chattering, before she managed to issue a spell that neutralized it. Water pooled at her feet.

"What would you like to do with the oracle bone?"

"I lied to the Empress," Gui said, making a succession of rapid sawing noises that expressed its glee. "I told her I would use it for the Feng and Shan rituals in a few years."

"You want it for another purpose." Qilan was intently focused on Gui's every move as they continued to circle around each other in the ancient hall.

"I will use it to destroy human beings," Gui said. "I'll start with the Emperor and Empress, all their servants in the Inner Palace, then the ministers, the court, then finally, all the people in this city! That's only a beginning. For humans are a scourge upon the earth, and they deserve to be eliminated."

"You seem to think this oracle bone would aid you in this?"

Gui snarled, baring its sharp teeth. Its foul breath made Qilan wince. "You can't fool me. I know this oracle bone belonged to Ao. It's only fair that I gain possession of it. It will make up for the humiliation I suffered in my previous incarnation as an ugly human."

"Are you sure you would know how to harness the bone's power?"

Gui stopped in its tracks then once again reared up to its full height, its eyes now gleaming. "I can see the fox in you. So you must understand why I hate. They hate us because we're not like them. So why should we not hate in return and destroy them?"

"I don't hate humans. You're the one who's been suffering for eons, trapped by your own hatred. No wonder your head has grown blacker and your neck is so thin. Let me feed you."

Gui gasped. "Feed me? How could you? How dare you presume?" The protuberances on its jaws jangled as it stretched its mouth open. It ceased its loud, effortful breathing momentarily. "You know I can simply pounce on you, and you'll be dead."

"You're probably right," Qilan replied nonchalantly.

Gui was caught off guard. "Aren't you afraid?" it hissed.

"I'm only agreeing with you."

"We can work together. Would be such a waste to kill you."

"You can't destroy me yet. I know how to harness the power of the oracle bone. You don't need just the bone. You need me as well."

"Such an exquisite mix of human and fox, such delicious energy. I must have your soul."

"Are you proposing to possess me?"

"It would be different than what I did with your father."

"How?"

"Co-operate with me or I will destroy you!"

"You used me to get to my father. He chose to let you possess him. But I refuse. You chose to become a demon in order to take revenge on humankind, but your hatred makes you weak. It's time for me to take you back to the Underworld."

Gui scratched the ground vigorously with its front claws. "You can't possibly succeed. Enough of this talk."

Qilan grabbed the cannabis rod from the altar. She bared her fangs, and flames shot out from her mouth. The rod ignited at the tip. She blew a strong wind at the cannabis rod. The smoke from it formed wisps resembling large snakes that moved quickly toward Gui. The coils of smoke wound themselves around the demon's body.

"By the powers of the Divine Ones, I bind you and break the curse." Qilan brought out the oracle bone. "Behold, Ao's plastron. A dream wants waking, a sky needs light."

"It's mine!" The demon struggled against the coils of smoke, freeing its front limbs, and lunged clumsily toward Qilan.

She could feel the plastron start to throb in her hands. The demon's cold energy began to sap hers as it held her in its suffocating embrace. Coldness crept over her.

The force of their contrary energies created a whirling torus. It took all of Qilan's energy to direct the tip of the oracle bone at the web of chairs where there was one tiny central opening. She needed to aim the oracle bone exactly at that opening. A violent tremor ensued as the chairs blocking the doorway disappeared and a powerful force pulled both Qilan and Gui through the portal.

The well. *So here it is, no longer just a dream. What next?* Qilan had to focus. But on what?

She had to put aside her reasoning mind and its attendant fears and tune into the darkness around her. Scanning with her fox eyes, she discovered countless holes along the inside of the well. They were almost perfectly round.

The oracle bone started to pulse strongly in her hands. The heat emanating from it was immense, and her fingers felt as if they were burning. Then the pulsing stopped almost as suddenly as it had begun. She wondered what the pulsing meant.

"Is this well an illusion?" she asked the oracle bone.

It pulsed again.

She thought of the time four years ago when she took the oracle bone away from Hsu the Elder's house. It had pulsed more gently then. It had given her visions of the future, the far future, when people and the city—everything—looked different. Then there was Ling's first experience with the plastron.

The plastron was a kind of oracle bone after all, but with its own mysterious ways of behaving. Qilan decided to ask it another question. "Can you choose whom or what you would respond to?"

A burst of pulses.

"Do you respond to what is most important to the one in possession of you?"

No response. Sometimes, when the plastron did not respond, Qilan wasn't sure what it meant.

Her mother's voice entered her mind. *Be deep and still and so perpetually present.*

This was a familiar phrase to Qilan, but where had she read it? She couldn't quite recall. She looked up. Far above her there appeared a glimmer of light. Was that sky? Maybe this was a well that opened up to the universe. If the well was a product of the mind, and it opened up to the universe ... then it wasn't a literal place. She'd entered the well when she uttered the inscription and the oracle bone had caused the portal to open.

In dreams, she had been able to sense her father's presence, but he was nowhere to be found now that she was here. Neither was there any sign of the demon. This reality was so different than her dreams.

In the midst of its dark depths are essences. Returning to the root is called stillness. Her mother's voice again. Qilan suddenly realized where those lines came from—the Xiang'er commentary to Laozi's teachings. What came after that last line? *Stillness is called "restoring destiny." The restoration of destiny is called "the constant."*

She pondered the meaning of these lines. She thought of the time, eleven years ago, when she had last seen her father the way he had been before he left for the temple, desperate to save her. Was that his destiny? If he hadn't left, if she hadn't needed to flee, she wouldn't have gone to Da Fa Temple. She wouldn't have rescued Ling, and that would have meant that Ling wouldn't be able to become Abbess of the temple some day. All that had occurred was interconnected.

The demon was poisoned by its hatred; that hatred insisted on its alienation from others. It struck Qilan how alienation and hatred led the demon to want to ingest and assimilate the souls of humans just at the cusp of their emergence into life. Gui practiced annihilation, not connection. She believed she had made the right choice not to separate herself from the demon. It meant overriding all of her survival instincts to welcome the demon's embrace as it attempted to annihilate her.

She felt a trace of sadness, but it was soon followed by a lifting of her spirits.

She asked herself if she would have done what her father did. Her answer was clearly no. She was a different kind of creature altogether. Having chosen to face the demon and join with it had led her to enter this dark well of her dreams. What was the darkness about? The only chance of discovering answers lay in her ability to attain stillness. She focused her mind wholeheartedly on that task. She had to quiet her mind to listen better. Finally, from the holes in the well came the softest hint of wailing. The longer she listened, the louder the sound became. It was not singular, she realized, but an eerie chorus of weeping. Qilan intuited that the holes must represent all the lost souls taken by Gui. This was their well of despair.

She understood what she needed to do next. She held the oracle bone close to her chest and said aloud, "If this well has arisen from my mind, and I feel constrained in it, then I would like to return to my original freedom. By doing so, may I also restore freedom to the souls of those imprisoned here with me." She held this wish close to her. The oracle bone throbbed in agreement. She took a deep breath and repeated, "A dream wants waking, a sky needs light."

She was back, but now in the front courtyard outside the ruined temple. When she looked into the dark interior of the temple, she saw that the lights had all been extinguished. She stared at the building. To her surprise, the whole edifice began to look hazy, its outlines becoming less definite until it disintegrated before her eyes.

She had a moment of panic and reached into her jacket to feel for the oracle bone. Not there. But her cloth bag was with her, next to her right foot, on the ground. She reached into the cloth bag and felt the outlines of the plastron.

Just then, her mother's voice spoke. *Return, my dear, return to Da Fa Temple. Quickly.*

The spell had been broken, but she had no way of knowing exactly what had happened. Her mind felt slightly muddled, as if she had been immersed in a deep sleep or stupor. She walked slowly, feeling slightly dizzy. Grateful when she reached her horse, Qilan leaned against the animal and sniffed, the familiar smell comforting her. She started to weep. She wasn't quite sure why.

The sun was halfway past the mid-point. Had she been in the well overnight—or longer? How much time had actually passed? Or was she returned back in time to the moment before she entered the temple?

No answers came, but that didn't matter now. She tucked her cloth bag into a side pocket of the saddlebag before mounting her steed and setting off in the direction of Chang'an.

The journey back went much faster. She didn't know if, in fact, she was riding the horse because it felt as if her mother was riding with her, sitting behind her on the saddle, and they travelled inordinately fast. Time did not seem to move at the same speed.

She didn't feel well. Her body began to be wracked by a searing cold that ate at her from the inside out.

THE INNER PALACE AT TAIJIGONG, NORTH CENTRAL CHANG'AN

Wu Zhao awoke with a start. She called out to her maid.

Ah Pu thought that the Empress had once again dreamed of the female ghosts. When she entered Wu Zhao's bedchambers, she was shocked to find that the Empress's body was elevated several cun above the kang.

"Help me, please!" she gasped. A blue mist lay on top of her.

Ah Pu screamed at the sight. Two guards rushed in and tried unsuccessfully to pry the invisible presence off the Empress. A third guard took a torch and waved it around the Empress but to no avail. As a shrill, piercing sound grew louder, the guards were flung against the walls. The curtain caught fire when the torch landed against it. The shrill sound stopped abruptly, and Wu Zhao was dropped back down onto the kang.

After the fire was extinguished, Wu Zhao looked sternly at the guards. "Do not report this to the Emperor. Anyone defying my order will be executed."

Two new guards were summoned to keep vigil outside the Empress's bedchamber. Ah Pu returned to her antechamber, shaken up and exhausted. Wu Zhao sat at her table, unable to return to sleep.

Who was responsible for tonight's mischief? Doubtless someone opposed to her power. Or someone against Xie's favoured position with her. A sorcerer hired by Li Zhi? This last possibility unnerved her. She hadn't heard anything further from Xie yet. He had refused to disclose where he was heading when he left the city.

Despite herself, she wept. She couldn't bear the thought that something awful had happened to Xie. She'd become attached to him. Her heart began to beat furiously. Without Xie, how could she bring about the Feng and Shan rituals? She needed his magic. She needed his potions, his spells.

She clasped her arms tightly in front of her body and rocked back and forth. After a long while, she stopped when she recalled the prophecy. *Yes, of course.* The prophecy that she would one day become the Emperor. She had to believe it. With or without Xie, she would succeed. She simply had to trust. Her destiny was already carved out for her. She continued to rock her body back and forth, whispering reassurances to herself.

THE VICE HAMLET,
EAST CENTRAL CHANG'AN

The full moon was slowly obscured and then turned red. The phenomenon lasted for almost a double hour. This instilled wonder and fear in people.

All activities came to a halt, and the city was thrown into chaos. Many shouted to chase the cursed shadow away. Some rushed out into the streets with pots and basins and hit them hard, creating a ruckus. People stopped what they were doing and went outdoors to watch the eclipse.

Everyone paid attention except one who sat motionless in the graveyard under the gingko tree. Around the form a cacophony of wails rose up from the ground. A handful of shopkeepers across from the graveyard swore that they saw slight wobbling forms rise up and glow in the dark night under that red moon.

The next morning, his manservants found Xie's body under the gingko, limp and desiccated. Around him, a massive amount of fluid had streamed throughout the graveyard, rivulets watering the ground.

DA CI'EN MONASTERY,
SOUTHEASTERN CHANG'AN

Harelip couldn't sleep. He got out of bed and made his way to the apothecary.

He lit one candle and took out his mala, then faced his Buddha statue and said a few rounds of mantras. He stared at the figure and wondered what to do about the drawing Xuanzang had entrusted to him.

There were preparations afoot. News was delivered to the monastery earlier that morning that there would be Feng and Shan rituals in less than two years' time. The Emperor and Empress wanted Da Ci'en Monastery to appoint a contingent of monks to be part of the entourage to support their ascension up Mount Tai.

Huili insisted that Harelip had to be part of the retinue. Taishan was the mountain associated with Imperial authority, with officialdom, and it was popular with devotees. No, this was not the mountain Harelip wanted to go to, especially as part of delegation that sanctioned the rule of an Emperor and Empress who, despite having made some decisions to the benefit of common folk, were also known to be selfish and cruel.

Xuanzang would never have wanted Harelip to do something that was repulsive and unnatural to him. Even though the great man himself sacrificed so much when he was unable to escape the city. *Distinguished personages can't have as much freedom as we anonymous ones*, thought Harelip. *Because they are constantly scrutinized.*

Compared to Xuanzang, Harelip felt like an imposter. He wasn't sure that life at the monastery was for him anymore. For one thing, he was no longer celibate—he sneaked out whenever he could to meet Ardhanari. An image of Ardhanari sleeping next to him flashed through his mind. How much longer would he be able to continue the affair? How long before someone from the monastery discovered his secret? He simply couldn't imagine how they could continue being together.

Wait, he pinched himself on the arm, *stop ruminating*. Maya approached and pawed at Harelip's ankles. It was not important whether he had known Xuanzang or any of the other monks better than they had known him. What was critical was that he knew himself.

Xuanzang never got his wish to return to live in nature. He was hampered by the wishes of the Emperor who was his patron. *But*, Harelip reasoned, *I am not Xuanzang, and I don't have to compare myself to him.*

He was not an imposter. He knew what he wanted. And he would be prepared to break free of the monastery, to go in search of what would make him happy. His heart and body yearned to be close to Ardhanari, and yet he knew he would never be happy remaining in Chang'an. He would come to resent Ardhanari. For the first time in his life, Harelip knew that he had to follow his spirit's deepest longing above all else.

Some day soon, before the Feng and Shan rituals, he would flee Chang'an. He was going to take the few important things he needed, including his Buddha statue, and head for Mount Hua. He would take his life in an entirely different direction than Xuanzang had.

DA FA TEMPLE,
WEST CENTRAL CHANG'AN

They were all in the front hall, clearing up the offering bowls, preparing the room for the mid-afternoon meditation, when they heard the loud thud outside, followed by a yelp like the sound of an animal in pain.

The Abbess looked at Sister Lizi and Ling. "You two, go investigate."

They recognized her immediately even though she was lying face down on the gravel. They carried Qilan in and saw that her face was scratched up, as if by some wild creature.

Sister Lizi put her face close to Qilan's nose and felt the slight breath on her cheek. "She's barely alive."

The Abbess was helped down from her seat on the dais and went to Qilan immediately. "Quickly, time is of the essence." She nodded to Sister Lizi.

Lizi uncorked a small vial and poured the liquid into Qilan's mouth. Within a few miao, Qilan opened her eyes—but the look was one of horror.

Ling touched Qilan's face and called out, "Sister Orchid ...

Qilan!" It seemed as if Qilan couldn't see her.

They carried her into the infirmary. A couple of nuns were assigned to watch over her.

"Where is her steed?" asked Ling.

No one had paid any attention to the missing horse. Ling walked across the courtyard and exited the temple. She looked around. Only a few people strolling by. She whistled, knowing the call to summon Qilan's horse.

She waited. And whistled again. She looked across the street at the wooded area and thought of the many times she and Qilan went there. A head popped up. A fox. Then the creature disappeared. Finally, the stallion came to her, and she led him down to the stables.

"What happened?" cried Old Chen.

Ling was tearful. "Qilan, she's ... hurt. Something's wrong with her." Ling stroked and patted the horse. The stallion didn't look hurt at all, but he seemed anxious. Ling spoke to him softly.

Old Chen took off the saddle. The saddlebag was tied only on one end, and the flap not even closed well. Out slipped the cloth bag, the oracle bone falling to the ground.

She gasped. "The plastron!"

Old Chen's eyebrows twitched. "You bring it to Sister Orchid."

She understood his meaning immediately and ran back in, sprinting into the infirmary, breathless.

Xu was there with another nun tending to Qilan whose lips looked drained of colour. She seemed to be sleeping, her belly rising and falling a near-imperceptible amount.

Ling sat down on the low stool in the corner, one hand pressed against the plastron nestled inside her tunic.

The older nun, known to Ling as Sanjiao, Triple Warmer, was in charge of the infirmary. She glanced at Ling in between inserting needles into Qilan's scalp. She mumbled to herself as she worked. "Curious, curious. She's been completely healthy all along, all these years here, and now this. Her pulses are ... I've never encountered such a problem before." Sanjiao frowned and shook her head.

Tears filled Ling's eyes, but she felt annoyed as well. She leaned forward, arms crossed, and held onto her elbows. "Sister Sanjiao, what do you mean? If you can't figure it out, who can?"

"Don't fuss, and don't be in the way," chided Xu, whose face turned a slight pink.

"Shush, shush, you two!" Sister Sanjiao looked worried.

Ling ignored Xu, refusing to meet her friend's gaze. She bent her head down and let the tears fall. They made dark spots on her tunic.

It seemed a long time before she heard Sister Sanjiao say to Xu, "Come with me to the apothecary." Ling raised her head and watched the two nuns leave. She rushed to Qilan's side and brought out the plastron.

"What happened? What has made you like this?" She sobbed and wrapped her arms around Qilan's body. "I cannot go on without you."

She placed the plastron in Qilan's right hand. "If this plastron is so powerful, can't you use it to come back?"

But nothing happened. She heard Sanjiao and Xu talking, their voices getting closer. Her heart was pounding hard in her chest. She had promised Qilan she would never reveal what she had told her. She had to keep the secret. But what if telling Sister Sanjiao might save Qilan's life?

She heard the nuns approach the infirmary, so she retrieved the plastron and slipped it back into her tunic.

"You best go tend to your duties." Xu's face showed her displeasure and her voice was stern.

Ling got up and ran away.

Sister Sanjiao patted Xu on the wrist. "You mustn't be so hard on her. You know how close she is to Sister Orchid."

Ling ran to the outer courtyard. She didn't know what to do. She spotted the Abbess in the small alcove, kneeling in front of the altar along the west wall. She watched the Abbess as she chanted, the frail nun's voice just barely audible from where she stood, but she recognized the mantra.

She listened to the soothing sounds with eyes closed.

Heaven and Earth
You and I
Nothing separates us all

Heaven and Earth
You and I
One

The Abbess finished chanting and noticed that Ling was watching her. She got up slowly and walked over to Ling. "My dear, you have been very distraught."

Ling started to feel her whole body tremble. "Is she, is she ..."

"She's in a trance. But I have been praying for her release."

Ling nodded but wasn't sure what to say.

Just then, a beautiful butterfly flitted from the shortest juniper to the camellia bush. She recalled that first lesson Qilan gave her when she'd transformed the caterpillar into a butterfly.

"Not all transformation is an illusion," she mumbled to herself.

The Abbess placed her right hand on Ling's back. "Sister Orchid has taught you well and prepared you for assuming the position of Abbess one day."

"I don't know if I—why would I want to be powerful? What is the point of having power?"

"The point, my dear, is so that you can inspire others and guide them. And to do good."

"But aren't the Emperor and Empress—isn't that power?"

"That, my child, is weakness. To be truly powerful is to be harmonious with everything else."

Ling breathed more easily from the gentle energy that the Abbess directed at her. She felt that energy radiate from the Abbess's hand, spread across her back, and move up her neck.

"Return to the infirmary, stay with her. I'm sure she can still sense your presence. I will give instructions to the others not to chase you out."

Ling felt encouraged by the Abbess's kind words. She bit her lower lip and bowed from the waist, placing her palms together, but keeping the plastron safely tucked in place with her right arm.

Returning to the infirmary, she was relieved that no one else was there. She gently moved the stool next to the bed where Qilan lay. She would chant the same words that the Abbess had uttered. She touched Qilan's hand with her own and began. She kept going for almost a double hour until startled by the bell ringing from the tower for the mid-afternoon meditation.

At the sound of the bell, Qilan opened her eyes and smiled.

"You have awakened me by chanting those lines."

Ling gasped with joy. "You are back!"

"No, Ling. I am going to leave you soon."

Ling gave a little cry, like a wounded animal.

"Listen well. When I entered the Demon Star Temple, I knew that Gui would meet me, expecting to defeat me. There had been some degree of fear existing in me all these years. That's why I had to wait eleven years—in order to master my own fear. Gui didn't expect me to use the oracle bone to absorb its energy and take it into me."

"You, you ..." Ling shivered with the shock of this revelation.

"Yes, I embraced Gui and took it with me through a portal. Then I entered the well that I've dreamt about all these years. Who knows how this happened? As in all things, it was a mystery. But I let myself remain there, without giving in to my fear.

"At first I didn't understand fully what had happened, whether or not I had succeeded. I felt quite ill when I emerged from the demon's lair. I believe it was my mother who helped me ride my horse back to Da Fa Temple, casting a spell for us to travel very quickly. She risked her life bringing me back to Chang'an.

"I could feel the chill and hatred of the demon trying to consume me, to conquer me, but it wasn't able to succeed. All the souls that Gui had taken into itself have been released. Including my father's. All except one. The one I am holding inside me. When I am finally released from this form, my soul will accompany Gui's soul back to the Underworld." Qilan beamed with a look of complete joy.

"I had to wake up—your voice reminded me of my ties to you," she continued. "The least I could do is to tell you this one last story and say goodbye. But, Ling, our parting is only temporary. It will be a long time before we meet again under different circumstances. Dear one, trust me, there will never be a permanent farewell between us."

Ling felt a sudden change inside her, a release from fear and anger. Without knowing what the future held for her, she now resolved that she would believe Qilan's words.

"You know why you had to stay behind at the temple?" Qilan asked. "So that you could be here when I returned."

Ling nodded and closed her eyes for a few miao. When she opened them, she saw that Qilan's form had altered. Her face was slowly changing, returning to her fox features, her body withering.

"Now, you cast the spell for me," Qilan said.

"Which spell?"

"The one I taught you at our favourite spot by the stream, just before I left. The one that ends life as we know it."

"You want me to end your life."

"Yes. Only then can I bring Gui back to the Underworld. But it is not really to end life, but to end the attachment to this physical manifestation. Life flows into death, and that death will generate new life."

"No, Qilan, I can't," Ling sobbed. "You saved me."

"Do it, Ling. Quickly. Don't delay. I can only hold Gui a little while longer, and if we wait too long, I will not only lose this life, but Gui as well. Do you understand?"

Ling swallowed hard. She understood. More importantly, she accepted. She touched the plastron and knew that it was now the right time to draw it out.

She placed it on top of Qilan's body and stepped back. She thought of what Qilan had taught her about casting spells. She had to have pure intent, the motivation to reduce suffering, to respect another's wishes.

Taking a deep breath, she held up her arms and called upon the Great Spirit of the Universe. She created a spiral of energy deep within her body, then uttered the spell in a low but firm voice charged with purity of intent and love. She kept repeating the spell, as the changes came into effect.

The room shook and the windows were blown open, causing a massive forceful wind to rush through. Ling stood firm and kept her gaze fixed on Qilan.

Qilan's body slowly began to disintegrate in front of Ling's eyes. She saw the desperate, writhing form of Gui only for an instant.

The room quieted down. Only the plastron remained on the bed. Then the sweet scent arrived, bringing Ling back to the first day she'd met Qilan. The scent that had wafted from Qilan's hair when she had been carried on the nun's back. It was the smell of apricots.

Ling's entire body was drenched with sweat. She shook with such force that it took her a great deal of effort to stay upright as she stumbled back outside again. The main courtyard was empty. All the nuns were in the meditation hall, chanting. Their combined voices rose up, soothing and harmonious.

Ling lay on the soft white gravel and looked up at the sky. It was true. She too had died, all that she had been, the lives she had led until now, this moment. She was a third kind of creature, just like Qilan had been. Still was. Somewhere in the universe out there, transformed.

She breathed deeply and felt her body welcome all the sensations on her skin—the last rays of the setting sun, the light breeze caressing her face—she was grateful for everything.

A thought whisper, clear as a bell, entered her mind.

Dear heart, we will meet again. Take care of the oracle bone until I return for it.

It was a glorious end to the day. She cried until laughter overcame her.

AUTHOR'S NOTES
AND
ACKNOWLEDGMENTS

This is a work of fiction. Although certain characters and events in this novel are based on historical figures and incidents, these have been altered to suit narrative purposes. Some known myths have also been borrowed and transformed beyond conventional understandings.

Chuanqi 傳奇 tales were a literary form/tradition that emerged during the mid-Tang Dynasty period; they are tales of marvels, and the term literally means "transmitting the strange."

The Heraclitus quote in the epigraph is from Guy Davenport's 1976 book, *Herakleitos & Diogenes*, San Francisco: Grey Fox Press, fragment 113.

The map of Chang'an in this novel is a fictionalized recreation of the city based on various details taken from *Daily Life in the Tang Dynasty* by Charles Benn (Westport: Greenwood, 2002) and the Wikipedia page: https://en.wikipedia.org/wiki/Chang%27an

The three sections of the novel have titles based on names of hexagrams from the Yijing:

蠱 Gu - Poison, based on Hexagram 18

復 Fu - Return, Hexagram 24

既濟 Ji Ji - Completion, Hexagram 63

Details about Chang'an and daily life during the Tang Dynasty were taken from *Daily Life in The Tang Dynasty* by Charles Benn.

Historical references about Wu Zhao and Li Zhi came from Denis Twitchett's chapters in *The Cambridge History of China: Sui and T'ang China* (Cambridge: Cambridge University Press, 1979) as well as C.P. Fitzgerald's *The Empress Wu* (Vancouver: University of British Columbia Press, 1968).

The system of dividing the twenty-four hours of the day into twelve double hours (using the animals of the Chinese zodiac) and the naming of the various seasons and lunar months were taken from *Chinese History: A Manual* by Endymion Wilkinson, revised and enlarged edition (Cambridge: Harvard University Asia Center, 2000).

In the Chinese system, a person is considered one sui when born, hence a year older than the western way of counting age. The age in sui takes into account the time spent in the womb.

The tale of Gui was inspired by the myth of Gui Xing 鬼星, who became the God of Literature in the Daoist pantheon. The character Xie was inspired by the Daoist sorcerer Guo Xingzhen who had been Wu Zhao's lover.

Langgan Elixir was mentioned in Stephen R. Bokenkamp's *Early Daoist Scriptures* (Berkeley: University of California Press, 1998), page 289.

The Verse for opening a Sutra—"The unsurpassed, profound and wonderful Dharma ..."—is one English version of a traditional gatha thought to have been spoken by Shakyamuni Buddha. This version was found in *The Vajra Prajna Paramita Sutra: A General Explanation* (California: Buddhist Text Translation Society, 2003).

"To become whole, let yourself be partial ..." is my paraphrase of Stephen Mitchell's translation of *Tao Te Ching*, Number 22 (New York: Harper Collins, 1988).

Zhuangzi 莊子 was a third-century BCE philosopher who told fables about famous people such as Confucius and Mencius to demonstrate his teachings. Irreverent and wise, Zhuangzi's allegories inspired many poets in later centuries. Several excerpts in the novel are paraphrased from *Zhuangzi: Basic Writings*, translated by Burton Watson (New

York: Columbia University Press, 2003).

Many details about Xuanzang were taken from *The Silk Road Journey with Xuanzang* by Sally Hovey Wriggins (Boulder, CO: Westview Press, 2004).

The first stanza of "Return to Gardens and Fields" by Tao Yuanming (365–427 CE) is translated by me based on the original as well an English translation by Richard C. Fang, *Gleanings from Tao Yuan-ming* (Hong Kong: Commercial Press, 1980), page 40.

Description of Torch Dragon, Zhulong 燭 龍 is my paraphrase from page 188 of *The Classic of Mountains and Seas* by Anne Birrell (London, UK: Penguin, 1999).

"The reeds flourish thus ..." are lines from a folk song, "The Reeds." My translation is based on translations by Yang Xianyi, Gladys Yang, and Hu Shiguang (*Selections from the Book of Songs*, Beijing: Panda Books, 1983).

For "Frolicking above the Graves" by Tao Yuanming, my translation is based on the original and an English translation by Richard C. Fang in *Gleanings from Tao Yuan-ming* (Hong Kong: Commercial Press, 1980), page 105.

The inscription on the oracle bone, "A dream wants waking, a sky needs light," is my translation of a couplet by Sweden Xiao, 夢要醒，天要光。

鼇, pronounced Ao, is a mythical marine turtle. I have created a new myth based on it.

The English translation of the Heart Sutra is taken from Red Pine's *the heart sutra* (Berkeley: Counterpoint Press, 2004).

The poem recited by Hamed the Turkish tea seller is my adaptation of a poem by Rabia Basri, eighth-century Sufi mystic, found in *Islamic Mystical Poetry*, edited by Mahmood Jamal (London, UK: Penguin, 2009), page 7.

The Zhuangzi fragment from *Autumn Floods*—based on Burton Watson's *Zhuangzi: Basic Writings* (New York: Columbia University Press, 2003) has been paraphrased as well as added to. "Time moves beyond the human" is a line I inserted, and it was inspired by a talk given by Professor Pheng Cheah (Department of Rhetoric at University of California, Berkeley) at a conference at UBC, on March 17, 2017 on "Worlding Literature."

The quote "Be like a virgin ..." is a paraphrase from the translation of Sun Tzu's *The Art of War: Translation, Essays and Commentary* (Boston: Shambhala, 2009), page 258.

Shangguan Yi's poem "Early Spring in Guilin Hall" is my adaptation based on Stephen Owen's translation in *Poetry of the Early T'ang* (New Haven: Yale University Press, 1977), pages 73–74.

Portions of Qilan's chant for exorcism are based on *The Great Petition for Sepulchral Pliants* translated by Peter Nickerson in Stephen R. Bokenkamp's *Early Daoist Scriptures* (Berkeley: University of California Press, 1998), pages 261–71.

"Be deep and still and so perpetually present" and "Returning to the root is stillness" and "In the midst of its dark depths are essences" are taken from Xiang'er Commentary in *Early Daoist Scriptures*, translated by Stephen R. Bokenkamp, pages 81, 101, and 113, respectively.

Many thanks to Arsenal Pulp Press for believing in this book—for all the great skill, dedication, and love everyone put into it. My appreciation to Dayaneetha De Silva and Cathy Stonehouse for reading an earlier version of the manuscript and to many friends and acquaintances who listened to me talk about this work.

One of the primary literary influences that seeded ideas for *Oracle Bone* was Pu Songling's *Strange Tales from a Chinese Studio*, translated by Herbert A. Giles (Tokyo: Tuttle, 2010). I owe a great deal to Pu's work. Daniel Hsieh's *Love and Women in Early Chinese Fiction* (Hong Kong: The Chinese University Press, 2008) was also an invaluable resource regarding the various stories of fox spirits created by male scholars of the literati class.

I owe a great debt to all the martial arts movies I watched as a child, teenager, and adult, for furnishing some of the narratives and tropes which I employed, referenced, and sometimes subverted in this novel. The Japanese TV movie *Onmyoji* was also influential.

Much appreciation to Dr Lawrence Chan who helped with providing some Traditional Chinese Medicine diagnostic details for Xuanzang the monk based on a known incident in which he had suffered prolonged chills while on a journey through the Tian Shan mountains. Dr Chan also provided feedback about the fight scene between Ling and Shan Hu at Prosperity Tavern—in addition to being a naturopath, he has many years of experience as a martial arts practitioner and instructor.

Thanks to Sweden Xiao who gave me permission to use his couplet 夢要醒，天要光。 and my translation for this novel.

Last but not least: To you, dear reader, who was willing to follow me on this journey.

AN EXCERPT FROM LYDIA KWA'S
The Walking Boy *

Jinzhe Jieqi, The Waking of Insects,
Second Lunar Month, 702 C.E.

MOUNT HUA,
270 LI EAST OF THE WESTERN CAPITAL CHANG'AN

At this time of the early morning, just as the perpetual lamp indicates the Hour of the Rabbit, everything exists in the bluish shadows before dawn, suspended between life and annihilation. The candles on the altar to Harelip's left flicker in the draft. His upright torso vibrates, swayed to and fro by an invisible wind. The sensations from the dream are still with him, the raspy dryness in the throat and the fickle heart rhythms. His hands clasped in his lap break out into a sweat. Last night he washed off the blood immediately after coughing it up, but the memory hasn't disappeared. He checks the height of the incense stick on the altar. Barely half. Why is time passing so slowly? He directs his gaze back to the ground. A dull ache spreads across his shoulders and he stifles a sigh. The jade pendant rests against his chest with the weight of regret. Ardhanari has probably spent all these years wondering what has become of him. Last night's dream took him by surprise, seeing his friend's face just as he had looked all those years ago.

The Walking Boy, a novel by Lydia Kwa, takes place chronologically after the events described in *Oracle Bone*. First published by Key Porter Books in 2005, a new edition of *The Walking Boy* will be published by Arsenal Pulp Press in 2018.

A narrow beam of light through the one window in the wooden shack caresses Baoshi's left cheek and tickles the fine hairs of his nostrils. He twitches his face then sneaks a look at Harelip sitting directly across from him. His Master is deep in concentration, head bowed and body showing no signs of slackening since they both began to sit before sunrise. Dust motes suspended in that beam of light are rushing toward him, with news of recent adventures in the magic realms. He smiles with pleasure.

Harelip's mind wanders through various incidents in his early life at Da Ci'en Monastery in Chang'an, learning from both Buddhist and Daoist medical texts. The meeting with Xuanzang who brought the sutras back from India. Then Xuanzang's death shortly after his translation project was completed. Two years later, preparations by his superiors to recommend him to the court, where Daoist influence was threatening to overshadow Buddhist sympathies. He was the perfect gambit, a young, intelligent monk who was a gifted healer. Oh, yes, a bit of a renegade but absolutely suited to his superiors' plans to increase their influence with Emperor Gaozong. That recommendation to the court was to happen at the same time as Gaozong and Wu Zhao's ascent up Mount Tai for the Feng and Shan rituals. That was the reign year Qianfeng. Well, he turned his back on all that when he didn't join that procession up the sacred mountain.

He even knows more about the world of Wu Zhao since she has become Nü Huang, Female Emperor. He hears news about the intrigues at court from the villagers below. When they make the trek up the mountain to see him with their ailments, they rattle off what they've heard without any suspicion that their hermit healer has his own secrets. Twelve years ago Wu Zhao usurped the throne from her son Li Zhe, and proclaimed herself Holy and Divine Emperor. That fact has been repeated to Harelip countless times, the tone of incredulity surprisingly fresh. These days, the villagers are harping on Nü Huang's affair with those two half-brothers. Imagine, they would say in hushed tones, in her seventies. Harelip often feels tempted to say to them, "Just how exciting can that be?" The villagers have been especially nervous ever since Nü Huang moved the court back from Luoyang to Chang'an last winter. Rumours are circulating that her health is failing.

Harelip clears his throat uneasily. He shouldn't let his mind drift aimlessly through such troublesome reminiscences. He looks up and notices that the incense stick has completely burned down, leaving a pile of grey ash. The perpetual lamp confirms the time. The Hour of the Dragon. He's surprised by growling sounds emanating from Baoshi's belly. That boy! He bends forward to gather up the pair of tiny bronze cymbals in front of his feet, strikes them together, and waits for the sound to fade away before striking the cymbals together a second time, then a third.

Baoshi raises his head at the sound of the cymbals and frowns. His loud stomach embarrasses him. These days, he never seems to go for very long before feeling gripped by monstrous hunger pangs. Only moments before, his mind had started to fantasize about a pig roasting above hot coals. He listens as Harelip recites the Heart Sutra.

"Whatever is form is emptiness, whatever is emptiness is form ..."

Baoshi's attention drifts back to the idea of the roast pig. When was the last time he had eaten suckling pig? Or any kind of pork for that matter? When he was still with his parents. Sadness lodges in his chest. Before too long, the final words of the sutra penetrate his daydreaming.

Their eyes meet. Together they emit sighs as if one were prompting the other, yet their furrowed brows are plagued with vastly different concerns. Harelip uncrosses his legs from the lotus position and groans. The two small hours of sitting were painstakingly slow this morning.

"Curse of old age! Wooden screws coming undone! How could a creaky wheel reach immortality? Will my body be nimble in that Pure Land?"

He and Baoshi rise up from their tattered cushions and turn their bodies to face the altar. They make their prostrations before the figure of Buddha, a modest wooden sculpture only two hands high whose sensuous red and gold robes are faded and chipped in places. Even Buddha is in need of repair, Harelip notes. He turns to face Baoshi and rests his gnarled fingers lightly on the boy's shoulders.

"Baoshi, I've taken care of you all these years."

"Yes, Master, I remember and I'm always grateful." He blushes, the memory still able to flood him with shame. He fidgets under Harelip's hands. That tone of voice is what Harelip uses when he's about to launch into a speech or a teaching. How much longer before their morning meal?

"My dear Baoshi, do you remember what I told you about my reason for coming to this mountain?"

"Yes, Master. You said you were fleeing for your life."

Harelip's cheeks flush red-hot. Would Wu Zhao have become so enraged by his absence at the Mount Tai ritual that she would have had him imprisoned or killed? Or exiled to Lingnan to the south? He'll never know for sure.

He nods to Baoshi, appreciating the firm jawline and the elegant cheekbones. What bright, curious eyes! And those lips, as yet untainted by carnal pleasures.

"I had a troubling dream last night. When I woke up, I knew I couldn't ignore it." He notices that Baoshi looks somewhat distracted.

Harelip chokes back the rush of feelings and hobbles over to the window to peer outside. A sparrow pecks at seeds on the ground, its hopping movements swift and urgent. He thinks to himself, he's nothing like this sparrow, utterly focused on picking out everything edible in its path. Instead, his mind is distracted by misgivings about the past. Had he made a mistake, fleeing to Mount Hua, without any consideration of Ardhanari's feelings all these years?

He can't answer his own question. He turns around to find Baoshi replenishing the oil in the perpetual lamp.

"Do you know what a novice on a pilgrimage is called?"

"No," Baoshi shakes his head vigorously.

"A walking boy."

Baoshi looks at his Master quizzically.

"I dreamed that you left the mountain and found your way to Chang'an. And you met this man Ardhanari. He was a special friend of mine before I fled the city." Harelip pauses before continuing. "You must become a walking boy for my sake. Leave this mountain, find Ardhanari, and bring him back to Mount Hua to see me." He means to sound firm, even confident, but his voice wavers.

"When?" Baoshi sits down, elbows on their small table, his hands cupped against his forehead.

"Not for another two or three months. When the ice on the paths has completely melted, and it's warm enough for easier travelling." As he finishes speaking, he shudders at the memory of his harrowing journey up the mountain in winter. To think that had been half a lifetime ago, and he has never left since then.

He joins Baoshi at the table and leans toward him. "Do you remember what I called you that first day we met?"

"You said that I'm a miracle of Heaven. I shall never forget." His ears burning with upset, he asks, "How long do I have to be away then?"

"Until you find Ardhanari and convince him to return with you. Can you accept this, my son? That I would ask you to set off on this pilgrimage based on a single dream? A dream I find so compelling I would sacrifice having you at my side." Harelip's body trembles with all the emotions he's holding in check.

"Master, I owe you my life. I will do what you ask, even though I'll be very sad to be away from you."

Harelip inhales loudly, sucking back his own urge to cry. "If you decide to assume a hermit's life on Mount Hua at the end of the pilgrimage, you'll be doing so of your own volition. You had no choice when you were placed in my care. You were a boy. Still a boy, really. When you go out into the world below, you'll be exposed to all kinds of possibilities, and that would allow you to discover what your true path will consist of. I must stay on the mountain for the sake of the villagers. Besides, in the dream, you were the one who met Ardhanari, not me."

Baoshi's belly offers another long growl. Harelip laughs. "Come, miracle of Heaven! We're taking up too much time talking about a pilgrimage that will begin many weeks from now, and here I am ignoring your hunger. Let's fill your belly before you faint from starvation."

Lydia Kwa is the author of the novels *This Place Called Absence* (shortlisted for the Books in Canada First Novel Award), *The Walking Boy* (shortlisted for the Ethel Wilson Fiction Prize), and *Pulse*, as well as two books of poetry, *The Colours of Heroines* and *sinuous*. She lives and works in Vancouver as a writer and psychologist. *lydiakwa.com*